Slowly, hesitantly, Paige examined the attic further. As the flashlight shone on the table near the inside wall, she heard movement. Startled, she backed up, frantically circling the flashlight to zero in on the noise. Suddenly, something large sprang from beneath the table, went flying through the air, then landed with a thud. It hopped up, sprinted across the room. Paige saw the thing pause at the tiny screenless window, throw it open as wide as it would go, then disappear out of it. She ran to the window, leaned out, and directed the beam of light downward. By that time the thing was halfway down the fire escape.

Paige was certain it was a child . . . a little girl . . .

A Whisper in the Attic

"A fast-moving tale that echoes Mary Higgins Clark's nail-biting novels . . ."
— *New Bedford Standard-Times*
(for *Down Will Come Baby*)

SPELLBINDING THRILLERS ...
TAUT SUSPENSE

☐ **A REASONABLE MADNESS by Fran Dorf.** Laura Wade was gorgeous and gentle, with a successful husband and three lovely children. She was also convinced her thoughts could kill ... "A riveting psychological thriller of murder and obsession." *Chicago Tribune*! (170407—$4.99)

☐ **THE HOUSE OF STAIRS by Ruth Rendell writing as Barbara Vine.** "Remarkable ... confirms (Barbara Vine's) reputation as one of the best novelists writing today."—P.D. James. Elizabeth Vetch moves into the grand, old house of her widowed aunt and plunges into a pit of murderous secrets 14 years old. (402111—$4.99)

☐ **GALLOWGLASS by Ruth Rendell writing as Barbara Vine.** In this stunning novel of erotic obsession, Barbara Vine illuminates the shadows of love cast by dark deeds. Her spell is gripping—and total. "Dazzling ... Barbara Vine's most penetrating foray yet into the dark mysteries of the heart's obsessions. (402561—$5.99)

☐ **BLINDSIDE by William Bayer.** Burned-out photographer Geoffrey Barnett follows a stunning young actress into a world of savage secrets, blackmail, and murder. "Smashing ... unstoppable entertainment." —*Kirkus Reviews* (166647—$4.95)

☐ **RINGERS by Tim Underwood.** The mob, a scam, and a Las Vegas horseplayer in a race for his life. (172256—$4.99)

Buy them at your local bookstore or use this convenient coupon for ordering.

NEW AMERICAN LIBRARY
P.O. Box 999, Bergenfield, New Jersey 07621

Please send me the books I have checked above.
I am enclosing $_____ (please add $2.00 to cover postage and handling).
Send check or money order (no cash or C.O.D.'s) or charge by Mastercard or VISA (with a $15.00 minimum). Prices and numbers are subject to change without notice.

Card #_____ Exp. Date _____
Signature_____
Name_____
Address_____
City _____ State _____ Zip Code _____
For faster service when ordering by credit card call **1-800-253-6476**

Allow a minimum of 4-6 weeks for delivery. This offer is subject to change without notice.

A Whisper in the Attic

Gloria Murphy

A SIGNET BOOK

SIGNET
Published by the Penguin Group
Penguin Books USA Inc., 375 Hudson Street,
New York, New York 10014, U.S.A.
Penguin Books Ltd, 27 Wrights Lane, London W8 5TZ, England
Penguin Books Australia Ltd, Ringwood, Victoria, Australia
Penguin Books Canada Ltd, 10 Alcorn Avenue,
Toronto, Ontario, Canada M4V 3B2
Penguin Books (N.Z.) Ltd, 182–190 Wairau Road,
Auckland 10, New Zealand

Penguin Books Ltd, Registered Offices: Harmondsworth, Middlesex,
England

First published by Signet, an imprint of New American Library,
a division of Penguin Books USA Inc.

First Printing, August, 1992
10 9 8 7 6 5 4 3 2

Copyright © Gloria Murphy, 1992
All rights reserved

 REGISTERED TRADEMARK—MARCA REGISTRADA

Printed in Canada

Without limiting the rights under copyright reserved above, no part
of this publication may be reproduced, stored in or introduced into
a retrieval system, or transmitted, in any form, or by any means
(electronic, mechanical, photocopying, recording, or otherwise),
without the prior written permission of both the copyright owner
and the above publisher of this book.

PUBLISHER'S NOTE
This is a work of fiction. Names, characters, places, and incidents
either are the product of the author's imagination or are used ficti-
tiously, and any resemblance to actual persons, living or dead,
events, or locales is entirely coincidental.

BOOKS ARE AVAILABLE AT QUANTITY DISCOUNTS WHEN USED TO PRO-
MOTE PRODUCTS OR SERVICES. FOR INFORMATION PLEASE WRITE TO
PREMIUM MARKETING DIVISION, PENGUIN BOOKS USA INC., 375 HUD-
SON STREET, NEW YORK, NEW YORK 10014.

If you purchased this book without a cover you should be aware that
this book is stolen property. It was reported as "unsold and destroyed" to the publisher and neither the author nor the publisher
has received any payment for this "stripped book."

*Dedicated to the memory
of
Bruce H. White
1952–1982*

Thank you:

Alice Martell, that bright and wonderfully aggressive agent . . . Audrey LaFehr, whose editorial know-how gave it just the right feel . . . Joe Murphy, the heroic attorney who was the first to play the courtroom scene. Laurie, Julie, Sheryl, Billy, and Danny Gitelman and Kate Murphy, my readers, my supporters, my critics . . . my children.

Prologue

She knew a lot for four years old, everyone said so. Mostly, she'd listen in or watch when she wasn't supposed to be doing either. But sometimes Mommy or Daddy would come out and tell her things. For instance, Mommy told her about the baby growing in her belly when her belly was so flat no one would have believed it could fit. And though neither of them talked about a name for the baby, Daddy started right in calling him My Boy.

But the biggest things made the smallest sense—just like the way it was with the punishments. Not that Mommy or Daddy would talk about *them*, not even with each other. Of course they didn't happen every day, not even every week, but when they did happen, they happened to Mommy: she was the bad one. And Daddy being the biggest and strongest and smartest was the one to spot the badness.

So this day when the girl came in from play to find him stretched in front of the television—rather than outside fixing one of those old cars—

and Mommy nowhere to be seen or heard, she knew it was another of those times. Daddy's attention moved from the noisy game show to the door where she was standing, and he spread his arms wide so she could run into them.

"How's Daddy's girl?" he asked, scooping her onto the sofa with him, and she smiled, hugged him hard the way he liked, and pressed wet kisses over his face and neck. She wanted to find out about Mommy, but didn't ask: he would tell it when he was good and ready. And it wasn't until after she put down a whole jelly sandwich and glass of milk and watched the rest of *The Price is Right* that he said, "Mommy's in the bedroom, want to take her in some lunch?"

She nodded and he took out a plate from the refrigerator, already fixed with thin slices of meat on lettuce leaves. He set it on a tray along with a knife, fork, napkin and a short white glass filled with the same violets that grew out back.

"See that she eats it all," he said. "My Boy needs it."

Just the mention of the baby made her happy—a real life dolly that eats and wets and cries, all hers to play with. And for maybe the hundredth time since she knew he was coming, she asked, "Can I take care of him when he comes, Daddy?"

He smiled: big white teeth ... the better to eat you with. But he answered his same good answer. "Who else better able than a sister?"

One, two, three ... three more months till My Boy was to be born, she reminded herself as she lifted the heavy tray and carried it toward her parents' bedroom. At the door, she stopped, took in a big breath, held it—she was never quite sure what she would see—then slowly turned the knob and pushed it open.

Mommy was on the bed with no clothes, her arms and legs spread apart and tied to the bed-posts with her own ripped panty hose. She was skinny except for the belly pumped round and hard like a basketball, and though her eyes were shut tight, she wasn't asleep. She looked her over—no black-and-blues, no bumps, no cuts, no blood. She let go her breath, then leaned over and kissed her cheek.

"Hi, Mommy."

She opened her eyes, and when she saw her, she smiled.

"Where's Boss?" she asked, using her pet name for Daddy.

"Watching television." She showed her the tray. "He cooked a lunch for you."

The woman examined the dish, then shook her head.

"You have to eat it, he'll be mad if you don't."

"I can't, you know I can't. I'll throw it up."

The girl cut off a piece of pale meat, then speared it with the fork and held it to her mother's lips.

"Just try a little bit," she said.

She pressed her lips together and turned her head away. "I can't, I won't, please don't make me." Then finally turning back to her daughter, her big purple-blue eyes all shining with tears: "Baby, could *you*?"

The girl made a groaning noise, stared at the food . . . she wasn't hungry, especially not hungry for *that*. But she raised the fork to her mouth, chewed the tough meat, swallowed it, then took more and more until it was gone and she thought she'd burst or maybe throw up though she'd never done either of those things in her life before.

As she began to leave, her mother's fingers reached out and tickled her palm.

"What would I do without you, baby?" she said in a whispery voice that sounded close to crying.

"Can I touch My Boy?"

Usually she didn't like her belly bothered, but this time she let her daughter place her hand on her stomach and move it round and round till she found the new place those baby feet were hiding. Finally after tracking down a whole bunch of kicks, the girl slid her hand away and lifted the tray with the now empty plate.

"The flowers," the mother said. "Be sure to tell Boss how much I like them."

Silence.

"Oh, come on, don't be like that. He's already doing sweet little things to say he's sorry. And once this is over, well, you know him, he'll probably go right out and buy us some silly gift then dance us both around the living room. Besides, it's really not so bad as it looks."

More silence.

"He loves you . . . you know that, don't you?"

She nodded.

"Well, he loves me, too, it's just that it shows different with big people."

It wasn't until late that night that Mommy started screaming so loud that it scared even Daddy. He untied her arms and legs from the bedposts, carried her to the car, and drove her off to the hospital.

The girl—now left alone in the bedroom—examined the bloody globs, then with her hands, swept them from the bedsheet into a green garbage bag, tied the strings, and buried it in the woods.

And no one talked about My Boy again. . . .

Chapter One

They wouldn't have considered spending the winter in Briarwood if Paige—in her first trimester of pregnancy—hadn't been assaulted less than fifty yards from their Manhattan co-op. Their building was three blocks east of Central Park, in what her best friend Brooke still insisted was a good neighborhood. But nowhere in the city seemed safe anymore to Paige. And though she wasn't a novice at handling confrontation—she traveled regularly through high crime areas as special education teacher for a five elementary-school district—she panicked when she saw the steel blade slip from the kid's shirtsleeve.

She screamed, kicked, walloped him with her purse, reacted the way police warn victims not to. But she stunned him enough to run and gratefully came through it unhurt: a superficial gash to her right shoulder and a few bruises and scrapes on her knees where she fell to the marble floor once safe inside her lobby.

But the real fear came later, once she realized

how close she'd come to losing another baby; the result was insomnia, nightmares, elevated blood pressure, and anxiety sustained by the daily horror stories of the city. Finally it was Dr. Lucas, her obstetrician, who pushed her to act. "Do whatever is necessary to get rid of this stress," he told her. "If you let it go on, you'll be risking the pregnancy."

Now it was several months later, midafternoon on a Friday, and she looked out the car window as they entered Route 9, the road that shadowed the Hudson River upstate to their country house. Jason had managed to duck out of the office early enough to avoid traffic. Paige, five feet seven and carrying comfortably small, thanks to Jason's thumb on her junk food intake, sank into the soft, leather-cushioned bucket seat, relieved to be temporarily rid of the city.

"I feel as though my pressure just dipped ten points."

"Good . . . let's hope the doctor confirms that," Jason said, flipping one of those green-visor caps over a shock of wiry hair the color of copper. "You did contact Lucas's referral, didn't you?"

"No emergency . . . I'll do it first thing tomorrow." If Jason was at times a little too managing, Paige overlooked it . . . he was also attentive, stable, resourceful, dependable—all qualities Paige had missed in a chaotic childhood that could claim no other family than a mother who'd paid attention only between boyfriends.

Jason had initially opposed relocating on the grounds that Paige would receive inferior medical care outside a major city. But thanks to Dr. Lucas's praise of Poughkeepsie Medical Cen-

ter—twenty minutes north of Briarwood—Jason
got past that. That the center's chief of obstet-
rics, Milton Barry, was a highly qualified former
classmate of Lucas's and—at his request—would
gladly take Paige as a private patient, was what
finally convinced him. What still concerned
Jason, though, was the seventy-mile commute to
work he'd be making twice daily over the next
five months.

"You'll be pretty isolated," he had argued.
"Most nights I won't get there till after eight . . .
maybe nine, depending on traffic."

Though they didn't know their neighbors
well—after all, what they'd originally wanted
from their country retreat was privacy—they did
have a nodding acquaintance with many of the
township people. "There's always the Beeders,"
Paige reminded him. "They seem like a nice
young couple, helpful . . . and they're not much
more than a quarter of a mile down the road.
We'll have a phone put in, of course, we can
even lease a car for me, and the hospital is
within easy distance. Besides, first babies are
only in a rush in the movies."

So, she had convinced Jason it was the right
move, the only logical move. But the truth was,
she wasn't sure herself it was. Though Paige
pooh-poohed it over and over again, unlike Jason,
who was introspective and if need be could fare
well without the company of another living soul,
Paige had, as long as she could remember, hated
being alone. Cutting herself off from Brooke,
who since buying into the adjacent building five
years earlier had become more a sister than a
friend, would not be easy.

But she was thirty-three, Jason was going on thirty-seven, and they were desperate to begin a family. If this is what was needed to get her back in control, then she'd do it.

The house—two living levels, a cellar, attic, and front porch that hugged the sides of the house—was a big old cow with chronic laryngitis, the kind of house that an amateur carpenter like Jason could work on indefinitely. The best part was the space—eleven acres of wooded land that extended to the grassy shores of the Hudson. The moment they pulled into the long unpaved driveway that circled toward the house, she knew that this was, indeed, the right therapy.

"Look at the yard, Jason . . . the foliage," she said, getting out of the car. A sudden gust of wind came along, standing up brilliantly colored leaves and marching them away while her thick, chestnut hair swept her shoulders, then wrapped her head like a snug cap. With her fingertips she plied back hair from her cheeks, tucking strands temporarily behind her ears. Though she and Jason had bought the property nearly two years earlier, until now they'd used it only during spring and summer—rarely after Labor Day, let alone into October. She crossed her arms over her chest, a chill seeping into her bones despite her thick-knit sweater.

"I suppose we should have the furnace looked at," she said.

Jason glanced at her over the trunk lid, his eyes hidden from her by the glossy brim of his cap. He lifted out two large leather bags from the car trunk and set them on the ground.

"Gas man was here two days ago. The furnace and water heater are in good shape. The phone will be connected first thing Monday. And the nearest car dealer out on the thruway has a good selection of rentals available. We'll go tomorrow, and you pick what you like ... What do you think of Eugene for a name? Strong yet simple."

"Not to disparage your father, but I dislike the whole business of namesakes," Paige said.

Eugene Bennett, her father-in-law, was a remarkably fit sixty-five-year-old who ran both family and business like the captain of a ship. From a dirt-poor young man who knew nothing about business, the respected patriarch had managed to work a two-acre farm into one of the biggest cattle ranches in southern Illinois.

Along with his wife Callah he had also produced four sons, all but one now ranchers like himself. Jason, the youngest, the smallest—jokingly referred to as the runt of the litter—at age seventeen sprang to five-ten, still was not to be compared in size to his brothers. But Jason was the one who thumbed his nose at the family ranch and moved East. He was also the only Bennett to go beyond high school.

"It's called continuity," he said.

"What's that?"

"Naming a kid after family. A way to keep the past generation alive, at least in one's memory."

"Maybe not having grown up in much of a family, I don't understand the hoopla made about names. But I would think continuity had more to do with the strength of the bond."

"I suppose you're right."

"And besides, your father already has a son who bears his name, and a grandson . . . and then aren't there some middle names thrown in somewhere too? I thought we'd give our child an original name, nothing to scuttle up his psyche."

Jason shrugged. "Okay, you sold me. Does that mean we can't use Jason, Jr.?"

A pained expression. "You're joking, right?"

He laughed—she picked up a fistful of leaves and tossed it at him. "I went to school with a Eugene. He sat in front of me straight through grammar school."

He shook the leaves out of his hair. "So?"

"His pleasures were reading the dictionary and eating insects."

"What kind of insects?"

"Any that came along." She reached through the back car window and lifted out the bag of tuna sandwiches on kaiser rolls and containers of cold milk Jason had insisted they pick up at the last decent roadside restaurant. "Jason, you were so right about the take-out, would you believe I'm hungry already? When did I last tell you how clever you are?"

He thought a moment, then slammed the trunk shut and pocketed the keys.

"A couple of weeks, at least." He put one suitcase under his arm, then lifting two others, gestured to his full arms. "Not so bad for a scrawny kid, huh?"

"You're not scrawny anymore. That was kid stuff."

"I still feel it. It's not a thing that lets go easily. Not after all that dirt goes in your face."

"Well, in that case, concentrate on your fine mind, a much worthier effort."

"So then you do think I'm scrawny?"

She ran ahead to the front door, opened her purse, and began rummaging through it.

"You didn't answer," he said, coming up the porch steps, waiting, then tossing her his set of keys.

Catching them, she picked out the long, straight-backed key and inserted it in the lock.

"So okay, you're not six-two."

"I'm not?"

"Look, if it helps any, you look good to me. Your body's perfect. I bet if you had reasonably long legs you'd be six feet."

"I'm the one told you that."

"Hmm, so you did." She turned and looked at him. "Hey, do you think you can take a paternity leave and stay up here full-time until the baby comes?"

"What would we do?"

"Talk, eat, play Scrabble, walk in the woods . . ."

"Fuck?"

"I guess . . . if that's what you want," she said, her lightheartedness suddenly gone.

She looked away from him, pushed open the front door, and stepped inside an alcove, beyond which was a room twice the size of their living room in the city. More than six hundred square feet of space and as a focal point, a marvelous stone fireplace with a raised hearth that filled an entire wall.

Off to the left was an eat-in kitchen that led to a cellar and back entrance. Though the kitchen had too little work and storage space, Paige loved the dining area with the bow window that looked out into the back woods.

The house was furnished with a conglomeration of styles, mostly late attic, early garage. Lots of wicker and brass and old books with missing covers that were standing on bookshelves Jason himself had built. Paige stepped a half-dozen feet into the living room, then stooped onto the colorful braided carpet, picked up something, then, creeping forward, reached again.

"I don't like this," she said.

"What?" he asked as he set down the bags.

She held up a fist, opening it to show Jason the acorns inside. "Squirrels?"

The insomnia didn't go away that night, not with the thought of little animals roaming freely around the house.

"Look at it logically," Jason said once they had settled in bed. "You like squirrels, right?"

"Sure, outdoors," Paige said. "Even ants, keep them outdoors and I have no argument with them. Take them indoors and they traumatize me. Ditto for a mice, lizards, spiders, you name it."

"What difference does it make where the creature is when you see it? The important issue here is the creature. Unless you corner it—which I have confidence you won't do—it'll turn and run in the other direction. Besides, if in fact a squirrel brought in those acorns, it would likely be out of the house by now."

She turned and eyed him dubiously. "You're only saying that to pacify me."

"No, not at all."

"What do you base your theory on?"

"The noise, squirrels—more so than other rodents—have highly proficient auditory systems. They hear voices, footsteps, they scamper, take off, run . . . By the time we turned on the alcove light, it was likely doing ninety out of here."

"How did it get out?"

"The way it got in. They have sort of a built-in radar that takes them right back—"

"This is a lot of purely invented crap, isn't it Jason?"

"Look, we'll get an exterminator out here tomorrow to check it. And if there're any openings in the foundation, I'll seal them. Meanwhile, it's important you sleep. Want a back rub?"

"Thanks, but no thanks."

Jason turned away so she couldn't actually tell he was put off, but odds were, he was. And why not? Just a few months ago, it wouldn't have dawned on her to refuse one of his delicious back rubs. But since that terrifying encounter . . . She could still see the despicable smile, the thin black mustache, the decaying teeth, a bottom front tooth missing . . . Why couldn't she get his face out of her head?

An hour and forty-five minutes later, she was still awake and thinking, but by then had managed to move on to better thoughts: the baby. Jason, who had been sleeping calmly beside her, suddenly swung around, part of the down quilt sailing to the floor. She reached over him, lifted the cover, and pulled it back over both of them, then touched her lips to his cheek.

Though it wasn't always so easy to see it—

what with her moods these days, she adored him—had ever since she mistakenly wandered into a civil liberties course her second year of City College and discovered the fresh-out-of school lawyer teaching it. He was wiry, only a few inches taller than she, but those astute blue eyes and that lopsided grin piqued her interest so, she maneuvered the class into her permanent schedule. And he'd been in her life ever since.

The rest of the night was a series of catnaps interrupted by a nightmare that disappeared from her consciousness the moment she woke . . . and scratching noises that came from the attic.

"I'm absolutely sure I heard something up there," Paige insisted over the blast of her hair dryer the next morning. After they exercised—Jason would jog, she walk—they would breakfast at the town diner, then pick up groceries at the general store.

"If you were nervous, you should have woken me," Jason said.

"What?"

"If you were nervous—"

She turned off the dryer. "No need to shout."

A hesitation, then quietly, "I was just asking, why didn't you wake me?"

"So you could have buttered my brain with another tall tale from the animal kingdom?"

"If you're referring to last night—"

"I am."

"I was simply trying—"

"I'm not questioning your motives, Jason."

"Then what?"

A sigh, then: "I simply don't enjoy being treated like an imbecile."

"I didn't."

"You did."

Jason grabbed a thermal-lined sweatshirt from his dresser drawer and put it on, then climbed into sweatpants. "Look, why don't you finish dressing," he said, heading to the door.

"Where're you going?"

"Outside."

"Wait up."

"Why? I'll just be—"

"Damn. Can't you just wait a sec? Jason, what do you think of Alexandra, Alie for short?"

From the diner, while they were waiting for honeydew melon and wheat waffles, Jason called Klondike Exterminators and Paige called Barry's secretary for a Monday afternoon appointment. At the general store, Otis Brown, an angular man with a circle of gray fuzz outlining his skull, recognized them immediately.

"Kinda late in the season for you folks, ain't it?" he said unsticking one of the grocery carts, then wheeling it to Paige.

"Well, not really," she said. "We're staying the winter, we thought it'd be nice to have the baby here." God, she was grinning stupidly like a schoolgirl, and she couldn't stop.

But Otis ignored it. "Don't suppose you'd be in the market for one of them midwives, Miz Bennett? Because if you are, the wife's real crackerjack at it—delivered a lot of little ones in the past years ... each one healthier than the one before. Now if ya'd like, I'll ask—"

"Thanks just the same," Jason interrupted finally. "She'll be going to the Poughkeepsie Medical Center."

He pressed his lips together, nodding. "A good hospital for sickness, but for givin' birth I'm not so sure. It's quite a ways from here."

"A twenty-minute drive," Jason said.

"Well, sure, going at top speed in good weather. I don't know 'bout the snow season though."

"They do plow up here, don't they?" Jason said, his voice a mixture of concern and irritation.

"Why sure they do."

"Then what's the problem?"

"Come on, Jason," Paige said pulling him aside. "Help me get the order." Once up the first aisle, she said, "You looked like you were about to bop him, what's wrong with you?"

"Nothing. I was just trying to make some sense out of the conversation. For all we knew, they might not have snowplows up here."

"I wish you'd relax, Jason. The old man was simply trying to drum up business for his wife."

At the car dealer Paige took an immediate liking to a sporty, two-seater, Mazda RX7, but Jason insisted on the Nissan Pathfinder.

"Is this the same man who said that I would pick the car?"

"That was before I thought about snow. This is a four-wheeler, it'll be perfect."

Paige examined the Nissan, frowning. "I don't know, it's so big and klutzy."

From behind, Jason reached around her, then

nuzzled his face into her hair so that his lips tickled her neckline. "So are you, honey," he whispered. "Do I love you less?"

Now doubly annoyed, she pulled away from him, biting back any urge to laugh away his teasing.

"Sorry, I just couldn't resist that. Paige, what about the name Robert? I know I've brought it up before but—"

"I told you I hate it." She folded her arms smugly at her chest and avoided eye contact. "And you're not sorry."

"I don't get it—how can you hate a simple name like Robert?"

No answer.

"Paige, come on, why so sensitive? Look, if I upset you, I swear to God, I'm sorry. Moreover, I think, pregnant or not, you look sensational." He looked down at his watch, then: "Look, if we don't get home soon, we'll miss the exterminator. If he leaves, I doubt we'll get him back before Monday. Who knows, maybe Tuesday. Will you please take the lousy four-wheeler?"

She looked at one car, then the other, and finally at Jason. "And if I won't?"

A deep sigh, then: "Why are you putting me through this?"

Jason followed Paige home to make sure she had no trouble handling the Pathfinder. "Well, what do you think?" he asked opening the door and helping her out.

She tilted both thumbs down. "So where's that exterminator?"

"Any minute, he promised me two o'clock. Want to take a walk?"

"And risk missing him?"

Clyde, the exterminator, looked to be no more than nineteen but handled himself like he'd been doing the work for years. It took him fifteen minutes to check through the house—when he came back to the kitchen, he shook his head.

"Found a couple of mouse droppings in the basement."

"Oh great," she said.

He dug a dirt-stained finger into long, scruffy hair and scratched his head.

"I put down packets of poison, the mice oughta be gone within a week. You see any after that, you let me know."

"What about the squirrel?"

He shrugged narrow shoulders. "None."

"I mentioned the acorns."

"Yeah, well, I can't explain that. I can only say what I found, or in this case, didn't find."

"Okay, maybe it wasn't a squirrel. But there was definitely something in that attic, I heard it."

"I checked up there thoroughly, ma'am. Now if there was any kind of animal, I woulda seen a dropping of some kind. All I can say is there wasn't any."

"Are you saying I imagined it?"

He put up his palms—fingers spread—and shook his head. "Hey, listen, I'm just saying, there's no sign—"

"Look," Jason interrupted, "since you're already here, why not put some poison in the attic. That way if there's anything—"

"Oh, no, I couldn't do that, sir."

"Why not?"

"Ya see, we're not allowed to kill squirrels."

"But you said, there is no squirrel."

"Sure, and I'll stick by that. But you want me to put something up there to kill a thing I'm not allowed to kill."

Paige tilted her head back, shaking it.

"I cannot believe this conversation," she said.

Jason raised his hand, quieting her.

"Look, let's take it slower, Clyde. Now, suppose, just suppose there were a squirrel up there?"

Clyde nodded.

"Are you saying I'd have to live with it?"

"No, sir, I'm not telling you that."

"Okay, then what do we do to get rid of it?"

"We set a trap and catch it. Then I take it and let it loose out in the woods."

Jason continued to tread gently. "Okay. Have we got one of those traps?"

"Sure, out in the truck. But you don't need it, you don't have a squirrel."

"Look Clyde, what I want is for you to set up one of those traps. Now if there's a squirrel, we'll catch it. On the other hand, if there's none, what have we lost?"

"Well, for one thing, money. It'll cost you plenty."

"Clyde, look, I pay you to do it, you do it."

It took Clyde about ten minutes to set up the wire cage—peanut butter on squares of Italian bread served as bait.

"When the animal smells the peanut butter," Clyde explained, "he goes inside. Then he has no choice but to step on this lever which activates the door hinge. And pow—the door slams shut!"

The edge of Clyde's hand slammed hard onto the tabletop, startling Paige. "That's all there is to it," he said. "He's trapped. That's when you call me. But I don't expect you'll be calling me. I figure, in a few weeks, maybe a month or two, I'll stop by to pick up the cage."

Between the mice and the squirrel cage, the bill came to a hundred seventy-five dollars.

"He's a crook," Paige said later, munching unsalted, unbuttered popcorn in bed.

Jason set down the legal brief he was reading and yawned.

"I suspect some of that was punitive damages. We did stomp around on his expertise."

"We city guys unquestionably have the art of the stomp. But I refuse to feel guilt, he asked for it. *You* believe I heard something upstairs, don't you, Jason?"

"There's a trap up there, isn't there?"

"You're avoiding my question."

"I don't see what difference—"

"Jason!"

"Of course I believe it."

She shot up from bed, tipping the bowl, the popcorn spilling over the sheet. "You don't. Damn you, I hate it when you say things just to shut me up!"

He heard her feet pound their way downstairs and out onto the porch. Sighing, he climbed into his jeans, grabbed her robe from the hook on the inside closet door, and followed her outdoors.

"Are you crazy—you'll catch cold," he said dropping the robe over her shoulders.

She shrugged it off, letting it fall to the porch floor. "Leave me alone," she said.

He leaned back against one of the railing poles, his hands stuffed in his pockets.

"I can't fucking win, can I?"

Silence.

"We come up here so you can mellow out and what happens—you're freaked by some kind of noise in the attic. And we can't be together for five minutes without you bitching at me. If I want to live with a manic-depressive, I can do it a hell of a lot easier in the city. I don't need the added hassle of commuting."

It was the commuting part that tickled her, so much so that laughter burst from her, catching her by surprise. And that followed with more laughter and Jason joining in.

"I do hate that car . . . truck, whatever it is," she said when she was finally able to speak.

He wrapped his arms around her, and she didn't wiggle away like she had found herself doing lately. . . .

"How about I use it till it snows. You use the Volvo."

She rested her head against his chest. She'd never before given much thought to the car she drove; her criterion was, simply, as long as it gets where she wants it to go. Then why this to-do about nothing? "It doesn't really matter," she said finally.

"You're sure?"

She nodded and when he looked down, there were tears on her cheeks. He cupped her chin, tilting it, forcing her to look at him.

"Damnit, Paige, tell me."

She took a deep breath. "I'm scared, Jason."

"Of what?"

"Of losing the baby."

"But you're not going to." He leaned down and kissed her.

She returned his kiss, but as soon as his hand dropped low, his fingers exploring, she pulled away.

"No, don't, Jason, please."

"Why?"

"The baby, it could hurt the fetus."

"But the doctor assured us—"

"Jason, I'm fat, I'm clumsy."

"You're neither, but you know that, too, don't you?" He began to walk inside.

"Look, if you really want to . . ."

He opened the screen door, stopped, and looked back. "Do I look that desperate?"

The fear was illogical . . . she thought about it later lying awake in bed. Though she had gone through a miscarriage the year before, it occurred in the fetus's most vulnerable stage, the first three months. Now she was at the end of her sixth month, and according to her amniocentesis and sonogram, was having absolutely no difficulty carrying what looked to be a healthy, well-developed fetus.

Not comfort enough—she and Jason were now living in a town that aside for an occasional fist-fight, drunk driving, or petty theft, hadn't had a crime in twelve years. But despite Jason's assurance and her common sense, the fear was there: like a dark spot that no matter how many times rubbed away, kept returning. The trick, she decided, was not to allow herself to dwell—

Her thoughts were interrupted by a faint rustling from above. She sat up, looked at Jason: sound asleep. No, she wouldn't wake him, not for this. By morning, the thing—whatever it was—would be trapped.

Pow . . .

Chapter Two

Up half the night, Paige didn't hear Jason dress and leave the house Sunday morning. But when she woke at nine, she found a note lying on his pillow: *Eight, go back to sleep—went for a run, then for newspaper and bagels.* The bagel shop was in Kingston—so she figured he'd be at least another half hour.

She rolled onto her back, then sat up immediately as she remembered the noise from the attic. Maybe she'd go upstairs, take a look herself—no, better wait for Jason. If there *was* something in the trap, better not to approach it alone. Instead, she headed for the toilet, concentrating on how nice it would be when someday she wouldn't have to urinate at every ill-timed juncture. My God, last night at least five times. So okay, surely a nuisance, but still reassurance that the baby was alive and well . . . busy doing aerobics on her bladder.

So see, Paige—the baby is fine, will continue to be fine . . . both you and Jason will see to it. That stupid smile again at her lips and she leaned

25

toward the vanity mirror over the bathroom sink. Her face had lately gotten fuller, slightly distorting features once described as graceful in her high school yearbook. And those dark eyes were now tarnished by deep underlying circles.

If she had a little girl, would she look like Paige? Not necessarily ... she hadn't looked at all like her mother. Instead, she pictured a baby boy with Jason's thin lips and wide jaw. Though the baby's sex had already been determined via tests, she and Jason had decided to wait out the information. Which of course meant they'd have to agree on two names, when so far they couldn't agree on one.

"You up, Paige?"

She rushed downstairs—more aware than usual of her graceless sprint. She went into his arms.

"Whoa," he said, nearly dropping the papers and bags he was carrying. "What'd I do?"

"You're up for the 'patience' award. How do you put up with my moods these days?"

He led the way to the kitchen and while she sat at the table watching, he began to put together breakfast.

"Pregnant women have a reputation for muddled emotions," he said. "Up, down, all over the place. When my mother was pregnant with me, she cried every morning when my father left for work. She was scared she wouldn't be able to handle the other kids while he was gone."

"Well, pregnant with two still in diapers, it's no wonder."

"But she managed, at least until he got home." Jason put a half grapefruit, a glass of low fat milk, and toasted bagel with a thin layer of cream cheese in front of Paige.

"Here, eat."

She looked at him as he began on his own breakfast. "Did you ever want to be a mother?"

"Funny."

"I'm not kidding, you're just so damn good at it."

"So will you be."

"I'm good with the children at work, but I don't suppose that's the same, is it?"

"Eat your grapefruit."

"I just don't know how to properly fuss and bother over children. Maybe I'm too selfish . . . Jason, you think I'm too selfish to be a good mother?"

"No I don't." He took the business section of the *New York Times* for himself and passed her a thin weekly. "Here, thought you might be interested in seeing some local stuff."

She took the paper, opened it to the second page, scanned the articles.

"What is this, trying to keep my news low-keyed? Church bazaars, street repairs, cub scout merit badges, school lunch menus?"

"You're out of the city, away from the crime. What's the point reading about it?"

"What about the book review, travel—"

He gathered up several sections of the *Times*, put them in front of her, then picked up his bagel.

"Oh, I almost forgot—the trap, Jason. I heard noises coming from there again last night . . ."

Jason looked at the bagel in his hand. "Could this maybe wait?" Then seeing the anxiousness on her face, he put it down and pushed back his chair. "Okay, let's get this over with."

She followed him to the attic, dropping behind as they reached the threshold.

"See anything?"

"Uh-uh. Empty."

She pushed ahead into the airless room: only two miniwindows available for ventilation, both closed. She sidestepped the clutter—old furniture and tools left behind by the former owners—moved closer to the cage, then brought her palm to her chest.

"Oh, shit."

He leaned in closer. "What?"

"The bait, Jason . . . where did it go?"

According to Clyde, who came out immediately after Jason's call from the phone booth outside Otis's market: "No way a squirrel coulda got to that bait without first steppin' on the lever."

"Has it occurred to you, the trap might be defective?" Jason said as they stood looking over the cage.

"Sure, but it's not. Here, I'll show you." He stuck the tip of a pencil on the lever and whisked his hand out before the door slammed, swallowing the pencil and snapping shut.

"Then what?" Jason asked.

"Has any other person maybe been up here, foolin' around with this cage?"

Jason's eyes followed Paige's eyes to the heavy door leading to a wrought-iron fire escape.

"Don't even think it," he said, going over to it. "There's no way. Look, it's bolted from inside." He tried to slide the thick, rusty bolt aside but couldn't budge it. "And it's stuck, as well. In fact, one of these days, I ought to replace the lock . . ."

"This is silly," Paige said to Clyde. "An animal took the bait. I hardly think an intruder would bother."

"Yeah, but—"

"But the trap didn't work," Jason interrupted. "Or alternatively, we have a super smart animal here."

Paige looked at him.

He shrugged, then began to check along the wall and molding for openings to the outside.

"Well, apparently it's figured out how to bypass the lever."

Before Paige left the attic, she also did some quick investigating of her own—in a flowerpot she discovered a half dozen more acorns. Another peanut butter bread chunk was set out, and Clyde stuffed industrial strength steel wool into the wires along the sides of the cage.

This time, no detours.

It was nearly nine o'clock when Paige got up Monday, another note beside her: *Phone company will hook up service. Checked trap—still empty, will look again tonight. How about Richard . . . Richie for short. What do you think?*

The empty trap was no surprise: since she hadn't slept well the night before, she had purposely listened for noises, but there had been none. It reminded her of a movie she had seen once on television: a rat so intelligent it actually frustrated the homeowner's attempts to exterminate it. And of course that recollection led her brain to flit around to other equally outrageous scenarios . . . Not fifteen minutes after the phone was in service, Paige was going on about it to Brooke.

"Doesn't sound like you're getting all the tranquility you bargained for," Brooke said.

"Oh, I will. First priority is getting rid of that high-level rodent. It's glorious here though, really, wait'll you see the fall landscape. When're you and Gary coming up?"

"Last we spoke, it was weekend after next."

"Do I catch something dark here?"

"I haven't talked to him in two days."

"Dare I ask, why?"

"The tickets to *Phantom* . . ."

"Oh right, you went Saturday. How did you like it?"

"Loved it passionately. Of course, Gary didn't arrive till intermission. Third time late in two weeks."

"He is a doctor."

"So the man keeps telling me . . . Should I bring my easel when I come?"

"Absolutely," Paige said, immediately falling in with the change of subject. "Hey, how about you send Gary back alone Sunday night. Stay a few extra days, just you and me—then drive back to the city with Jason whenever you're in the mood. You'll be able to paint to your heart's content . . . I won't come near you." Paige respected Brooke's strict ten to three o'clock work schedule, and since taking leave from her own job with the city schools, had gone out of her way not to violate it.

"Oooooo," Brooke now purred and Paige could picture the heavy red-lipped pout that drew in the attention of every man who saw it—that is, with occasionally the exception of Gary.

It even drew Paige's attention when she—rushing to hail a taxi—crashed into Brooke that bleak rainy day Brooke moved into the next building. As a result, painting and artist landed facedown in the mud. And though Paige tried to salvage the canvas while her new, teary neighbor showered in her bathroom, the piece was ruined. But despite their abrupt beginning they became steady friends.

"Sounds wonderful," Brooke said finally, "but I've got a commission to do—a portrait that needs to be finished in three weeks. Rain check?"

"I could arrange it."

As Paige put down the phone, she smiled in anticipation of the visit. That damn squirrel had better be gone by then. It wasn't until she was securing the Nissan Pathfinder's safety belt across her lap, getting ready to head to her four o'clock doctor's appointment, that she saw it—or at least she saw something. It moved quickly—like a streak or shadow, the kind of thing the mind catches when the eye blinks.

She continued to stare at the same spot, now only a patch of dry grass leading from the house, and the base of the fire escape to the woods. She looked to the second-floor wrought-iron balcony outside their locked bedroom window, then directed her attention to the third-floor attic: the door was bolted from inside. Permanently bolted by default . . . she had seen it herself.

It must have been the squirrel. Of course. It mounts the fire escape, then crawls through some inconspicuous hole, inside. She and Jason would check for openings again tonight.

Dr. Milton Barry wore flimsy, horn-rimmed glasses, the kind of frames usually found on second-pair-free racks. His shiny, baggy brown trousers under a short wrinkled lab coat reflected the same total disregard for fashion.

The examination over and Paige back in street clothes, she took a chair in his office. He handed her a Lamaze schedule—she looked it over, then folded it into her purse. A pink slip pulled loose from the back.

"What's this about?"

"Some kind of social event, I think. My nurse, Lenore—she's the one who handles the class— has a couple of women from each new group organize a family social, there's usually something every few months. You'll find the people up here friendly."

She smiled. "Good. Oh, and before you begin, I ask that you not reveal the baby's sex. Jason and I want to wait."

"Got it. Well, the baby is doing fine, you listened to the heartbeat yourself."

She nodded.

"And as for you ... well your pressure is definitely higher than I want it to be. You look like you could use more sleep."

"That's why I'm in the country."

"So?"

She shrugged. "Give me time."

"Okay, but if you want to talk to someone about it . . . Sometimes it helps."

"There is no 'it,' not really. I'm just one of those worriers."

"Yeah, about what?"

"What do pregnant women worry about?"

"Uh-uh, my question."

She paused, then: "Is the baby healthy?"

"I already told you it is."

"But things can happen, you're not God."

"You want God to deliver this baby?"

"Is he on staff?"

He smiled, and she approved of it . . . and him.

"Look I don't mean to kvetch," she said finally. "It's just that—Did you ever look forward to something so much you figured it must carry a jinx along with it? Just because it's far too good a thing to happen to anyone, let alone you."

"You feel the baby's jinxed?"

"It or me. You read my file—I miscarried once and a few months ago I was assaulted by a kid, stoned and holding a knife to me. The baby could have been killed."

"It wasn't."

"But it could have been. Everything is hung in such delicate balance. How do you know—"

"You don't. Surely you knew that before the assault."

"Yes, well, of course." She laughed, sighed. "I must sound like a simpleton."

He shook his head, his hand rested at his chin.

"Basic stuff, but we tend not to pay much attention, at least not until something's at stake."

"My marriage is at stake." Out of nowhere, the statement had come, and not even in proper context. His hand waved back, encouraging her to go on.

"I was referring to our sex life," she said, deciding at this point, she might as well say it. "I don't have the same desire these days. I'm not quite sure why. Other than my being so afraid. For the baby, and I guess in some odd way, for myself. Whenever I feel the touching is about to go further, I back off."

"The assault, did the kid try—"

"No, nothing like that. In fact, he didn't have much opportunity to do anything. I just looked at him and freaked ... punched, kicked like a madwoman, ran, I barely remember it. So why now should I be so turned off? Normally—" she stopped with a smile.

"Actually I could name a number of reasons for your sudden disinterest, the most likely one being, pregnancy. While most women have no problem enjoying intercourse throughout the gestation period, others—for various reasons— find it distasteful. To some, the pregnant body is just not sexy, in fact, one woman told me that the sex act would violate the purity of the fetus's incubator."

"I can't imagine any such hogwash going on in my subconscious, but ... Do you think I need a therapist?"

"Well, maybe I'd suggest it if you weren't only a few months from delivery. It seems to me," he said, a smile touching his lips, "I mean, particularly where we're dealing with a healthy libido— this should all straighten out quite nicely by itself."

By the time she got out of the doctor's office,

it was rainy and dismal, and her cheeks had yet to cool off. *Oh, what a big mouth have I.* Whatever possessed her to tell him about their sexual problems?

She stopped at the market on her way home, picked up a Jackie Collins paperback along with a box of sugared donut holes, a pound bag of Hershey Kisses, and a cylinder of Pringles.

Jason wouldn't be there to scrutinize her diet and so what if she and the baby felt like being bad.

The broom is alive, damnit it is! A long, thick-handled body and a fat yellow face kissing the floorboards. "Stop that noise, get up and stand on your butt," she shouted, but it wouldn't, couldn't cease sweeping. Nothing to worry about, or was it? This is silly, Paige . . . silly, dumb, maybe even a dream. She generated massive power to her brain, pushing it to snap awake, but not a budge.

She leaned over, tried to grab the broom handle, to put a stop to the nonsense, but the straw face turned into his ugly face, and his hot tongue whisked to her ankles, licking them, burning them. She wanted to scream, but her voice lodged somewhere deep in her throat. She was being swept backward, further and further . . . swaying, stumbling over her feet. Oh, God—watch out for the baby, don't let me fall!

Her hands spread protectively across her stomach, her eyes strained to penetrate the total blackness. But she didn't move—she concentrated on the sweeping noises coming from above . . . from the attic. Her heart hammering, she sat up, fumbled to find the lamp, and turned it on.

She looked around her: a couple of foil candy wrappers on the mattress, the potato chips container and paperback on the bedside table, the clock . . . Only six-thirty—Jason wouldn't be home for a while.

Finally, she raised her eyes, her stare reaching the ceiling. Something was up there . . . would she stay here and wait, not knowing what? Or would she march upstairs like a reasonable adult, open the door, and look inside. If she then felt threatened . . . well the phone was working, she could always call Clyde.

Armed with flashlight, she climbed the stairs, stopped at the landing, and biting down her bottom lip, flung the door open. Though the light was aimed on the trap, she couldn't see in . . . She took several steps, moving closer to it: empty . . . again, the bait was gone. She swung around, her unsteady hands bouncing the bright beam across the room and into the corners. Nothing . . . And the strange sweeping noise—could it be possible, it was gone too?

Slowly, hesitantly, she examined the room further. As the light hit the table near the inside wall, she heard movement. Startled, she backed up, temporarily losing her balance. Steadying herself, she circled the flashlight frantically to zero in on the noise. Suddenly something large sprang from beneath the table, went flying through the air, then landed with a thud. It hopped up, sprinted across the room. Though Paige tried to follow the rapid movement with her light, she couldn't, not until she saw the thing pause at the tiny screenless window, throw it open as wide as it would go, then disappear out of it. Paige ran to the window and leaning out, directed the beam of light down.

By that time, the thing was halfway down the fire escape, and she was certain it was a child.

She took just enough time to jam the cylinder of chips into her yellow slicker jacket pocket, then carrying the flashlight, headed into the darkness. Though the rain had settled to a thin drizzle, the wind had risen, sticking soggy leaves at her ankles, and when she forgot to duck, slapping vines at her face. She had no idea where she should go, but on impulse, started toward the river.

Paige thought she had spotted the child twice, but like an animal having the definite edge in its own habitat, within moments it darted behind a tree or bush and was again gone. The more reasonable thing would be to go back, telephone the police, let them come out and search. Deciding to do just that, she turned quickly toward the house, then felt something hard whip across her scalp. She sank . . .

"Paige, Paige, hear me, Paige?" Each word got closer and louder, taking her quickly back to the wet floor of the woods. She opened her eyes and saw Jason bending over her holding a lantern.

"Are you okay, what happened?" he asked.

"I don't know." She put her hand to the side of her head and felt a lump the size of a chestnut. "I guess I got hit." She gestured to the tree beside her. "I think a branch."

"What're you doing out here?" She sat up, but he tried to stop her. "Wait, maybe I ought to—"

"No, I'm okay, really. Here, help me up." She

leaned on his arm, paused a moment, then stood up taking her flashlight with her. "Jason, there's a kid out here."

"What kid?"

"I don't know, the one from the attic."

He looked at her oddly. "Maybe you ought to see a doctor."

"I don't need . . ." She dug a hand in her pocket, then, coming up empty, shined the light along the ground where she'd been lying. "The Pringles are missing, Jason."

"You're making no sense."

"I am, you're just not following me. Potato chips. I took them along because with them, I thought I'd have a better chance of getting him to come to me."

"There's really a kid?"

"That's what I've been trying to tell you."

"If there is, why didn't he at least stop and help you?" But not waiting for an answer, he put his arm firmly around her shoulders, directing her toward the house. "Come on, you're drenched, full of mud, let's get you back."

"But what about—"

"We'll call the police."

Jason first called the Briarwood Police Department, which consisted of the sheriff and one deputy. Then to Paige: "Honey, I think that lump ought to be looked at by a doctor. Why don't we hop in the car, take a ride down to the—"

"I told you, I'm fine, I'm not going anywhere. With the exception maybe of the shower."

"You still haven't explained, what were you doing out there to begin with?"

"I saw the child run from the attic."

"So that was a reason to go out at night in this weather?"

"What did you want me to do, ignore that I saw something?"

"No, I'd just like you to consider your own well-being first. You could have telephoned for help."

"I didn't think I needed it."

"Great. And you're the one so worried about this baby?"

"What does that mean?"

"I'm just pointing out how dumb it was to go out in the woods at night in this fucking miserable weather. You could have gotten sick, injured yourself seriously, even been attacked by an animal . . . Not to mention how you scared the shit out of me: I come home, my ass dragging, to find the house lit up like a night-time doubleheader at Yankee Stadium, the doors unlocked, the bed filled with caloric crap, and my pregnant wife nowhere to be found. What am I supposed to think?"

"Okay, which is it?"

"Pardon?"

"Which sin would you have me serve penance for—playing in the rain, wasting energy, or eating junk food? Who knows, maybe they're all interconnected. Look, I'm heading to the shower. When the sheriff comes, call me. I think I should go with him."

"Why?"

"I don't know, maybe I can help. Jason, it's a little child out there alone."

"Boy or girl?"

"I couldn't tell, does it matter?"

"No, just curious. It's hard to believe a kid was stowed away in our attic, and we had not an inkling. So much for squirrels, I guess." Not waiting for a reply, he shook his head, then raising his hand in a compromise: "Look, Paige, I'm going to give your obstetrician a call. Let him decide if you ought to be checked."

She took a deep sigh. "All right, if you want. But tell him I feel fine . . . no pain, no dizziness, no sleepiness, no nausea."

Dr. Barry announced a split decision—though he didn't think it necessary that Paige see him, she was to call immediately if anything out of the ordinary occurred, particularly any sign of discomfort or staining. In any event, it would certainly be wise for Paige to take to bed for the remainder of the evening.

But there was no need to battle the issue further—by the time Paige stepped out of the shower, she was already in doubt—*was* it possible the baby had been injured in the fall? She hadn't fallen very hard—the leaves had cushioned her, and the injury to her head, though definitely the result of something hard hitting it, was minor. . . .

The real question was how it had happened. A low-hanging tree branch swinging into her? No, she strongly doubted it was that. Could the kid have hit her? What kind of a kid—*A silly question, Paige—a frightened kid, that's what kind.*

But still, a little shiver skipped along her

neckline. If the child would attack her once, would he again? The second attack within months, though one could hardly compare this episode with the other: This time she was the one pursuing, and the child was the one running, trying to escape a strange adult. Wouldn't she as a child have done the same herself? Still, for now, she was agreeable to letting Jason fetch her pajamas, brush off and smooth out the bedsheet and cover, and prepare her a steaming bowl of chicken vegetable soup.

Sheriff Buldoon did show, but without his deputy. After hearing how Paige had seen the child escape the attic, he spent the better part of the evening searching the property, then at about eleven-thirty, rang the front bell. Jason went for it, insisting Paige stay put.

"Well?" she said when Jason got back.

"He went over the whole area, all the way down to the river and back, but didn't spot a thing. He figures the kid must have been scared off, gone elsewhere."

"But who is it?"

"He has no clue."

"I don't understand—how can a young child be missing and the police not even be aware of it? I mean, if we were in the city, okay sure . . . But out here?"

He shrugged, turned off the lamp, got into bed, pulling the covers over both of them.

"Thought at all about the name Richard?" he asked.

"Yes, I don't like it."

"Why?"

"I don't know, somebody I didn't like. I think

Richie, no, Rich. But I can't recall who he was, or for that matter, how I knew him. Watch now, it'll drive me crazy trying to remember."

Several times during the night, Paige got up, went to the window, and peered out into the blackness. Not that she expected to see anything ... or hear anything. Certainly no more scratching or sweeping ... The child was out there somewhere, likely cold, hungry, and scared silly, not apt to find even close to the shelter of a warm attic.

She also thought about the name Rich. ... She could remember two guys named Richard from high school, neither of whom she knew well. And the bagger at the grocers in the city. No one, though, who would trigger such a bad feeling ...

Chapter Three

Finding the bakery bag empty, Paige settled for bran buds and milk. As she ate, she looked out the kitchen window, again thinking about the night before and again astonished that a child had actually been hiding out in their attic. Deliberately picking discomfort, solitude, dust, and spiderwebs over whatever it was he or she had left behind. How long had the youngster been there, and now that Paige had pretty much scared him away, where would he go? Though the sheriff hadn't been able to find him, Paige was willing to bet that he was still in the area.

Well, at least the rain had stopped, and though it was chilly, the sun would provide some warmth. . . . By late afternoon, according to last night's weather report, the temperature would dip. . . . There were three bagels left in the bag yesterday, she had noticed when she'd straightened up the kitchen before leaving for her doctor's appointment. Could Jason have eaten all of them?

She went to the back door, tried the knob—

locked. Not that a locked door was proof of anything: this youngster seemed to know the ins
and outs around here better than she or Jason.
Paige walked through the house searching: attic,
basement, closets, cupboards, crannies, even
under beds. . . . Satisfied no one was hiding inside, she went around again, this time locking
doors and windows.

Finally she fished the thermal bag from the
army chest in one of the upstairs bedrooms and
took it to the kitchen. *Well, Paige, what do you
say to a solo barbecue in October? Dress warm and
take along a book.* She paused a moment, remembering the lump on her head, then went to the
hall closet and took out her tennis racket. A little
protection wouldn't be such a bad idea.

She waited until one o'clock, then headed out,
setting up station at a weeping willow about
forty yards from the river, just about where the
trees and bush cleared way for the sun. And
though she was a middling to dreadful cook—
Jason was far better at it than she—she'd taken
pains to fix potato salad. Now, the coals white-
hot on the little fold-up grill she brought along,
Paige plunked two franks on the grate.

She pushed her shades up on her nose, lay
back on the blanket, opened her paperback . . .

Startled because she'd heard not even the
faintest rustle of leaves—there had been only a
shift in the sun disturbing the shadow on the
page of the book. She turned in time to see the
bare right hand scoop, first one frankfurter, then
another off the fire.

"Watch it!" Paige shouted getting to her feet.

She leapt back into the woods and though Paige instinctively began to chase her, she stopped abruptly: it would only scare her more. Standing at one of the trees, Paige listened: silence. The girl—tall, skinny, looked to be about ten, eleven—had stopped somewhere, and surely she would be listening, too.

"My name is Paige," she said finally. "Paige Bennett. And I didn't mean to scare you. You took me by surprise, I was worried you'd burn yourself on the grill." A pause, then, "Did you?"

She waited: nothing.

"The hot dogs were for you anyway, at least one of them was. But if you want both, not a problem. I imagine you get pretty hungry living out here."

More silence. Paige waited, then beginning to feel a little spooked, walked back to the blanket and sat. Her throat was dry—she cleared it as one of her hands reached out and closed firmly around the handle of the tennis racket.

"Actually what I had in mind was a picnic, ever go on one? I thought it'd be a good way to get to know one another, you know, lots of chow and girl talk." She let go of the racket and lifted the thermal bag and began to unzip it. "Let's see, I brought potato salad, cold root beer, fruit, and about a dozen peanut butter cracker sandwiches."

A long pause, then: "So you think I'm pushy, huh? I suppose I should blame that on desperation. You see, I'm kind of new around here, haven't any friends—that is, except for Jason. He's my husband and he goes off to the city most days, leaving me alone. Besides, what I really had in mind was a girlfriend, I haven't any of those."

Paige sighed. "Now you must be thinking, 'Oh gosh, what a jabberjaw!' Right?"

She sat silently for nearly fifteen minutes. Finally she stood up and emptied the grill, extinguishing live embers with dirt and the heels of her sneakers.

"I wish you would trust me a little," Paige said folding the blanket, then hooking the handles of the thermal bag over one arm. "Sure, I'm a stranger so maybe it's a lot to ask so soon ... But if you'd come out of hiding and talk to me, I promise not to push you to do anything you don't want to do."

Still nothing. "Well, I guess I'll leave now, go back to the house ... but if you should change your mind, want to talk, whatever, you know where to find me. I mean, just come on over anytime. Knock on the door, ring the bell ..."

Her arms full, Paige turned toward the house, and had only gotten a dozen steps when from behind she felt a tug at the food bag, then two strong arms tangling about her ankles.... She tripped—the grill, blanket, racket, and bag scattering as her arms sprang forward to find leverage. Her hands butted a tree, halting the fall.

She turned in time to see the girl snatch the bag from the ground. Without thinking, Paige leaned forward, grabbed the bag, and yanked it away, then sent it sailing into the woods. She grasped the girl's arm, dragging her toward her: dark blue eyes stared up at her, so dark, they startled Paige and she nearly released her.

But instead she hung on and stared back, examining the child's face—her fine features screwed-up so tightly they seemed ready to burst. And the dirt. She had never seen so much dirt, even embedded in the child's arched eyebrows and in her long hair that was pulled back, encircled in elastic, and hanging in a snarled clump down her back.

"Damnit," Paige said. "Why'd you do that, I could have fallen. I would have given you the food had you asked!"

Silence, staring.

"Say something."

The child pulled away, kicked wildly—her torn sneaker twice smacking Paige's leg—but Paige dodged the blows and punches, got behind the girl and using all her strength clasped both her hands tightly over the girl's smaller hands. Then leaving the picnic supplies where they'd fallen, Paige, continuing to use maximum pressure so as not to let her get away, headed toward the house.

Fifteen minutes later, within twenty feet of the back door and out of breath, she stopped and looked at the girl.

"I've already gone back on my word, haven't I?"

No response.

"I said I wouldn't push you into anything, and here I am reeling you in like the day's catch. I couldn't possibly need a friend that badly, could I? Besides, you've won, I've had it. You're as strong as a wildcat, and I'm tired. Would you believe, exhausted? Well, if you get hungry, the food's where I tossed it. I'm sure you'll find it—

that is, if you refuse to come inside and eat at a table."

Paige released the little hands—the child stood there watching her as she turned and headed inside.

She wasn't kidding about being tired. Though she knew she had to tell the sheriff to come back, find the child, and take her into custody, what would a few more hours hurt? Paige climbed the stairs to the master bedroom, fell across the bed. She had to report it, what else could she do, continue to play cat and mouse while a frightened little girl ran around out there on her property?

Soon it would be cold, too cold, and unless she managed her way inside the house again . . . Besides, the girl had to belong somewhere, someone had to be looking for her. . . . *Relax, Paige, what's gotten into you anyway? Why so concerned when it's simply a matter of notifying the authorities?* Soon she'd be too busy looking after her own. . . . And if she knew anything at all about kids from teaching, it was, how difficult they could sometimes be. In fact, didn't she run away from home once herself? But she had been much younger, more likely she had wandered off . . . and as usual, Mother wasn't watching.

She must have been awake awhile, but her eyes were closed, her mind filtering disconnected snatches of thought, when suddenly she felt or heard something—she wasn't sure which—but her eyelids opened: the child was standing there, her back pressed against the bedroom wall, watching her. . . . How long had she been there? And the doors and windows were locked, so how did she get in? *Easy, easy, don't move too fast, say the wrong thing, talk too loud. Don't scare her.*

Quietly, slowly, she sat up in bed, drawing forward her legs and with more difficulty than she'd ever had before, crossing them into a lap in front of her.

"It's getting harder and harder for me to pull this off," she said, gesturing toward her extended belly. "The mysterious person rolled up inside here seems to be getting in the way."

Silence while Paige glanced at the clock, then back at the girl.

"I guess I *was* tired, I was resting nearly two hours. How long have you been here?"

Paige got up, went to the bathroom, urinated, washed her hands, came out. The child was still in the same spot. "I'm going downstairs to fix dinner," Paige said. "Want to come?" She didn't wait for an answer, just led the way, aware that her frightened visitor was following about ten seconds behind.

She went to the refrigerator, took out fresh vegetables, then at the sink, washed her hands again.

"Want to wash up?"

Instead the child ran over to her, snatched a raw carrot off the countertop. Paige caught her hand as she withdrew.

"Wait, the carrot's dirty, first let me scrape it." She uncoiled the tight fingers from around the vegetable and that's when she noticed the run of blisters on the girl's right thumb and across her palm.

Oh, shit, the grill . . .

*   *   *

After a good deal of urging, the girl allowed Paige to wash her hand, smear the burn with antibiotic ointment, then wrap it. Though she refused to be cleaned further, she barged into the bathroom, then sat on the toilet, watching Paige shower.

"When I was young," Paige spoke from behind the sliding glass doors, "way younger than you are now, I liked to watch my mother get ready for dates—shower, makeup, manicure, dress, the works. I hated that she left me alone, but I suppose I could understand her wanting to be glamorous, go to glamorous places. We were poor, the kind of poor that often registers your belly on empty and makes it hurt."

Paige stepped out of the shower, wrapped a towel around her body, and another around her head like a turban.

"Here I am confiding all these things about myself, and you haven't so much as told me your name. I'm not complaining . . ." She shrugged. "I bet you spotted that lie. Okay, so I am complaining some, just don't feel you need to listen."

Dinner was salad and pasta with store-bought spaghetti sauce. It was after six when the girl finished, lifted the plate and—Paige thought for pure effect—licked it clean, then at Paige's urging relented enough to run a damp napkin over her mouth and chin. Paige pulled her chair closer and leaned in toward the girl.

"The truth is, I must find out who you are. I mean, maybe *I* don't have to know, but the police do. You see, it would be wrong for me to simply do nothing. I'm sure there're people out there frantic, looking everywhere for you—your mom, dad?"

The child squeezed her eyes shut, then clapped her hands over her ears, refusing to listen. Paige waited a few minutes, then pried her hands away.

"Well, someone then, surely you belong to someone. Look, you're not to worry—sure, we'll need to locate your family, but that doesn't mean you'll be forced to go back to them. Not if there's good reason you shouldn't. There are laws designed to protect children, you'll be given choices. Please trust me." The child, now on the edge of her seat, watched as Paige stood and backed up toward the telephone on the kitchen wall. Would she run? Had it been foolish to warn her?

Maybe . . . but Paige had not been prepared for the attack when she lifted the telephone receiver. The child sprang from the chair, dived to the floor, wrapped her arms tightly around Paige's calves.

Paige dropped the receiver, sank to her knees, and tried to take control of the child's hands, which had now begun jetting in every direction and seemed multiplied by a hundred.

"Stop it! I said, stop it!"

The game plan finally exhausted, the girl let go.

"I can't keep you here, it's not that simple, there are laws and I need to follow them."

The girl's eyes filled and though Paige was never before trapped emotionally by a student's hurts or tears, this time she felt so tight a drawing on her chest, she could barely stand it. She reached out her arms, and the girl moved into them, burying her head in Paige's bosom, her head pressing deeper and deeper as though she were trying to crawl right inside. And mumbling words ... After several minutes Paige drew back, reached for a terrycloth towel, then using a corner of it, wiped the tears and dirt from the child's face.

"Now say it so I can understand."

"Finders Keepers," the girl said.

Finders keepers, losers weepers, Paige remembered the taunting little phrase from her own childhood. And it meant whatever a person might find was his for the keeping. She looked into the wide blue eyes, and her heart ached.

"Operator here, can I help you?—"

Paige sighed and looked at the phone receiver now swinging freely by the curled cord, then lifting it with her as she stood back up, replaced it in the cradle.

Paige questioned the girl, and though she was unresponsive to all else, she did admit to the name Lily. By the time Jason came home at nine, Paige had made up the spare bedroom next to theirs, given Lily a nightgown of hers to wear, and put her to bed. But it wasn't until he had finished dinner that she brought it up.

"There's something—"

"Hey, what do you say one of these weekends I buy a bunch of tomatoes, straight off the vine, some fresh garlic, and make a big pot of spaghetti sauce," he said. "It might be a good time when Brooke and Gary come—"

"Okay."

"Not that this stuff wasn't good, but—"

"Please, Jason, Francesco Rinaldi never stands on ceremony. Homemade sounds terrific. Now would you listen?"

"Sorry, go ahead."

"She's here, Jason. She came by herself. Of course, I went out into the woods this afternoon to find her, my plot was to take her back, but she fought me so, I finally—"

He put down his fork, raised his hands.

"Whoa, wait, slow down. Are we talking here about the kid from the attic?"

Paige nodded. "One and the same. Her name's Lily, she has the deepest blue eyes I've ever seen. And there's something about her, Jason, something so vulnerable."

He looked around, leaned his chair back, glanced into the living room, then back.

"Okay, I give up. Where is she?"

"Right now, sleeping in the spare room next to ours. I wanted you to meet her, but she could barely keep her eyes open. I figured you could meet her tomorrow."

He shook his head, as though to clear his brain.

"Let's back up here a little. How did this all happen?"

"Well, it's kind of complicated. You might say we've become fast friends."

"Where does she come from?"

"I don't know."

He took his napkin off his lap and tossed it on his plate. "These fast friendships apparently leave a thing or two to be desired. Well, what did the sheriff say?"

"Nothing."

"What, nothing?"

"Well, as I said, it's complicated. I get the feeling that if there is someone out there looking for her, she doesn't want to be found. It could be a case of abuse, in fact, I think it's likely."

Little lines creased his forehead, then smoothed away. "You didn't call the sheriff, did you?"

She shook her head.

He stood up, went to the phone, and began to lift the receiver; she followed after him, reached over his shoulder, pressing the receiver back in the cradle.

"Just hold it, will you? What will one lousy day hurt? Besides I haven't noticed any great concern on the sheriff's part, he might have checked back today to see if she showed up." Paige took his hand. "Come upstairs, I want you to see."

"What's there to see?"

"Please, just come."

She had left a night-light going so they saw immediately that the bed was empty.

"Great," he said, backing out.

"Wait, shhh," she said, her hands going to her lips. "Look." She pointed to the corner where she heard movement. Lily was rolled in a ball—that is, all but one thin leg that hung freely and swept the floor like a timing device.

They walked closer—Paige pulled the quilt off the bed and spread it over her. She had a flash of herself as a child sleeping on a floor. A tiny room and a very hard floor ... That's all she could remember.

"What's with the hand?" he whispered.

"She burnt herself."

"How?"

"A picnic. She took the hot dogs off the grill."

"With her hand?"

A sigh, then she nodded.

"Christ, she's filthy."

"Tomorrow."

"What—"

"Shhh." She took his arm and backed him out of the room.

"What about tomorrow?" he said once in the hallway.

"Nothing. Just that maybe she'll trust me enough to let me give her a bath."

"And if not?"

"I don't know, I guess she'll stay dirty another day."

"Is this therapy straight from the old college textbook—water phobics?"

"Hilarious, my nose is running from laughter." She went into their bedroom and Jason came after her.

"What's happening here, am I wrong or are you suggesting we keep this kid?"

"I'm not suggesting anything at all like that. But what's a couple of days—"

"Hold it, right there. Tomorrow, I call the sheriff, no ifs, ands, or buts. It's contributing to the delinquency of a minor to do otherwise, a misdemeanor."

She switched on the light in their bedroom and she led the way in.

"I have no problem with that, I've not lost my mind totally." She rested her hands on her stomach, in a protective gesture. "After all, we have our own little person to think about. But who knows, maybe they'll need someone to watch her temporarily while they try to locate her parents or guardian."

"That's what children's services are geared for. Why should our hard-earned tax dollars go for something never put to use?"

She turned away, took off her shirt and bra then rummaged through the bureau drawer till she came up with pajamas. He went up to her, nuzzling her bare shoulder, her neck.

"Come on, Paige, so you have a soft spot for the kid, no problem. But I don't want you forgetting how important it is that you take it easy, get your blood pressure to a safe level."

She nodded. "You're right, I know it. I was thinking earlier how difficult kids are, particularly at her age."

"And particularly ones that come from a fucked-up world, the kind of world that forces them to run away, steal food, break into houses, sleep on floors."

"You don't have to spell it out. I'm aware of what an emotionally disturbed child is."

"So okay, you've dealt with them at school, but only in a teaching capacity and only in a specialized environment, surrounded by a whole damned support system designed to keep the kid in his place. And best of all, you always got to leave when the bell rang.

"You don't need this aggravation, honey, especially not now when your condition's so precarious. Your first obligation is to our kid. Come on, let me talk to him." He stretched his arms around her, his hands gently caressing her stomach.

She could feel herself begin to loosen. "Stop with the *him*?" she said finally.

"Him, her, whatever. Get rid of these, will you?" He took the pajamas from her hand and tossed them on the floor, then turned her around, his hand barely touching her breast before he stopped.

"What's this?" he said.

She looked down to see a large purple mark on her breast. "Looks like a bruise."

"Did I do it?"

"No, of course not."

"Then how—"

"I don't know." Before he could say or do more, she reached down for her pajama top, put it on, then moved away. "I went to the doctor's yesterday. What with all the commotion last night, I didn't have time to tell you."

A pause, then he headed for the closet, one hand loosening his shirt and necktie.

"Yeah, I forgot it myself. Well, what did he say?"

"Everything's fine, my blood pressure's still a bit high. Jason, I asked him about our . . . my problem."

Jason yanked the tie and it whizzed free of his shirt collar; he draped it over a tie bar on the door, then turned and looked at her.

She extended her hands, palms up. "You know. My sudden disinterest in sex."

"You talked to him about *us*?"

"It was about me really, not you. According to him, it's not uncommon for pregnant women to go through this kind of thing. Not feeling especially sexy."

"So what does that mean?"

"Just that once I have the baby, things will likely go back to normal."

"I see. Well, if he says so . . ."

"What, don't you believe that?"

"I don't know what I believe these days, Paige. I just know you've been like this since that attack." He studied her a moment, then: "Paige, did that sleaze do more to you than what you've told me?"

"No, Jason! How could you think I'd lie about that?"

He shook his head. "Look, forget I even said it."

"Fuck, shit, piss, scum, asshole, bastard, bitch . . . Fuck, shit, piss, scum, asshole—" The young girl's sweet muffled voice came from beneath the covers, the words obviously meant for no one's ears but her own. Paige tiptoed quietly away from the door, no need for Lily to know she'd even heard.

She had just come from the toilet, second trip. In the interim, Jason had taken full custody of the bed. With great care she removed his arm, then his leg—he grunted amicably as she forced his limbs to remain on his side of the mattress—then climbed in beside him. As she lay back on her pillow, she felt pain sear through her breast.

Her breasts were supersensitive, that's how it was with pregnancy. It certainly wasn't Lily's fault that when she hugged Paige, her head pressed her hard enough to cause a bruise. But

judging by Jason's apprehension about Lily even
being here, she doubted he'd see it so simply.

But when you hit the bottom line, Jason was
right. Even on a short-term basis—which is certainly all Paige had thought about—Lily would
require time, patience, maybe more than she was
willing to give. Troubled youngsters could be
fiercely possessive, draining one's energy and
even then, sometimes you just couldn't get
through. . . . Certainly judging by her vocabulary, she was furious.

Chapter Four

Paige awoke to the aroma of eggs frying and by the time she'd returned from the bathroom, Lily was carefully placing a breakfast tray on her bedside table. She turned to Paige and held out her hands to show she had washed them.

Paige smiled, then looked over the food.

"Golly, I'm impressed with this spread. Who taught you to cook like this?"

Lily shrugged, picked up the fork, then pushing her to sit on the bed, handed it to her.

"These home fries look wonderful, smell it, too. I usually try to stay away from fatty—" The corners of Lily's mouth sank, and Paige took the fork from her hand. "Well, I don't suppose it'll hurt this once."

Lily backed herself up to the wall, then slid to the floor, ready to watch her.

"What about you, aren't you eating?"

"I did."

"Oh." Paige nodded, pleased to hear the child finally respond to her speaking. She took a bite, another bite, then remembered that Jason was calling the sheriff, probably had already called him. She looked at the clock, then at Lily. She'd have to tell her before the sheriff came, before . . . The phone rang.

Startled, Lily jumped to her feet, and Paige grabbed the receiver. "Hello."

"Paige, honey . . . me."

"ESP."

"What?"

"Nothing. Did you?"

"I did," Jason said. "The sheriff is checking his computer for kids reported missing in the area. In fact, he ought to be on his way to the house soon to talk to her."

"I doubt she will—"

"Will what?"

"You know . . . talk."

"She's there, listening?"

"You could say."

"Well, even if she refuses to cooperate, he can get down a description and take a photograph to send out on the wires. And would you believe that the county doesn't have a children's services?"

"Oh?"

"Well, what they do normally—not that this sort of thing is a normal occurrence—is find a temporary home for the kid. According to the sheriff, one of the town women will surely volunteer. If it goes too long, the state will—"

"If one of the townswomen will do it, why not me? It'll keep me busy, maybe stop me from worrying about the baby. And it'll keep me from being lonely."

A pause, a deep sigh, then: "I'm not nuts about

the idea, but you already know that. Look, Paige, if you want to do it so damned badly, then go ahead, do it. It looks like my only hope now is the sheriff will know where the kid belongs, in which case this entire conversation will be moot."

She put down the receiver. She had tried to be careful in what she said, knowing Lily was right there listening. But apparently she hadn't been careful enough: Lily ran to her, took her hand, pulled her to her feet, then in a frenzy, toward the doorway.

"Hey, wait, no, stop it," Paige said, but Lily ignored her. "What're you doing?" Paige managed to yank away finally, then cupping her hands firmly over the girl's shoulders, sat her down on the bed, forcing eye contact. "Listen to me, Lily, I want you to relax. I want you to take a deep breath . . . hear me, a nice deep breath."

Lily did it.

"That's a girl, now another . . ."

After a while Paige could see the calm begin to register through the girl's features. Could she possibly know the sheriff was coming to the house? Paige hadn't said anything that would have led her to believe that. . . . But still she had to tell her before—The phone rang again, and Lily jumped.

"It's all right, Lily."

Paige lifted the receiver, spoke into it . . . Someone looking for a Susan Lewis . . . She found herself relieved at it being a wrong number, she wasn't quite ready to let Lily go when they were just beginning to make progress.

*   *   *

It was strange—she hadn't known for certain she wanted the child to stay before she suggested it to Jason on the telephone. And true, he wasn't thrilled at the prospect. But for all his grumblings, when she stuck solid to what she wanted, he invariably backed off. This time she would stick solid. After all, what was so wrong with keeping the girl around awhile?

She'd like to have someone to do for, someone to keep her from being lonely and dwelling on her own silly ghosts. And she did have extensive training with children, likely more than any of the town's women. . . . Besides, what were a couple of days, a week at most? Surely, the police wire would pick up something immediately on a child that age.

Sheriff Frank Bulldoon was fiftyish, barrel-chested with a short thick neck that got lost somewhere in his brown suede jacket. Paige wondered if the Bull in his name stood for bull-frog, which was what he looked like.

He followed her to the living room, his eyes scanning the room.

"Where is she?"

"Upstairs. I wanted us to talk first."

"Well, your husband told me—"

"Sheriff, I'd like to keep her here. I mean, temporarily, until you find out where she belongs."

"That's not exactly what your husband explained to me this morning."

"Jason tends to worry about me, in this case, without much cause. With me being pregnant, he was afraid caring for the child would be too much of a strain."

"I'm inclined to go along with him. The little

girl's likely a runaway, they're usually a tough lot, sometimes too tough for the parents themselves to handle, which might account for her being on her own to start with. In any event, not really the type of kid a lady in a family way would want as a house guest."

"I'm a special education teacher, which means I teach children with learning disabilities, physical and emotional handicaps. More important, Lily and I have already begun to make friends."

"Lily, huh?" He took out a notebook and jotted it down. "Know her last name?"

"No, but if given more time, I believe she'll tell me. In fact, that's why I wanted to talk to you. I think it'd be better if you didn't try to fire questions at her just yet. She's frightened and when she's frightened, she pretty much loses it, acts out, whatever. One thing is for certain, she won't answer your questions."

"So you're suggesting *you* be the one to get information from her?"

"That's right. As soon as I know something, I will, of course, contact you."

"What about a description? I'll need that. And a picture of her would help."

"At this moment, she's a mess, I mean, filthy. I made a deal with her—I get you to go away and she gets into a hot soapy bathtub. Once she's washed and into clean clothes, I'm certain she'll have no objection to me taking a few pictures with my Polaroid. One of which I promise to drop off at your office later this afternoon."

He rubbed his chin with his hand, then nodded.

"Okay, looks like you're pretty much the expert on kids. If you think this way will work better, we'll try it. Get me her approximate height, weight, identifying marks, that kind of thing, too."

"Not a problem."

"I hope this sits well with the mister. I mean, from what he said on the telephone earlier . . . But he's your husband, I guess you're the one knows him best."

Paige let the sheriff out, then headed for the stairs. She tried to call Jason to give him an update, but according to his secretary, Pat, he was still out at lunch. She left a message for him to get back to her, then went to hunt up some bubble bath, she was sure she had some of that strawberry stuff tucked away in the linen closet.

Get ready, Lily, this could be fun.

It was the Bernstein file and he was certain he'd left it somewhere in the co-op—just where, he wasn't sure. Already annoyed at the prospect of the kid staying on longer, wading through the mess in the apartment—fruits of Paige's dubious housekeeping skills—didn't improve his spirits any.

He thumbed through the dozens of magazines and papers scattered on Paige's dresser, his dresser, then the bookcase in the den. It was the first time he had ever misplaced a file. What with the move, all the goings on this last week, more accurate to say, the last few miserable months . . . Damnit, it just didn't seem fair.

When they were first married, Paige wasn't ready for kids, and though he was, he understood her need for more time. Heck, she hadn't even begun college—let alone a career—until she was twenty-three, and had managed to save a few dollars to help her with her education.

Unlike Jason, Paige had had to scrape for everything as a kid; she'd never even owned a lousy bicycle. When the spectacular coed from his civil liberties class confided that to him on their first coffee date, he was shocked. In Springfield, Illinois, even the kid from the poorest neighborhoods had a bike. So though it might have been a bit excessive of him—giving a gift of a ten-speed trail bike on a second date—he would have done handsprings right along Fifth Avenue if it would have put one of those saucy, seductive smiles on the face that by then wouldn't leave his thoughts.

By the time Jason heard the noise at the apartment door, the knocking had turned to banging. Surprised, he ran to the door and opened it. Brooke was standing there, the handles of a wicker basket circling one arm. She wore stonewashed jeans, a black halter top beneath an opened white cotton shirt . . . her long straight blond hair reached the small of her back. She swept inside, putting the basket on the floor.

"Hey, what's this?"

"No greeting?"

"Of course." He smiled, leaned over, pecked her cheek, then: "How's it going, neighbor. How's Gary? How'd you know I was here?"

"Lots of hows . . . Actually I saw you pass from my window. I thought maybe you'd stop and visit. Then I was standing here knocking so long, I thought maybe you ducked out the back way."

"Don't you work these hours?"

"I do, but I don't like to be rigid, after all, there are such things as extenuating circumstances."

"Well, as you can see, Paige isn't with me. In fact, I just stopped by to pick up a file. Speaking of which, I haven't found it yet."

She sank down on the floor like a kid, grabbed his hands and gently tugged. "Come."

"What're you doing?"

"A picnic lunch for two." She gestured to the basket.

"You're kidding, right?"

"Would I kid you? Look here . . ." She opened the basket top and took out a small red-and-white checkered cloth, spread it on the carpet, then a box of chicken wings, two egg rolls, pork fried rice, sweet and sour sauce, hot mustard. . . .

"You know it's my favorite."

"Ah so. Tell me, do they have Chinese food up your way?"

"Not so you could tell."

She smiled, then brought out a wine bottle, along with two crystal glasses. "In that case, sit—"

"Wine, hey no, I don't think—I'll pass. Truth is, I do have to get back to the office."

A pout . . . "Must you be so boringly uptight?" She extended her arms behind her, leaning her weight on them. "What you need, my boy, is a little fire put in you."

A pause, then: "What I need is to find that file."

"Jason, it's only a lunch. Eat up, then I promise to help you find that file."

"You mean that? I'll hold you to it."

With her finger, she drew a cross on her chest. "Swear to God, hope to die . . . Now come on."

"Does this need to be on the floor? I mean, we've got a perfectly good table—"

"Jason, will you get down here!"

Jason slipped out of his suit jacket, loosened his tie, and rolled up his shirtsleeves. . . . "Okay, but only one glass of wine."

They ate, he talked, mostly about how roughgoing it had been these last months. And now in the country, how this kid strolled right in, about to disrupt their lives even more. After they had both downed their third glass of wine, Brooke ran her tongue over her lips, slipped off her shirt, and as though it were the most natural thing in the world to do, unhooked her halter top and tossed it aside.

It wasn't until Paige took her out of the tub and blew her hair dry that she really looked at her. Oh sure, she was a pretty little thing—you could tell that even with dirt caked on an inch thick—But once she was clean, her natural rosy-colored cheeks, lips, were startling against white skin . . . and her hair wasn't yellow but gold, the kind of pale gold that seldom lasts beyond age three . . .

"You smell good," Paige said as she hunted through drawers, looking for clothes that might come close to fitting Lily. She was tall, but Paige was far taller . . . and of course, she was looking in her pre-pregnant clothes for a one-size-fits-all waistband. That's when she thought of Jason's sweats. Though he was a couple of inches taller than Paige, his legs were shorter. And the sweatpants—if she remembered right—had ties at the waist and elastic at the ankles.

"What do you think?" Paige said later as Lily stood in front of a full-length mirror dressed in a mismatch: Jason's sweatpants, Paige's shirt. Lily looked at her reflection as though she hadn't seen it before or if she had, it wasn't something she remembered.

"Hmmm, too baggy to be chic, you say? I think I'm inclined to agree. So once we get a couple of pictures, I say we consider some serious clothes shopping."

She looked uncomfortable for the picture-taking, as though that, too, were a foreign experience. Paige put one photograph in an envelope to deliver to the sheriff on their way shopping.

Paige hadn't planned on pepperoni pizza, but after all that walking they needed somewhere to collapse, and the aroma from Pizza Hut was apparent in every corner of the shopping mall. So by the time they got home with a minimum of a dozen bags it was nearly seven and Jason's car was already in the driveway.

"Where've you been?" he said, his voice failing to hide his annoyance.

Paige put the bags on the living room buffet, then taking the remaining bags from Lily's arms, put those there, too.

"I didn't expect you this early."

"Still I figured you'd be here."

"It's seven o'clock, Jason, not midnight."

"You could have left a note."

"I expected to be home before you. Look, how about I fix you some dinner?"

"No, not now. I'd like to talk, that's the reason I left the city early." He looked at Lily who had backed into the kitchen and was staring at him from in there.

Paige looked at her, then at the buffet.

"Lily, why don't you take the bags upstairs to your room. Maybe you'll want to try on your new clothes before you put them away."

It took two trips and Jason waited until Lily disappeared upstairs for the second time before he said, "My sweats?"

She shrugged.

"Looks like you bought up the stores."

"I guess I did go a little overboard. It was such fun, Jason. You know, I never had a chance to shop in a girl's clothing store, just walk around and pick out something I liked."

"Never?"

"The few things I got, my mother bought at some secondhand shop in the Village. They were hideous and never the right size." Actually, Paige never got to pick her own clothes until she was old enough to work and buy them herself. And by then she was past girl sizes and shopping in discount stores.

He nodded his head. "Look, I really don't mean to put a damper on your fun, but the more I think about it, the more I think it's a bad idea keeping her here. I don't know that it's safe."

"Safe? She's the one who's been hurt."

"You forget, she already hurt you . . . that first night in the woods when she hit you over the head."

"We don't know that for sure."

"No, but still we know it. Don't we?"

Paige nodded. "Okay, but she was scared."

"That's no excuse."

"Of course it is, it's the best excuse. When you're frightened, you behave irrationally, you sometimes do things you normally wouldn't think to do."

She noticed the slight raise of his eyebrow. So he didn't agree—still she was in no mood for this to turn into a full-fledged discussion. She sank down on the sofa beside him.

"Enough about Lily. What is it you wanted to talk about?"

"What?"

"You know, you wanted to talk."

He shook his head. "Nah, not important."

"Are you sure?"

He was sure. What was it he was going to tell her anyway: that that afternoon he had betrayed her, fucked her best friend right in their own home? In fact, fucked her twice to make up for his record three-month celibacy? And now a load of remorse was exploding his insides. . . . And he was looking to dump some grief on her. . . .

Fifteen minutes later she put a chef's salad on the table in front of him.

"What's wrong?" she asked.

"Nothing, why?"

"I don't know. You seem preoccupied."

He shook his head and put a napkin in his lap. He picked up the bottle of dressing, uncapped it, and poured some over the salad. "It looks good," he said, then looking across at her empty place setting: "What about you and the kid?"

"We ate out." She pulled up a chair and sat.

He might not be admitting it, but he was definitely bothered by something. Could this still have to do with Lily staying? She reached over and laid her hand on his. "You should have seen her face in the restaurant, Jason," she said, "and at the stores. I think it was a first for her."

"I see you got her to bathe, she certainly looks a hell of a lot better. What about talking, did she open up to you, tell you her last name, where she comes from?"

"I learned she's eleven, her birthday was September 6. She's tall for her age, isn't she?"

"That's it?"

"Give me a chance. Look, it wouldn't be so terrible for you to reach out a little, too. Right now you've got her scared half to death. If for no other reason to be kind, she *is* a guest in our home."

"I never said a word to her."

"Maybe that's the problem. She's quite sensitive, she picked up immediately that you don't approve of her. She probably sees you as a threat."

"To her?"

"She's a kid, that's how she perceives your attitude."

"Okay, okay, I get the point. I'll watch it."

The baby moved—she smiled, quickly picking up and placing his hand on her stomach. "Feel. No wait." She moved his hand trying to locate where the baby's limbs had disappeared to. . . . "Right there."

He waited a moment, felt a rumbling, then a grin filled his face.

"Whoa, that felt like some pretty fancy footwork. It's all pretty magical, isn't it? I mean, him being in there with you."

Though she had been feeling movement for a while, every time the baby kicked or changed position, it still managed to startle and amaze her. She smiled. "By the way, if this is a girl, Jason, I can't guarantee she won't come out swinging furiously at you. I mean, how many times have you referred to this beautiful unborn child as a he? Or come up with boys' names exclusively?"

"Funny you should mention that, I notice you coming up with only girls' names."

"Simply trying to keep it fair."

"I see. Well, if it's a slight, it's not intentional. Maybe I'm just better at thinking boy. That's all we ever had around our house. Girls were those strange people we met at school: delicate, emotional, secretive, definitely more complicated." He leaned over, kissed Paige, then stood up and taking her hands, pulled her up beside him. "Come on, watch me welcome the kid proper."

"You mean it?"

"What do you think I am, uncivil?"

When they got to the top landing, he put his arm out, stopping her. "Listen."

"Fuck, shit, bitch, asshole, piss—"

"That's her," he said.

"I know."

"Then you've heard it before?"

"She's angry, scared, she does it when she's alone, or when she thinks she's alone. Children swear, it's not exactly unheard of."

"Not like that, and not normal kids."

That wasn't at all true, but again she wanted to avoid an argument.

"Please, Jason," she said.

"Okay, okay."

She was sitting on the bare floor against the closet door and the shopping bags were on top of the dresser, unopened. When they stepped up to the doorway, she straightened up and looked from one of them to the other.

"Hi, I'm Jason," he said. "Paige tells me you're going to stay awhile, at least until we find your folks."

Silence.

"You play games?"

More silence.

"Yeah, neither do I."

"What about Scrabble?" Paige said.

Jason nodded. "She's right, I do play Scrabble."

The phone rang—Lily jumped.

"I'll get it," Jason said, retreating to their bedroom.

Enlisting Lily's help, Paige began to unpack the bags, removing tags, then folding the new clothes into empty dresser drawers. When Jason didn't get back within five minutes, Paige went after him. He was sitting on the bed, no longer on the telephone.

"Who was it? Why didn't you come back?"

"Sit down," he said.

"Something's wrong. Your father?"

"No, it's her." His thumb directed to the next room. "It was the sheriff. He knows who she is."

"So soon?"

"Apparently she lived about a hundred and

fifty miles northwest of here. In Laurel Canyon. Her disappearance was quite publicized."

"Then why didn't he know immediately?"

He shrugged. "He didn't put it together. By now, everyone assumed she was dead."

A sudden cold went through her, and she hugged her arms tightly at her chest. "Why would they think that?"

"Her father was Maynard Parks. Ring a bell?"

"No, should it?"

"The story made the *Times*. I remember reading it. According to neighbors, the father was some kind of monster, beat up the mother regularly. Anna Parks didn't have friends, but the people who knew her casually liked her well enough. In fact, other than her inability to leave him, no one had a bad word to say about her. Hospital records show the woman suffered fifteen broken bones during a thirteen-year period. Well, finally, I guess she decided to strike back. She cooked him a fine dinner . . . while he was eating it, she killed him."

Paige drew in her breath.

"A real messy kind of killing, too."

"Messy, how?"

"She used a sickle. Decapitated, limbs severed—"

"Don't tell me more. Oh my God. And Lily saw that?"

"Apparently."

"When?"

"Are you ready for this? It was nearly a year ago. It happened during a major snowstorm, the kid ran off into the night before help could arrive. The town searched for days, actually weeks, they didn't stop searching till spring thaw . . . Meanwhile the mother was given a twenty-five-year prison sentence."

"Seems pretty steep, I mean under those circumstances."

He shrugged. "As I recall, she had a young schmuck defend her—a freebie public defender, probably straight out of law school. He pled her guilty, threw her on the mercy of the court, not even a legal defense—no trial, let alone a jury trial."

Paige shook her head; it took a moment for her voice to come out. "Jason, where do you suppose Lily's been? "I mean, in our attic all that time?"

He shrugged.

"And the monster, Jason, she was barely ten years old then, what did he do to *her*?"

It was late when they finally turned in. She had put Lily to bed, then she and Jason talked. . . . Though she wasn't sorry she'd decided to keep Lily temporarily, to do what she could for her, the news from the sheriff really hit a nerve within her. And though Jason clearly had more reservations about keeping Lily, to his credit, he didn't voice them. That night, both of them only wanted to weep for her.

The next step would be a trip to the women's prison in Albany: tomorrow morning Jason would visit Anna Parks, tell her about Lily, and ask about her nearest friends or relatives. Someone she trusted to take care of her daughter.

To face twenty-five years in prison—what must it be like? Maybe thinking her child was dead, it might not have made much difference.

But it would now—Lily growing up without her there to see it happen. But the monster wouldn't see it happen either ... that would have to be satisfaction enough.

Fifteen broken bones in thirteen years ... *What happened that night, Anna, why was that night different from the others?*

Chapter Five

As had become routine since moving to Briar-wood, Jason ran three miles, showered, then left the house before six; this morning, though, he headed the opposite direction to Albany. By eight-thirty, he'd had breakfast, called his secretary, Pat, to rearrange appointments, then via Sheriff Buldoon's office, made arrangements to see Anna Parks before the prison's normal scheduled visiting hours.

Not being a criminal lawyer, he hadn't been inside many prisons, but the few he'd been in, he'd found claustrophobic. This one, despite its reputation for being the best women's facility in the state, seemed no different. The guard ushered him through a tunneled hallway into a small one-windowed room containing a single wooden table and two straight-backed chairs. Anna Parks was sitting, waiting. The guard backed up, stepped outside the room.

Jason studied the woman as he walked to her. He sat across from her. She had blond frizzled hair, plain features. He looked at her hands, they looked rough and blunt, uncomely hands that had seen their share of work. Remembering the newspaper accounts of the case, he knew that those worn hands could generate a mighty amount of muscle, enough to kill a two-hundred pound man.

Though she couldn't have been much older than Paige, she had a weariness about her that made her seem twice as old. Jason wondered what she'd looked like before those paper-thin lines crept in and settled around her thin-lipped mouth. Before she woke up one morning and decided she had to kill her husband . . .

"I'm Jason Bennett," he said finally. "I don't know what they told you."

She shook her head. "Nothing really. Are you a lawyer?"

"I am, but I'm not here in that capacity."

She waited.

"My wife and I live in Manhattan, but we have a second home in Briarwood—it's about a two-hour's drive from where you lived in Laurel Canyon. Not long ago we opened the country house, moved in for the winter. Well, to make it a short story, we found your daughter living in our attic."

Her breath caught, and her eyes got wide—they were the same deep blue as Lily's eyes, but without the luster. Then leaning forward, she placed a hand on his arm.

"How is she, my baby?"

"When we found her, she was dirty, scared . . . She's still scared and she doesn't talk much. But considering what she's been through, she's done remarkably well. We stayed at the house lots of weekends this summer, but she hid her tracks. I imagine she was hungry now and then, but she somehow managed."

"Oh, I knew she would, she's a real tough one, not at all like her mommy."

He didn't know what to say to that—apparently Anna's toughness had festered for years, come out in one manic spurt.

"My wife . . . well, we're taking care of her. But naturally, it's only temporary, we wanted to find out first where she belonged."

"And now you think I can . . ."

"Well, not you, but family members. Sisters, brothers, cousins, grandparents?"

"There are none."

"Not one relative, or maybe even a good friend? I mean, if it's the distance that's bothering you, not to worry. We'll be glad to spring for any airfare—"

"No one, Mr. Bennett. I would tell you—"

He sat back, wondering how in hell he had gotten himself so deeply into this—so okay, he knew how, the better question was why? But apparently she was unable to read his thoughts because she asked, "Isn't there some way you and your wife could keep her? My baby's a strong girl—she cleans house, cooks, even shovels snow. She's a smart one, too, you won't find one smarter."

"Wait, hold it, time out." He shook his head. "Look, I'm sure she's all that, probably more, but it's out of the question. We're expecting a baby ourselves in a couple months. And forgive me," he said, "but I find it incredible how quick you are to want to hand her to strangers. I mean, you don't know me ... or my wife and you haven't an inkling of what Lily thinks about any of this."

"Oh, she wants to be with you, or is it your wife she wants to be with? One or the other, maybe both."

"What makes you say so?"

"Because she's with you, isn't she? You wouldn't have found her, caught her, not if Lily didn't want you to."

Jason studied the woman for a few moments, a little stunned at the extent of the confidence she had in her kid. But still, why the hell was she flaunting it at him?

He didn't bother asking. Instead he said, "I'll look into alternative homes for her. When it's decided where she'll be going, I'll see to it that you're notified."

She nodded, tears in her eyes. "Tell her not to worry about me. I don't mind it here at all. Some of the women are tough, mean, too, as tough and mean as lots of men I've known, but if you look to your own business, you can get by okay."

"Do you want to see her?"

She took a deep breath, then: "No, I don't. What good can come of her seeing me locked away?"

Jason stood up, began going toward the door, then came back.

"Why did your lawyer plead you guilty?"

"Because I am guilty."

Paige hadn't been completely honest with Lily—though the child knew the sheriff had come to the house, she didn't know that the Po-

laroid picture she took was for him. So now how
did Paige tell her that as a result of a police
probe, they knew who she was? Maybe it would
be better to wait till Jason spoke to the mother,
until Paige had something more concrete to say
to her . . .

All this was going through her mind while the
aroma of freshly perked coffee drew her downstairs. She glanced at the clock—eleven. She
hadn't slept so late since before she was married,
and come to think of it, she hadn't felt so rested
in weeks.

Lily didn't see her come downstairs, she was
too busy digging a short-edged vacuum cleaner
nozzle deep into the sofa lining. Paige—one of
those lick-and-a-promise housekeepers—couldn't
remember ever using that particular vacuum at-
tachment. When Lily saw her watching, she
pressed her heel on the power button and the
machine shut off.

"The place looks wonderful, Lily," Paige said,
looking around the large room, smiling. "I ap-
preciate all your help, really . . . but you don't
have to do this."

Silence.

"Did I smell coffee?" She walked toward the
kitchen, but Lily ran ahead, took out a plate covered with foil from the warm oven, and removing the foil, set it on the table. "Will you stop
this? You're spoiling me. Before you know it, I'll
metamorphose into some giant slug who spends
her days simply waiting for meals."

"Did *she* bring you food?"

It was her first attempt at conversation, in

fact, her first question. "She . . . who?" Paige asked.

"You said your mother went on dates and you stayed home, hungry? Well, did she bring back food?"

"Well, no, not really."

"Why?"

Paige shrugged. "I guess she didn't think to." Paige's thoughts went to her mother, she hated it when they did. Adele Adler, stricken with Alzheimer's four years earlier lived in a nursing home in Hyde Park. Though Paige took financial responsibility for her care and visited twice a year, it was strictly out of duty. In any event, her mother didn't recognize her, not even once on those visits.

"What about your father?" Lily asked.

"Pardon?"

"Why didn't he feed you?"

"He couldn't, he wasn't around. He ran off when I was very young, maybe three or four. I don't remember him."

Three, four—before kindergarten . . . She remembered the old lady across the street, the one who would give her peanut butter and saltines in a cellophane bag. She remembered the Puerto Rican girl up the street, the one who whenever she passed the front stoop would make funny faces to make her laugh. . . .

But not her father, she didn't remember him. . . .

Jason surprised them when he came into the kitchen. Lily did her usual shuffle, ball, back-step, retreating quickly away from him, in this instance, to the stairway.

"Lily," Paige called after her, but she moved quickly up the stairs, disappearing from sight.

"I thought I'd fill you in," he said. Then noticing the food in front of her: "Jesus, Paige, why not make it easy—run a sludge hose straight to your arteries?"

Paige looked at the remains of eggs and potatoes, then pushed the greasy plate aside.

"I admit it, I've been bad. But tomorrow, it's back to grain and fruit and all the good-for-me stuff. Jason, you should see how Lily tries to look after me, cooks, helps with the housecleaning . . . Do you think she does it because I'm pregnant?"

"I don't know, maybe. Look, I haven't much time, do you want to hear about it?"

A pause, then: "Of course. Tell me, what's her mother like?"

"Beaten down, alone, like she's not had much of a life. According to her, she has no family, no friends. But I'm inclined to disbelieve her on that end. Most people have someone."

"I suppose." She sounded so doubtful, Jason wondered if she wasn't comparing it to her own lack of family.

"In any event," he said, "I thought I'd check it out."

"Why would she lie about it?"

"Maybe she views it that no one wants to know her. I've already asked Pat to check out state agencies. To see what kind of alternatives there are for Lily in case there really is no one. The sheriff sees no problem with me doing that."

"And her, Lily's mother?"

"As far as she's concerned, her daughter hand-picked us. Or, at least handpicked you."

"Really, how so?"

"If she didn't want to be found, she wouldn't have been."

Paige shook her head. "What an odd thing for her to have said. However, it's not true. She was found out because she drags her leg in her sleep. And those silly acorns."

Of course, her spot to sleep was directly above their bed. Something Lily would be apt to know if she'd been in the attic as long as he thought she had been. All those long summer weekends—was it possible she'd been listening to them?

Hold the paranoia, Jason.

That afternoon Paige received four telephone calls from newspapers, one from the *New York Times*. It seemed Lily's unexpected arrival in Briarwood had big human interest appeal. Nonetheless, Paige refused any statements, pictures or interviews on Lily's behalf, seeing publicity as having no benefit for Lily.

Finally, to escape the intrusion, Paige and Lily went outdoors for a walk through the woods. When they got near the river, she took hold of both Lily's hands—the burned one still blistered but no longer bandaged—and said, "Jason visited your mother this morning."

Her mouth opened, her muscles tensed.

"Now before you go getting yourself worked-up, let me tell you about it."

Lily spread her hand across her chest. "How?"

"I gave the sheriff one of those pictures of you,

and I did it because it was necessary. Of course it didn't take him long to find out who you are. Apparently, a lot of people were worried, searched a long time for you. Your mother—"

"She killed him, Paige, I hate her!" She slapped her hands over her mouth.

Paige put her arm around her, hugging her close, then finally pulled back. "I know you don't mean that, Lily. What you're feeling is anger, hurt, maybe even fear, a whole lot of bad, confused feelings. Your mother already admitted what she did to the police."

"She did?"

Paige nodded.

A long, uncomfortable silence, then Lily asked, "What did they do to her?"

"She's in a prison in Albany. Not such a bad place, at least as far as prisons go."

Swallowing hard. "How long will they keep her there?"

"The sentence? A while, Lily, a long while."

Her eyes filled, and her lips pressed tightly.

"What about me?"

"Come on, let's sit and talk about you." They sat by a tree, Paige's arm again around her. "Jason and I are going to find a home for you, Lily. A wonderful home with people who will care about you."

"No, I don't want that, I want to stay with you." A few tears finally let go, but Lily turned her head, and with her fist, pushed them aside.

Paige ran her sleeve over her own eyes.

"Look at me, will you? You've got me all weepy now. Lily, I'm so sorry, but it's not possible for us to keep you." She put her hand to her stomach and took in a deep breath. "The baby is due in less than three months."

"I wouldn't hurt it."

"Oh, no, of course you wouldn't hurt it, that's not what I meant. Look, how about we don't think of you leaving, at least, not yet. It'll take time to find the right home for you anyway. So let's just hang loose and enjoy being together. And speaking of fun, when I looked through Sunday's paper last, I noticed a Goldie Hawn picture playing at the highway cinema. Now I don't know about you, but she makes me laugh. But to go laugh alone, well, it's nowhere near the fun. How about you and I—"

"Paige?"

"Yes, sweetheart."

"Why doesn't Jason like me?"

"What kind of alternatives are we talking about, Jason?" Paige asked that night at dinner after going on about the persistent press—she had received several more telephone calls by then, and one reporter actually came to their front door. Lily had eaten much earlier and gone upstairs with the three Plastic Man comic books Paige bought at CVS after the movie let out.

"I don't really know, but Pat ought to have some information for us by tomorrow. Did you tell Lily about my visit with her mother?"

"Earlier. What I really wanted was to wait awhile, but I didn't dare chance it. I wouldn't be at all surprised to hear something or other pop up on the television news."

"How did she react?"

"She's angry at her mother, but that's understandable—as bad as things get, a kid will never opt for the breakup of her family. And though Lily knows her father originally caused what happened, her mother was the one who took the final action." Paige shook her head. "She said if she can't live with her mother, she wants to stay with us."

"Why doesn't that surprise me?"

"Oh, Jason, you can hardly fault her for feeling that. But not to worry, I told her it wasn't possible. Isn't she bright for eleven, Jason? So perceptive, too."

"I suppose. Look, what do you want me to say—I'm happy she's here, I wish she could stay indefinitely? Well, forgive me, I don't feel that. We're having a kid ourselves, our first, something we've been trying to do for five years now. What, is it so wrong that I want to enjoy the anticipation of our baby?"

"Lily's not taking away from that."

"Even in this temporary situation, she'll be needing a lot of attention, are you up to it?"

"Okay, sure, she's been through hell and back, I won't try to argue that. But considering what she's gone through, she's not as messed-up as one might expect."

"Sure, every kid has a trucker's vocabulary."

"Give me a break, we're not going to convict her on the number of four-letter words she knows, are we? I mean, so far, she hasn't come up with one I haven't heard. Of course, with your refined vocabulary, who knows!"

"Okay, so strike that. But damnit, re-read your textbooks, Paige, no kid comes out of heavy duty slime without severe adhesion problems. She saw the mother beaten up time after time. Finally she sees her murder him, cut him up into pieces no less. And you said it yourself, what might the spineless bastard have done to *her*, to his own daughter?"

Yes, Jason, all quite true and all more reasons why we can't simply walk away from her. But she didn't say that to him—instead she said, "I know you're right. But still thousands of kids are abused, and they don't all carry signs saying so on their chest. Heck, if you want to dissect things all that much, I led a pretty sorry existence as a kid myself. So did I turn out so tragic?"

"You can't step in her shoes."

"Funny thing is, I can't seem to step anywhere else these days. Besides, what are you suggesting we do with her, throw her out?"

"No, of course not. I was just voicing my—"

"No need to, Jason. I'm not deaf. Lily isn't either."

"Is it my fault Jason's mad?" Lily asked outright the next morning as they walked through the woods. The truth was, Paige hadn't spoken one word to him since the argument at dinner the night before.

"Why do you ask that?"

Lily shrugged, stopped, then knelt down and picked a handful of dry leaves.

"If Jason and I argue, it's our responsibility, not yours. It means *we* can't agree. What it is we can't agree on is really not important, the problem still lies with us."

"Are you going to throw him away?"

Paige stopped, looked at her. "People don't throw people away, especially not those they care about."

"Do you care about me?"

She nodded. "I do."

Lily closed her hand on the leaves, crushing them, then let the tiny pieces sail off.

"So you can't throw me away, right?"

"Right."

They stood there a while longer, then Paige said, "Lily, I know your father abused your mother for many years. . . . What about you? Did he do anything—"

She turned away. "I don't want to talk about that. Please don't make me."

Paige took the girl's hand in hers, and they began walking.

"I would never force you to talk about it, sweetheart. But if you should change your mind and want to talk, don't forget I'm here."

Paige hadn't even sat down to dinner with him that night. Now that they were both in the same bed, each lay secluded, curled up as far from the center of the king-sized mattress as possible. Never before in their marriage had they carried an argument to the no-speaking level, and she didn't know about him, but she hated it.

She rolled over in bed—he was facing away from her. She reached out, caressed the back of his neck.

"Jason we must talk."

Silence.

"I had this idea. Actually it came to me yesterday, and I've been thinking about it since."

He rolled over, dug his elbow in his pillow, supported his head with the flat of his hand. "Go on, I'm listening," he said.

"What if we could find her a home, a good home."

"Isn't that what we were doing?"

"Not really. Pat's going to find out—if she hasn't already—what we both know. Lily is not adoptable, at least not unless her mother relinquishes rights. But even putting that aside, eleven-year-olds don't make good candidates for adoption. People want babies, little children they can mold to their own specifications. They don't want one with a background, particularly one like Lily's."

He shook his head. "Look, I'm not about to tell you it's not tough to place an older kid, sure it is. But it happens. Besides, there's always the option of foster care."

"Yes, good ol' foster care. A system that places and switches around children like they were so many coat hangers in a closet. Do you know how many people go into that just for the money? Or for more perverse reasons that I need not mention?"

"Wow, I'd say that's a mighty broad brush."

He was right, she *was* being unfair. Through teaching she'd had a fair amount of contact with social services, foster care included, and knew that most of the people involved were trying their best to turn around near impossible situations. Still her opinion of the system she had formed as a kid would likely not change.

"When I was a kid, I had a friend who lived in a foster home," she said. "She lived a couple of doors from me. The people were fall-on-your-face alcoholics. How they ever qualified as guardians to a seven-year-old, is still a mystery to me. Marie would race home every day after school to clean house, it was either that or get beaten."

"You never mentioned her."

"I hadn't thought about her until Lily arrived. Anyway, she lived there less than a year. After a particularly violent beating, she landed in the hospital. Finally, the system moved her on, and I never saw her again."

"It stinks, Paige. But it doesn't mean there aren't some decent people who take in kids."

"You're right, I'm sure there are. But then there is the question, how qualified are they to parent? Particularly to parent a kid who needs it as much as Lily."

Silence, then: "You said you had an idea."

"What about her living with Anna?"

"Her mother?"

"Well, what better person? People said she was okay, her biggest fault being not walking out on the monster years before, when it all began. And best of all, it's Lily's mother. Sure, Lily's angry at her, but underneath all that anger, she loves her."

"A slight hitch. She's got twenty-four years of prison, twelve if she makes parole. Lily will be twenty-two by then."

"I hate it when you pretend not to know what I'm talking about. I'm suggesting that you appeal Anna's case. Wasn't it you who said she had lousy representation? There is a good legal defense for what she did, isn't there?"

Jason nodded. "One of the oldest in the books—self-defense. What's happened is, the battered wife syndrome went and extended the self-defense theory."

"How?"

"In theory, a battered wife need not show she's immediately threatened, only that there's a pattern of continued abuse such that her life is in constant danger. And the barrier that prevents her escape from the situation does not necessarily need to be a physical one, it can be psychological."

"She might have won with that defense, right?"

"Possibly, no one knows that for certain."

"If she had a good lawyer, one who had at least put up a fight. But he didn't . . . Isn't that in itself grounds for appeal?"

"A lawyer would have had to make a grave error, acted irresponsibly for the court even to consider it. . . . And then the question is, would it have made a difference to the outcome of the case had the error not been made? In this instance, who knows? The bottom line is, did she kill her husband?" He was thoughtful a moment, then: "Besides, it's not exactly something one lawyer wants to do to another."

"I don't suppose it is, but what about Anna? She was beaten over and over again, broken bones, broken spirit, a total loss of dignity, and she never even got to tell her story in court. Where're her rights?"

"She wasted them pleading guilty. Unless . . . listen, I'm not a criminal lawyer. I haven't done that kind of work since law school, and then only two six-month internships for the D.A."

Paige moved up next to him, placed her palm against his cheek. "Either way, you're one of the smartest people I know ... and when it comes to appellate courts, you know your way around them better than any other attorney in the city. If anyone can find a flaw in the handling of a case, it's you."

"Did I tell you that?"

She leaned over, kissed him. "Well, yes ... but I heard it from other sources, too. Jason, you said she wasted her rights pleading guilty. Then you stopped with unless. Unless what?"

"I was going to say, unless she was incompetent to make such a decision."

"You mean, insane?"

"Insane will do for want of a better word."

"But she wasn't, was she?"

He shook his head, shrugged. "I don't know. How many sane people you know would hack up a body like that?"

"I believe people can be driven by extreme fear, temporarily go off the deep end."

He rubbed his forehead. "What I need to do is discuss it with someone with criminal experience."

"Then you will do it?"

"I'll look into it."

"Can I tell Lily?"

"No.

"You're right, why get her hopes up? Jason, can I enroll her in school, just for now?"

He sighed. "I want her to see a therapist on a regular basis."

"I'll find someone right away, I'd like her checked by a physician as well. . . ."

"And if she causes you trouble, extra work, or worry, you've got to promise—"

"If she takes too much out of me, I'll hire someone for a few hours a day, but—trust me—that won't be an issue. She's a help with cooking, the chores, wonderful company for me, and the bottom line is, I like having her around."

Jason lay back on the pillow, his elbows extended and his clasped hands beneath his head. For the first night since that episode with Brooke, he was able to push it from his mind.

Instead he thought about the case: so big deal—he would be doing a little *pro bono* work for a kid who didn't seem to have much of anything. He'd been relatively lucky in his career, wasn't it about time he paid a little dues? Though he didn't have much criminal law experience, he remembered liking it. In fact, if the pay in the D.A.'s office hadn't been so miserable and *he* hadn't been so propelled by greed, he might have stayed on longer. In any event, if he needed to pick brains, his office had plenty available.

If only he didn't mind having Lily living with them. All temporary-arrangement business set aside, by the looks of things, she might still be with them when the baby arrived, maybe until they returned to the city in April. So like it or not, he'd do well to make the best of it. Tomorrow was Saturday, an opportunity for him and the kid to work out some compromise.

Brad . . . Bradley, a thought, maybe . . . No, the more he thought it, the more he didn't like it.

Chapter Six

It was seven A.M. when Jason stepped out of his shower, dressed, and tiptoed into Lily's bedroom, where he found her blankets and linens untouched and her, along with other bedding, on the floor. She sat up, hugging a flowered quilt to her.

"Sorry," he said. "Didn't mean to scare you—"

Silence.

"Listen, I thought maybe you'd like to run with me. I usually do a few miles in the morning."

More silence.

"Later we'll have breakfast."

"What about Paige?"

"Yeah, well, Paige likes to sleep late these days and that's good. With the baby coming, she could use the rest. I thought it'd be a good chance for you and me to get to know one another. Looks like you may be around here awhile."

She stood up, still holding the quilt and standing on a foam rubber mat with a flannel sheet covering it.

He motioned with his hand. "Not too bad a bed if you like floors. Paige make it up for you?"

She nodded.

"Not a bad lady, huh?" There it was, they had something in common—Paige.

Another nod.

"Maybe when we get back we can fix her breakfast, bring it up to her in bed."

Lily stooped to pick her jeans from the floor.

"Put on sweats, why don't you? I'm sure Paige bought you some." He opened the top dresser drawer, looked through the clothes, then pulled out a bright blue two-piece sweatsuit and tossed it to her. "Here, wear this, it'll make you feel like the real McCoy."

"McCoy?"

"You know, the real thing. Like a runner, an athlete." He backed out of the room and held up his palm. "I'll meet you downstairs in, let's say, five?"

She was down in less than two, which meant she hadn't bothered to wash. She rushed to the cabinet over the dishwasher, opened it, and on tiptoes took down a bag of Oreos, then digging her hand in the bag, came out with a handful of cookies.

"Hey, what're you doing?" he said grabbing the bag away. "You don't need this kind of garbage, least of all do you need it at breakfast. Where did we get this junk?" He looked into the cabinet and counted two more bags of cookies and a box of Ring Dings. He removed the cookies from her hand and tossed them into the trash pail, then directed her toward the back door. "Come on, after the run, you'll eat real food."

But she yanked her arm from his and dug in her heels.

They stared at each other, neither moving. Finally he turned, went out the door, and it wasn't until a few minutes passed that she relented and followed after him. They had gone more than a half a mile in silence when Jason broke stride and looked back at her—she looked out of breath so he stopped.

"Want to rest a little?"

He went to a tree, sat down, and she slid down similarly against another tree.

"You like exercise?"

Silence.

"I suppose that's a dumb question. Most kids exercise without even knowing it. For instance, how did you get all the way here from Laurel Canyon?"

More silence.

"Not giving out information, is that it? Well, I figure you hitched a ride, at least part of the way, but I bet you did a lot of hiking in the process. You know what's got me curious? What you ate while you were here. During the spring and summer months, we might have left food behind, but when we closed the house for the winter, we cleared out the cupboards. Other than a bag of white bread left for—" He stopped and smiled. "Okay, so you beat the birds to the bread crumbs, but still that's hardly enough to survive a winter."

"I ate."

"Yeah, what?"

"Why do you want to know?"

"Just curious to see how smart you are. Your mother seems to think you're a real whiz."

She stared at him, then stood up. "Come on, I'll show you." This time she led the running right to the river. She stopped at a big oak on the riverbank.

"Fished, huh?"

She bent down: near the base of the trunk was a thick rope encircling it. She took hold of the slack and pulled ... then taking hold of more slack, pulled again. And Jason watched the water agitate as an object beneath came closer to the bank.

"Now I'm seriously impressed, what's this, some kind of trap? Lobsters, crab, crayfish?"

The cage came out—it was a wire trap, similar to the one in their attic but this one looked as though she might have put it together herself. She leaned over, lifted it up and onto the grass. No lobsters, no crab, no crayfish. Inside it were two squirrels and three black rats.

"I don't get it."

"I catch them, I drown them, I eat them."

They hadn't said a word on the way back to the house. Once they were in the kitchen, Lily got out the potatoes, then butter and eggs and onions from the fridge.

"If you want to eat garbage, fine, but do me a favor, don't make it for Paige."

"Why not?"

"Because I said so."

"But she likes it."

"I said, no."

"You rule her."

"That's ridiculous. I don't rule anyone. Look, I'm not about to argue this with you ... Let's just leave it at—since it's my house, you do what I say to do."

"Jason!"

He turned. So did Lily, but Paige looked only at him.

"What's going on?" she asked.

"Not a thing."

"Obviously it was something—"

He walked out the kitchen, through the living room, out the front door. She went after him, catching up to him at the bottom of the porch stairs.

"Jason, will you wait?"

He slowed his step and they began to walk together. "What was going on in there?" she asked.

"You won't believe how she fed herself."

"When?"

"Last winter, of course."

"Oh. Okay, how did she?"

"She ate squirrels and rats."

Her eyes widened in surprise, then turned to disbelief. "Oh, come on, Jason. How would you know that?"

"She told me, showed me—a bunch of rodents drowned in a cage by the river."

The instant revulsion sent a shudder rippling right through her, but she pushed back the horror of it, held fast to the practical, rational explanation.

"That's it, nothing to add?" Jason asked.

"I don't get it. Are you asking, does it turn my stomach? Of course it does. But she had to survive, didn't she? People have resorted to *cannibalism* in order to survive."

"Sure, you do whatever is necessary. But there's a river, what about fish?"

"Maybe she didn't have a pole."

"She managed to put together a wire trap with a snap-shut door apparatus. If she could handle that, surely she could handle a lousy fishing pole."

"Maybe she doesn't like fish, most kids don't."

"No, they like rats."

"Jason, you're being unreasonable, not at all like yourself. Correct me if I'm wrong—you agree it was a question of life or death, yet you're angry that she chose to eat rats over fish?"

He stopped walking, raised one hand, and clasped the back of his neck and rubbed it.

"The whole thing does sound a bit absurd, doesn't it?"

"Thank goodness you see it."

"It really wasn't so much the choice of food, Paige, not that it didn't shake me down to my toes. But she took a perverse pleasure in seeing me shook."

"Don't we all play those games occasionally? Personally, I take great delight in rattling you. I love to get a gander at that bewildered puss of yours."

He screwed up his face. "You mean this one?"

"No, that's the idiot puss." She started to run and he chased her down the driveway, across the lawn, toward the street, catching her finally by the scruff of her collar before she could make it across. "Okay, have kindness, Jason?" Louder, "Jason!"

"Paige?"

"Yes?"

"You've got to talk to her about food."

With her arms still high, ready for attack: "I'm sure she won't eat any more rats."

"No, but she likes to eat crap and I notice you like to eat it with her."

She sighed and brought her arms to her sides.

"All right. Oh, Jason, what do you think of the name Brittany?"

"Naw, too trendy," he said. "What about Michael?"

"As an alternative?"

"Don't be smart."

A few moments of silence as they walked together toward the house, then: "My mother once dated a guy named Michael."

"So?

"Just wondering what came first—my father leaving or my mother's boyfriends?"

"Didn't you ever ask her?"

"I did, but she'd never talk about it. Let's forget about the name Michael."

"Okay, nix Michael." He put his arm around Paige. "Look, promise you'll talk to Lily, okay? I don't want the baby born addicted to sugar. And I don't want you fat with hardening arteries."

Jason went off somewhere, presumably to give her an opportunity alone with Lily. She found her in the kitchen, preparing breakfast. Paige turned off the gas jet under the frying pan, then took her hand.

"Come, sweetheart, we've got to talk."

"Are you mad at me?"

"No, why should I be?"

"Because of Jason."

"Jason's not angry, at least not now he isn't."

"I saw him chasing you outside."

A pause, then: "You were watching?"

"I had to make sure he wouldn't hurt you."

Was she comparing their innocent roughhousing in the yard to her parents' fights? Though there was nothing even remotely violent in Jason and her play, could she have witnessed a similar scene that *had* turned violent?

"We were playing, Lily. Besides, Jason would never hurt me . . . or you. That doesn't mean he doesn't sometimes get rattled and shout a little now and then. We all do that."

The child gestured to the pan on the stove. "He won't let you eat it, will he?"

"He's right about it. Greasy food is not good for me."

"But you like it."

"Oh, yes, I know I like it. Unfortunately I like lots of things not good for me.

"Is it bad for me?"

"Too much isn't good for anyone. But there comes a time when a person ought to clean up her act, follow a healthier diet. Particularly when that person is eating for a baby, too. That's why Jason is so insistent."

"When?" she said.

Paige looked at her.

"The baby," Lily said. "When will it come?"

Finally, she was curious about the baby. Paige smiled, and with her hand, beckoned her closer. "Want to feel it?"

She came over, at first, skeptical, then let

Paige take her hand in hers and press it to Paige's stomach. Her eyes grew rounder and larger and her whole expression changed to wonder as she felt the baby move beneath her hand.

"I'm due the seventh of January."

Lily stayed like that for several minutes before she pulled her hand away ... and then—it seemed to Paige—only reluctantly. She went to the stove, lifted the frying pan from the burner, brought it to the garbage pail, and emptied the contents.

"Lily, you didn't have to do that, you could have—"

"Nope, if you won't, I won't either."

Paige went to the cabinet, took out two bowls, then poured bran and low-fat milk into both. She set one in front of herself, then slid the other across the table to Lily.

"Here you go, try it."

Lily took a spoonful.

"Well?" Paige asked as she took one herself.

"I hate it."

Paige laughed, swallowed quickly—too quickly, then pressed a napkin to her mouth, unable to stop laughing. Finally she took a deep breath and said, "Me too."

"You hate it, too?"

She nodded. "I don't know why I eat it, other than I buy it for Jason and it's always here. . . . We'll have to look around the grocery store this afternoon, find some tastier cereal, maybe something with a touch of sugar. Oops, better watch it, be sure to beep out that word when we're around Jason."

Lily smiled, it was the first time Paige had seen her smile.

Brooke called that night at nine.

"Where in hell you been?" she asked Paige.

"Right here, why?"

"You haven't called since Monday."

"I figured if you missed me enough, you'd pick up the telephone. So Saturday night home in the city, why aren't you out?"

"Gary had to cover for another resident, you know how the little club operates, tit for tat. But it *is* freeing up next weekend for our visit, so I'm not doing any of my complaining aloud. And speaking of visitors, I hear you have one already."

"Oh, and who told you that?"

"Jason, I spoke to him Tuesday, maybe Wednesday."

"He phoned?"

"No, I saw him outside the building."

"Oh. Well, what'd he tell you?"

"Only that it's female and dirty and curses like a bandit."

"Damn him."

"Did he lie?"

"Not about the female part and since then, she's bathed. Actually she's beautiful."

"Really? How long will she be staying?"

"Did Jason tell you more?"

"Is there more?"

"After years of abuse, the mother murdered the father. When Lily saw it, she ran, didn't stop."

"Oh my, that's horrible."

"It gets worse. She cut off his limbs, decapitated him."

"My God, is it wise to keep this kid?"

"Do you think she'd be here if it wasn't? Give Jason and me the benefit of having a little smarts. Why is it people hear this and automatically cop an attitude?"

"What people besides me?"

"Mostly the press. They call up and ask the most ridiculous questions."

"Like what?"

"Well for one—am I worried about the effect her environment has had on her."

"What did you answer?"

"I didn't. I hung up."

"What would you have answered?"

"Well, sure I worry. There's no way she'll walk away untouched by it all. She'll need therapy . . . and for quite some time I expect. But if the question was meant to imply that the child will play out the parents' script some day, then my answer is no. Children—particularly those as tough and bright as Lily—are amazingly resilient. They also respond amazingly well to kindness and caring. I want to see that she gets those in ample doses."

"Well, you've got to admit the whole scene with the mother is terrifying."

"Think how it was for Lily actually witnessing it. Either way, you can't blame her for her mother's mistake."

"Excuse me . . . mistake? Did I hear you call it a mistake?"

"The husband smashed fifteen of her bones in thirteen years, wouldn't you say that's enough?"

"What ever happened to 'get the hell out'?"

Paige didn't bother telling Brooke that Jason would be representing Lily's mother on appeal. She'd tell her next time they spoke, assuming Brooke got past her blame-the-victim attitude.

"What were you doing at the other house?" Paige asked Jason later that night, lying in bed.

"How'd you know I was there?"

A skulking tone with a look to match. "Spies."

"Oh?" He shifted uneasily, repositioned his pillow, bunched it, flattened it.

"Brooke. She told me she saw you outside."

Silence.

"Aren't you going to ask?"

"What?"

"If she and Gary are coming out?"

"Well, are they?"

"Sounds pretty firm to me."

More silence.

She raised her head a little and looked at him.

"Jason, are you paying attention?"

"I heard you—good, great. I'll make the pasta sauce."

"Okay," she said. But he wasn't getting off that easily. Going back to her original question, she asked, "So, tell me, what were you doing there?"

"Doing where?"

"Why do I feel like I'm talking to myself? At the house, Jason, what were you doing there?"

"Oh that. A file. I left the Bernstein file on the entryway table."

"Jason?"

"Yeah?"

"What if Anna's case is not decided by the time we go back to the city in April?"

"Hopefully It will be. I intend to push, ask for a speedy disposition based on Lily's homeless situation."

"But suppose it isn't?"

"Then we'll have to find Lily another home. And quick. By the way, Anna Parks had two siblings."

"Had?"

"The brother's dead. The sister, Nora Kalish, lived in the next county away in Windy Creek— at least she did till the murder. She moved soon after, didn't even wait for her sister's sentencing."

"That's odd, don't you think?"

"Even odder, Anna denies she has a sister."

"Maybe they didn't get along. Or maybe she's protecting her."

Jason raised his head and looked at her. "Protecting her from what?"

"The notoriety, the press. I certainly got a quick lesson in their relentless arrogance."

"But it still doesn't explain why she wouldn't want her only child to be with family."

A sigh. "I don't know," Paige said. "Maybe I should go back to the original theory of them not getting along. In any event, why didn't you tell me about her earlier?"

"I thought maybe I'd find her first."

"Suppose you can't, Jason?"

"Then the kid's here I guess."

"What about taking Lily back to the city with us?"

"Forget it, it's not even an issue. We've got six

rooms, one of them just converted to a nursery. Even if we wanted to, which *I* don't, we wouldn't have space."

She didn't look at him or answer him. Of course he was right about the space. He had more sense than to say it, but he was clearly relieved at what he perceived to be his "out."

"Don't forget about this afternoon," Paige said as Jason began to tiptoe out the next morning.

He stopped and turned: "What's this afternoon?"

"The Lamaze picnic."

"What time?"

"Two."

"What about Lily?"

"What about her?"

"We leaving her here alone?"

"It's to acquaint families, Jason. That usually includes children."

"Okay. Well, I'll be back in a while."

"Going for the newspapers?"

"After my run."

"What about taking Lily to the store with you? I'm sure she's up."

"No."

"Why not?"

"Because I want to relax."

"And you can't if she's with you?"

"Damnit, Paige, can't you give me a little space?"

It was held at a farmhouse between Pough-keepsie and Briarwood; and including kids, Jason claimed he counted sixty-five heads. Lily hung on to the sleeve of Paige's cardigan as though she were afraid to sever their connection. There were about fifteen women, all in different stages of pregnancy. Though there were three barbecue pits loaded with thick sirloins, hamburgers, and frankfurters blazing outside, tables laden with chips, pasta salads, breads, and cheeses were set up in a big old barn.

"Cholesterol heaven," Jason whispered.

"Shush. Jason, what do you think of Brooke?"

He did one of those double takes. "Why would you ask that?"

"I thought it'd be a good name—What, did you think I was asking your opinion of Brooke?"

"I don't know what I thought. It just sounded like . . ." He stopped, then: "Look, as for the name, it's okay I guess."

She took his hand in hers. "I like it. Maybe we ought to put it on our 'possible' list—"

"You're Paige Bennett, aren't you?"

Paige looked at the woman standing in front of her. She had short dark hair cut pixieish, a style Paige hadn't seen in years. Her full rosy cheeks pumped even higher when she smiled.

"Hi there, remember us, your neighbors, Ruthanne Beeder, and my Charlie," she said extending a plump arm to a tall, thin, balding man at her side. "We met once at the post office."

"Hi, how are you?" Paige turned. "This is Jason." While the men shook hands, Paige put her hand on Ruthanne's arm. "I'm sorry I didn't recognize you right off."

"Well, who would at this stage," she said chuckling. "I look like Elsie the cow." She turned to the side and stretched her knit top tight over her bulging stomach. "Look-see, forty-five pounds. Not that I have any real hope it's all in here."

"When're you due?"

"Three weeks, give or take a few days."

"I would think you'd be done with Lamaze by now?"

"Oh, yeah, we already took the last session. I just like to be around pregnant bellies, it makes me feel less grotesque. Not that you're much good for my ego—I can barely tell you're expecting."

"Well, I am in my seventh month. But I try to watch it, or I should say Jason does. You must be chomping at the bit being so close to term. It sometimes seems like I'll never get there."

Ruthanne laughed. "You'll remember those words come midnight feedings."

"We're so eager, even those kinds of words don't scare us."

"Spoken like a first-time mother."

With that, Paige smiled, looked down at Lily and just as she began to introduce her, Ruthanne said, "Oh, my, this must be the little girl you found living in your house?"

Paige glanced at Jason.

"Ah hah, that look wasn't wasted," Ruthanne chided. "But I'm afraid this isn't Manhattan, very little goes on here that doesn't get chewed up by the local gossip exchange. Of course, the reports don't always have full or even correct information—for instance, nowhere in the report did it say Lily was so beautiful. Oh, to die for that hair."

Paige smiled—she wasn't sure what she was expecting, but Ruthanne's directness was a wel-

come surprise. However, Lily still stood beside
her looking as somber as ever.

"How would you like to meet my little boy,"
Ruthanne said. "I suspect he's a little bit
younger than you are but . . . Charlie, quick go
find Roger so we can introduce these two."

Roger, who was only nine, was a speck shorter
than Lily but had at least fifteen pounds on her.
He also had a smile as big and friendly as his
mother's. After introductions and several
promptings on both ends, the children went off
to play.

"I predict—he'll be a linebacker for the
Giants," Jason said, shaking his head as the
dark-haired boy ran off with Lily.

"Twelve pounds, six ounces at birth," Charlie
said.

"Ohmygosh," Paige said to Ruthanne. "Ce-
sarean?"

"Natural."

"I won't ask if you felt it."

"Well, Lamaze did help some, that's why I
took the refresher course. Not that I wouldn't
choose to be zonked unconscious over any wishy-
washy breathing technique. But in this day and
age, obstetricians aren't so free with drugs."

Paige smiled. "I was beginning to think women
around here stayed away from medical
facilities."

"Really, what made you think that?"

"Otis Brown, the grocer—"

"Say no more, he's an old loon and so is his
wife. Other than their daughter's baby who was
born when the daughter was not yet fourteen
and an emergency in a car about ten years back,

I don't know of any baby she's delivered. But to hear him tell it, you'd think she delivered half the county's babies." Ruthanne looked over at the barbecue pits—a long line was beginning to form.

"Look, I don't know about you, but that aroma is just too wonderful. I've got to get a plate—" She stopped and pointed to a crowd beginning to gather near the hen house. "Hmmm, I wonder what's happening there," she said.

Paige looked over, but before she could spot Lily in the crowd, she heard her screams. She raced toward them, followed by Ruthanne and the men. When she got to the edge of the crowd, Paige pushed her way inside: Lily—blood smeared over her clothes, trembling—was standing alone, her arms stretched out, pushing away the adults trying to help her. *Oh dear, God, what happened?*

Seeing Paige, with Jason right behind, the other adults backed off. "The blood—" Paige began as Jason started to lift Lily in his arms. . . .

"Hey, it's okay, mister." A boy about thirteen came forward to stop him. "It's not her blood." He gestured toward a hen on the ground with a broken neck.

Paige sucked in her breath, then moved in closer to Lily. "Sweetheart, how did this happen?"

No answer.

Jason looked at the boy, who now seemed a bit agitated as though maybe he should have shut up and stayed out of it to begin with. But Paige was pleased to see Jason not let him off the hook.

"Come on, let's have it," he demanded.

A pause, shifting his stance, then: "Two kids did it," he said finally.

"Who were they?"

"Don't know their names, but I seen them around before. They hang out at Just Fun, that video game room over in the mall. They're maybe about fourteen, fifteen."

"Can you point them out to me now?"

"Uh, uh, they ran off. I don't think either of them belonged here at the party." He looked at another boy at the fringe of the crowd who nodded concurrence.

Jason sighed. "Okay, tell me about it."

The boy's round shoulders—like two rubber balls—bounced high, then low.

"All I saw was they started to call her names. You know, gross names having to do with her folks."

Paige, who was now cradling Lily in her arms, held her tighter as though that in itself would stop her hurt. *What names, Lily?* Damnit, how did they even know who she was? Ruthanne knew right off, didn't she, so why not them, too? But what was it with kids? Why was it that kids always had to dig whatever the wound, even deeper? Like bats radaring in to suck blood.

"And?" Jason asked.

"She ran into the hen house to get away from 'em, but they followed her in, still shoutin' out names. Next thing anyone knew, they came flying out of there like they did something real bad and weren't about to stick around." His chin tilted toward Lily. "And her, she was at the doorway screaming like crazy."

Paige spotted Roger in the growing crowd, he looked like he was about to cry.

"Kids!" Ruthanne said as Jason helped the silent child into the back seat of the car. Paige got in next to her, her arm around her. "Are they getting more sadistic these days or is it just my imagination?"

She sat on the axis of the merry-go-round . . . the axis spinning so fast she could no longer feel movement—only the people standing on the outer circle went around. And so ugly were those people, she wondered if they hadn't got locked into one of those silly mirrors you see hanging in the fun house at the amusement park.

Their arms stretched out, further and further . . . like plastic men from an old comic book, and she had all she could do to concentrate, to keep herself shrunk into that tiny black center dot so their bristly hands couldn't touch her. She shut out the sound of their deep voices, refusing to hear, but their mouths twisted and turned so grotesquely, she knew that evil was surely vomiting up from their souls. . . .

Suddenly the one with the missing tooth shot into her with such force, he snapped her neck! The blood, oh God, the blood!

Paige jumped up in the bed.

"No! Don't, no!"

Jason was up, his arms flailing, groping until they reached her. . . .

"What, honey?" With one arm, he reached out and turned on the bedside lamp . . . "What is it, Paige—the baby?"

She shook her head, took a long deep breath.

"No, no. Just a nightmare."

"Want to tell me?"

"I don't know, I don't remember."

"None of it?"

"Somewhere in there I think my neck snapped. . . ." She brought her hand to the base of her throat, her spread hand encircling it. "I guess it was what went on this afternoon. It got to me."

It had gotten to Jason, too . . . double time. Now, Paige already back to sleep and him wide awake, he thought about it more. When he was about seven he saw a high school kid kill a cat, put the sucker in a plastic bag, smother it—a real sick son of a bitch.

In any event, Paige had tried like hell to get Lily to open up when they got home, to get the sight of that dead hen out of her system. . . . But Lily clammed up and went off to her room to be alone.

It hadn't discouraged Paige though, she genuinely believed if given the time, she would get through to her. Now she was even having *her* nightmares.

Chapter Seven

First thing Monday morning, Paige telephoned the Laurel Canyon Board of Education and giving Sheriff Buldoon's name and address as authorization, asked that Lily's school and medical records be forwarded to the Briarwood elementary school. Next, she telephoned Ruthanne for the name of a good pediatrician.

"Most parents around here take their kids to Doc Healy over in Waring, that's about ten miles south of here. In the past forty-two years he's taken care of most every kid-related sore throat, ear infection, and belly ache in town."

"My gosh, how old is he?"

"Pretty near seventy. But don't let that scare you, he keeps up. In fact, he's had a number of articles published recently in medical journals. What's wrong, is Lily sick?"

"Oh no, she's fine, in fact, I'm registering her in school today. I'd just feel better if she had a physical, she hasn't been near a doctor in more than a year. And then, too, it won't hurt to have someone up here when the baby comes."

"I'm putting on tea, you come over when you get her settled in school."

"Well, I don't know—"

"You have something better to do?"

"No, not really . . ."

"Then come, I insist."

Paige got off the phone and watched as Lily reached for the box of Froot Loops and refilled her cereal bowl. With designer jeans and a lilac angora sweater over a blue turtleneck, high-topped sneakers, and swinging blond ponytails, she looked like she stepped out of a young people's fashion magazine. Such a profound change from the dirty, frightened girl of only a week ago. Paige looked at the clock.

"What do you say, almost ready?"

"Do I have to go?"

"Yes."

"They're not going to like me."

"Who're they?"

"Teachers, students."

"Why not?"

She shrugged. "I don't know, they just won't."

Despite her earlier uncertainty, once she reached school she didn't let it show: though she hadn't attended classes since her disappearance a year ago, both the guidance counselor and Paige thought—and Lily agreed—that she be placed with the children her age in the sixth grade, and given the opportunity to catch up on the work missed.

And when an attractive student named Heidi came to the school office to escort Lily to her homeroom, Paige watched them head away. There were definite signs among children, body language—and as a teacher, Paige had become fairly apt at interpretation. By the time the two girls had reached the end of the long corridor, though Lily seemed not to have spoken more than a few sentences, the escort was looking at her with what seemed to be admiration and she was chattering away as though she were the one trying to impress Lily. Definitely, not the standard new-student scenario.

Paige couldn't help but grin—if only *she* had had that kind of natural charisma at age eleven.

It wasn't that Jason expected Anna Parks to throw her arms around his neck, nothing that dramatic, but at least she could show some positive reaction for his time and bother. Instead, Anna Parks, after hearing him out, refused his legal help.

"Just leave it all the way it is," she said. "I don't want to change my plea."

"Why not?"

"I told you, I'm guilty, isn't that enough? A person ought to be held responsible for what he does."

"But there were extenuating circumstances. Don't you get it? Your husband didn't have a right to beat on you for all those years. So finally you went a little mad. A person will do that—accept something over and over again, then suddenly that very act infuriates him beyond reason. For that period of time, he loses control, does unspeakable things he may later not even remember doing."

"I knew exactly what I was doing."

"He might even have gone after Lily."

She looked up, her features suddenly taut as though she had just learned Maynard was still alive.

"What do you mean?"

"I mean he beat you, why not beat Lily as well? Did he?"

With a sigh, she pressed her lips together, shut her eyes, then shook her head. "No, thank God, not that."

"But you were afraid he would, weren't you? I mean, what was to prevent him from turning on her? And what could you have done to protect her?"

"Look, I already told you—Please, can't you leave me alone, let me be?"

He stood up, picking up the transcript and files he'd gotten from courthouse records.

"What about your sister?" he said.

She spun around. "What are you talking about, I don't have—"

"Please save the bullshit. I know you have a sister, what I don't know is where she is."

Silence, then: "I don't want you looking for her."

"Why not?"

"Because we don't talk. I don't know where she is, and I don't care to know."

"Does it have to do with Maynard's death?"

"No, it has to do with our hating one another. We've never had much use for each other, even as kids. And I'll tell you one thing right now: I don't want my baby living with her ... under any circumstances! Do you understand?"

Jason nodded, a little surprised to see the outburst brought on by the mere mention of her sister.

"Look, I'm leaving now," he said finally. "Again, you got a lousy deal in court, and I'd like to try to get you a better one. You take some time to think it through. While you're at it though, maybe you'd do well to stop concentrating on Anna and put some thought to Lily. She's floundering around out there, alone, eleven years old trying to act thirty. If you owe her nothing else, you owe her a reasonable effort to get the hell out of here. *She* needs you, the ladies club here can make it without you."

"But I can't, I mean . . ."

"Like I said, think about it."

Paige was still feeling good when she walked into Ruthanne's large rambling cape.

"How'd she do first day?" Ruthanne asked as she showed Paige to the bathroom, and then, at Paige's insistence, through the baby nursery so she could admire the Disney character wallpaper.

Finally they went into a big country kitchen with crisp red-and-white-checkered tiebacks at the two bay windows. The table was set with a Corning teapot, matching cups and saucers, and a plate of Danish. Ruthanne poured tea and after an appreciative study of the pastry, Paige selected a strawberry cheese tart.

"Actually, she did swell, though I doubt she'd admit it. Lily tends to put herself down—for instance, I don't think she has any inkling of how pretty or likable she is."

"Well, my Roger can attest to it. He definitely

took to her. In fact, so much so, she was included
in his last night's prayers."

Paige laughed, then in a serious tone: "Ruthanne, do you know Hillary Egan?"

"Hillary? Of course. In fact, their farmhouse
abuts my family's house. My dad's dead now, my
two brothers are off in the service, but despite
the size, Mom won't budge from there. I imagine
it's pretty much the same with old Mr. Egan."

"Tell me something about Hillary."

"Well, the Egans adopted her when she was
four, maybe five. I'd bet they were well into their
forties at the time, and, I always assumed, unable to have children of their own. Hillary and
I went to school together, not that we actually
hung out—she was two years ahead of me, not a
very pretty girl, but as brainy as they come. Always winning some kind of scholastic medal or
award, making her folks, the school, and the
whole darn town, proud. Why do you ask?"

"I got her name from the school guidance
counselor. I asked for a recommendation of a
child psychologist—I prefer one close by so Lily
can get there by herself after school. Apparently,
the board of education doesn't employ one, but
they've used Hillary's services on the rare occa-
sions they've needed one. However, I'm told
she's not actually a child specialist, more a gen-
eralist—which I guess makes me a little leery."

"What's wrong with Lily? She's not still upset
by that cruel episode that happened yesterday,
is she?"

"Oh, no, not that. Actually there's nothing
specific. We just want her to see someone on a
regular basis, some other adult besides me and

Jason who she might want to confide in. I'm sure you're aware of what her life was like in Laurel Canyon. And though she does amazingly well considering it, these things don't just disappear."

"Maybe it's the difference between city and country folk. If there were no concrete problems staring me in the face, I'd be willing to believe that there was simply no problem and get on with it, while you'd be apt to go on with the hunt."

"In other words, I'm paranoid."

"I didn't say that."

Paige laughed. "It's okay, I'm afraid these days that label seems right on target. High blood pressure, nightmares, fears, the whole works—a couple of months ago I was walking along outside my building . . . got attacked by some kid with a knife."

"Oh my God!"

Paige put up her hands. "No, it's okay, really, he didn't hurt me—at least not physically. I'm just left with the residuals. And it's the reason Jason and I decided to come to the country."

Ruthanne shook her head. "I don't know how people live in the city, especially these days with all the crime. I'd be scared to set foot out the door alone."

"I used to think nothing of it. Hopefully I'll go back to that blissful state. But with respect to Lily's therapy, it's more Jason's paranoia than mine. Either way, with what Lily's been through, it will definitely be beneficial." She gestured to the last bite of her pastry.

"Ruthanne, where did you buy this stuff, it's fantastic."

Ruthanne smiled. "Homemade."

"You're kidding."

"Uh, uh, I'll give you the recipe."

"Oh no, don't waste it on me. When it comes to anything remotely domestic, I'm a washout. If you don't believe it, Jason will be only too glad to verify it in writing. But getting back to Hillary, does she have her own practice?"

"Not really. Not many people in Briarwood would think to go to a psychologist, and then if they would, I doubt they'd choose someone they knew most of their lives."

"Why doesn't she open an office in a larger city? Poughkeepsie's not that far."

"Well, maybe there she'd get patients, but she really doesn't have time to work outside the home, what with taking care of her father. Actually, it's kind of a sad story. Here," she said, lifting a pineapple danish onto Paige's plate, "try this one and I'll tell you."

Helmut Ravin—dark, good-looking—at age thirty-three, was one of Manhattan's up-and-coming criminal attorneys. His tactics were occasionally criticized, but his record of wins was phenomenal. Although Jason was usually put off by the young attorney's cockiness, he temporarily set aside those feelings and cornered him in the law firm's library to ask his advice on Anna Parks' case.

Jason attempted to give him a brief synopsis; partway through, Helmut raised his palm to cut him off. "Was she psychologically tested before the arraignment?"

"According to the file, no."

"Good. Forget the appeal, at least for now. Go for postconviction relief."

Jason hadn't considered that. He would be asking the lower court to admit an error had been made to negate Anna Parks due process. He would be asking the court to withdraw the sentence and allow Anna to withdraw her plea. Essentially to start from scratch.

"I hadn't really thought in that direction," he said. "What about time limitations? It's been nearly a year since the arraignment."

"You worry too much, Bennett, you know that?"

Jason took that to mean, no problem, or if there was one, not a problem so severe he couldn't beat it. "What you're suggesting is I plead her insane," he said.

"Only in so far as to get her a trial. 'The lady was in deep shock when she stood before you, Your Honor, therefore incapable of making any kind of rational decision as to her defense. Or why else would she have pled guilty when she had a viable out? Blah, blah, blah, blah.' If the Court backs off, gives you what you want, then go for it." He raised his arms in a showy shrug. "Use whatever defense makes you happy."

Jason had to admit it sounded fairly reasonable. "Any recommendation of who to use for the psychiatric workup?"

Helmut snagged a large book from a top shelf, then holding it, sank into a chair and raised his feet onto a cluttered table.

"Use M.C. Wendell. He's got degrees coming out his asshole. He's affiliated with eight psychiatric hospitals, graduated with honors from top medical schools. And, one better, women jurors wet their panties when they see him."

Jason picked a pen and notepad from his pocket and jotted the name down.

"Suppose the client won't cooperate?"

Helmut opened the book in his lap, scanned the table of contents, then: "Why wouldn't she?"

"Right now she seems to be reveling in her guilt. I intend to turn her around on that. But the question is, can I proceed on her behalf without her consent?"

"You do what you have to do. In fact, if you can't change her mind in time, there's always the option of having her not show for the hearing."

"Go forward without her there?"

"It can be arranged."

"I don't quite follow . . ."

A smile. "It's simple. Facilitate a screw-up."

Apparently Jason's ignorance showed big-time.

Helmut waved away his comment as unimportant for now, and Jason wasn't about to pursue it, not wanting to be privy to any of his underhanded operations. By the time the court date arrived, Anna Parks would simply have to agree to fight for her freedom.

Helmut snapped the law book shut, pulled his feet off the table, and stood up—apparently ending the discussion.

"I think I've given you enough to get you going," he said.

Jason felt like slugging the arrogant prick. But instead he thanked him for his help, and in truth, he had been a help. Certainly his idea of going directly to the trial court for relief was an interesting one. Not that his chances were that good—from where he stood, it was strictly a long shot. But even if it failed, he'd walk away with a hell of a nice record to take up on appeal. And better still—if it succeeded, it would save enormous time getting Anna to trial.

He'd talk to Wendell right away, set up a psychiatric evaluation ... Best to let Anna think it was part of prison protocol, at least until he had her cooperation. And the public defender, the one who did such a poor job defending Anna Parks ... the more he considered that fiasco, the surer he was that he'd need to put the poor sap's rocks on the chopping block.

Hillary Egan always used the free hour when the physical therapist was busy with Father to read the current issues of her psychiatric journals. Only then, and the times when Otis Brown stopped by for his and Father's nightly checker game, could she be sure that the darn buzzer wouldn't assault her eardrums. So when the telephone rang at 10:15 A.M., interrupting her concentration, she was irked and had a little difficulty keeping it from her voice.

"Yes, hello."

"Hillary Egan please," the voice said.

"Speaking."

"Hi, Paige Bennett here. I'm sorry, is this a bad time?"

Was that name familiar? "No, not a bad time at

all," she said finally. "What can I do for you, Miss Bennett?"

"Please call me Paige. I need a psychologist and though I'm told you currently don't have a formal practice, I thought maybe ... The local school tells me you did some evaluations for them."

"Well, yes I did. Is this for yourself?"

"No, the patient would be an eleven-year-old. Her name is Lily."

"Then it's your daughter?"

"Not really. Maybe we could set up a time to meet, it would be easier to explain."

"Well, actually ... Could you come over now?"

The moment Hillary put down the phone, she remembered where she'd heard the name Paige Bennett. From Otis, of course. It embarrassed her to think of the old man's suggestive stares and stealthy touches—if not for Father counting so on Otis's visits, she would have chased him out the door months ago. But as it was, she tried to be politic. She'd gently sweep his damp hand away like it was an insect who'd lighted on her white cotton blouse—careful not to let it squash and leave a spot. Then pretend to be interested in his grocery store gossip.

But this bit of news wasn't simply gossip—it had also made front page of the local paper and page seven of the *Times* a day or two later—and it had indeed caught her interest. The Bennetts were the summer couple who'd found the little girl in the attic. She had been living in the house perhaps a year without anyone knowing or even suspecting. And then, her tragic background ...

Lord, what a web of horror surely to be found in that child's head.

What Hillary wouldn't do for the opportunity to work with her ...

The phys. ed. teacher had assigned the two softball team captains. Lily was second pick on the Blue Team, but that was only because Heidi, Lily's escort to classes, was first, and she saw to it that Lily was next. Once the teams were chosen, Heidi took the team captain aside and told her to let Lily pitch.

"No way, I'm pitching myself," Sandy said, swinging her thick, long red braid over her shoulder.

"Let her, she's new."

"So what? I don't even know she *can* pitch."

"She says she can."

"So does everyone say that. There's no one here doesn't like to pitch, except for maybe Cricket who'd rather be in the stands. What's so great about this girl?"

"Did I say there was?"

"Well, you act it. You made a big deal about me picking her for the team."

"She's new, that's all, it doesn't hurt to be nice."

Sandy fingered the smooth ends of her braid. "I was nice already," she said. "Now I'm pitching."

"Come on you guys, get on with it, will you?"

The other team captain stood with her fists on her hips, registering annoyance. Sandy turned quickly—flipping her braid off her shoulder, letting it tumble midway down her back.

"Okay, chill out, relax," she called back. Dismissing Heidi, she handed out assignments: the new girl got right field and number nine on the batting roster. And Sandy didn't miss the shit-assed stare she got in return ... wow, what nerve, who did she think she was anyhow?

It had taken Paige only five minutes to get to Hillary's farmhouse. Ruthanne was right, she wasn't attractive, but then again, she didn't seem to try to be: wire glasses, not a trace of makeup, and limp brown hair so short and uneven it looked as though she'd suddenly gotten fed up and clipped it herself.

"Feel free to call me Hillary," she said, showing her to a chair and sitting across from her. "First I want to tell you, I am aware of the circumstances here, at least to some extent. I didn't put it together until I got off the phone with you and remembered several days ago hearing the story. I'm afraid not too much goes on in this town that doesn't get reported in some detail." She put a palm to her nearly flat chest. "Not that you should ever think that I would—"

"Oh no, don't worry, I wouldn't expect that you and the town gossip exchange are in any way related."

"It's just that people around here don't understand there's such a thing as privileged information and professionalism."

"Well I'm a special education teacher in the city so I have a good handle on where you're coming from. Tell me," Paige said, eager to know more about her professional background, "have you worked with many children?"

"When I practiced in Boston, I'd say a third of my patients were children. Having worked with them yourself, though, you'll understand when I say the privacy we just spoke of obviously applies there, too. If I'm to make a significant difference, the youngster must feel his or her secrets are secure with me. Don't misunderstand, I'd be willing to talk with you about Lily, but the discussion would be of a general nature, no specifics. In other words, without the girl's permission, I cannot and will not divulge her confidences."

"That's not a problem, really. In fact, Lily and I communicate quite well ourselves, that is, if you consider the short time we've known each other."

"Good. Then she's receptive."

"Well, I can't say for sure. She views me as a friend, I don't know she'll view a therapist the same."

"Leave that to me. Once she realizes that during her time with me, I exist only for her and have no intention of lining up on the side of authority or the enemy—usually in a child's mind, those two are interchangeable—she'll relax. You'd be amazed how very much the same it is with adults: they need to feel total loyalty."

Paige was a little surprised to hear such a degree of passion and commitment in Hillary's voice. But she couldn't disagree with anything she'd said. In fact, she wondered how a doctor so devoted to her profession could bear to put her practice on hold while she stayed home nursing an elderly father.

"Then you will take her on?" she asked finally.

Hillary stopped, then her palm again resting on her chest, she smiled and nodded. "I guess that's what I've been saying, haven't I? Of course, I'll need as much information on her as you have. And then, well, then we'll schedule her to begin."

"How often do you think?"

"I think twice a week, on some weeks, more. But if that's—"

"No, that's fine. Whatever you think. But I would prefer it right after school."

"Of course . . . now let's see, elementary school gets out at two-thirty and I'm within a ten-, fifteen-minute walking distance, so excluding today, why don't we make it at three Mondays and Wednesdays."

By the time Paige Bennett left the house it was past eleven: the physical therapist had left and Father's buzzer was already bleating. But even that nuisance didn't take away from the exhilaration Hillary felt. And though she had purposely pushed aside any conflicts she might run into vis-à-vis Father's care and the child's sessions, once she responded to Father's call, she came downstairs, sat at the kitchen table and reflected on the entire picture.

She would have gladly brought in hired help—in fact, that was what she had planned originally after Father's illness and her return to Briarwood. But just the mention of strangers bathing him, feeding him, and changing his soiled diapers nearly caused Lester Egan a coronary. Since her mother's death and the stroke three years earlier that left Father paralyzed on his entire right side and unable to speak, all he wanted was Hillary. No fill-ins, no substitutes.

Perhaps it would have been easier to refuse him if he and mother hadn't been so wonderful, hadn't saved her from the sterility of the orphanage: surely no one else had seen beyond the sallow complexion, the pinched features, the skinniness of that lonely little girl. Or if they hadn't encouraged her quick mind, rejoiced in her achievements, and paid for seven years of education and a trip abroad for graduation ... But they did all that, and now with her fancy psychology degrees gathering dust in the attic, she knew what she was letting Father do to her was wrong, that it was already feeding resentment. But how to stop it?

Now suddenly she was getting a chance to do what she loved most, and she mustn't let it elude her—not for her sake, not for Father's. Her only option was to disconnect the buzzer—only for that hour twice a week, the time he was usually busy reading the local paper or watching daytime television serials. And it wasn't as though his calls had anything to do with medical emergencies. . . .

Why, the last time Father was checked, his blood pressure was actually lower than hers.

It was the first time the three of them had sat together for a meal. Paige went out of her way to prepare an especially good dinner, with Lily's cooking know-how being a definite advantage. She had telephoned Jason earlier so he was aware of the arrangements she'd made with Hillary Egan, and they had decided to present a united front—together, to tell Lily about it over dinner.

"This chicken is good," Jason said. "What's the sauce?"

Paige smiled. "A secret sauce, Lily gave me the recipe."

"Using edible ingredients, I hope?"

"Jason!"

He smiled, tapping Lily's arm in a show of comradery. "What's with you girls, no sense of humor?"

"We have plenty. Give us a joke, we'll laugh," Paige answered. "Oh, you'll be pleased to know, Lily had her physical this afternoon, and she's fine."

"I told you I was," Lily said.

"Well, sometimes we're better off leaving those things to experts," Jason said. "Which leads me to—" he looked at Paige and she frowned and took over.

"Lily, I met with a woman today named Hillary Egan, she's a psychologist here in town."

Lily stopped chewing and looked at her.

"Jason and I talked it over, and we thought it'd be a good idea for you to see her."

"Why?"

"Because it's nice to have someone to talk to."

"I have you," she said, ignoring Jason.

"Of course, you do. But when you tell me something, I look at it, well let's say from a biased perspective. In other words, because I care so much about you, it interferes with my ability to give a detached opinion. When you confide in a therapist it's different. She can analyze what you say objectively, not allow emotions to get in the way. That objectivity might be very useful to you."

Lily turned to Jason. "You think I'm crazy, right?"

"What I think is, you've been through a lot of hell in your young life, and when you go through something like that, you don't exit it without hauling away some nightmares. Even though you might choose to think otherwise."

"I don't want to see her."

"Lily," Paige interrupted, "I want you to meet Hillary. Give her a chance. I think you'll like her."

Silence.

"Okay?"

"I won't tell her anything. I'll just sit there."

"That's your choice. But if you change your mind and confide in her, she won't tell me or Jason what it is you tell her."

"Why not?"

"Because she respects your privacy. She's your doctor, not mine, not Jason's—whatever you say to her, stays strictly between you two."

Lily thought about it, then nodded.

"Good, on to something else," Jason said. "What about school, how were your classes?"

"Okay."

"What are your favorite subjects?"

She thought a minute. "Math and phys. ed."

"Yeah, why?"

"Because I'm good at them."

Jason nodded. "I can't argue that logic."

She looked at Paige. "The phys. ed. teacher

said to bring in deodorant, soap, foot powder, a bath towel, and sweats. We're supposed to shower every day after gym and bring the towel and sweats home to be washed once a week."

"What're you doing in gym these days?" Jason asked.

"Softball. Some girl went nuts."

"Oh?" Paige said.

"After the game, in the shower. She screamed, cried, so loud the teacher heard her from out in the supply room. They had to take her to the nurse's office."

"How awful, was it a fight?"

"Uh, uh, she was alone in the shower stall."

"Do you think it was drug-related?"

"No. I tried to see, but couldn't. Kids were blocking the way."

"Maybe the water scalded her."

Lily shrugged. "When her mother came to pick her up, I saw the girl run to the car. That's when I noticed her braid was gone, like it had been chopped right off. Paige, why would she do that to her hair? Do you think she went crazy?"

"There's something about the way she says things," Jason said to Paige that night in bed. "Do you notice it?"

"Notice what?"

"The way she told us about that kid freaking. Almost like she was just reciting information, not like there might have been a real person involved. Or if there was, she could really give a shit."

"Oh, Jason, you know how heartless children are, unless they know a victim personally—and in this case, we don't even know what really happened—they're not big on sympathy. Actually, they're not so different from adults. We put up barriers and God knows Lily's had more reason than most to shut off her emotions."

"Maybe."

"It makes perfect sense, and it's one reason this therapy idea is good."

"You mean to say I had a good idea?"

She smiled. "Don't let it go to your head. Oh, and don't think I didn't notice how hard you tried with her tonight. I think her response was positive, don't you?"

"Okay, but I wouldn't get too optimistic. She'd still rather I pack my bags and move out. Incidentally, my visit with Anna Parks today didn't go well."

Paige sat up in bed. "Why, what happened?"

"For one, she didn't want my representation."

"Why not?"

"She's got this thing about needing to take her just punishment."

"Where does Lily fit into these martyrly needs?"

"That's what I tried to stress. In any event, I'm moving on the issue without her consent. By the time I get close to the hearing, I hope to have her cooperating. Meanwhile, I asked about her sister, Nora."

"Oh?"

"She doesn't know where she is, doesn't much care . . . apparently there's a lot of bad feeling there. And she made it abundantly clear that Lily is not to live with her."

"Well, I guess we have to respect her wishes

when it comes to that. Maybe she knows something about the sister we don't."

"Like what?"

"Maybe she's a bitch, maybe she has a mean
temper . . . maybe, I don't know, Jason."

"May . . . be?" he said as he laid his hand on
the back of her neck, his fingers gently massaging
. . . She closed her eyes, determined to clear her
mind of everything else, relax, and lose herself
in the sensation. She felt his lips touch her neck,
twin whispers dancing along her skin . . . A
shiver ran around her stomach as his tongue
flicked her neck, her chest; cool air suddenly
flowed onto her breasts as her nightgown
lowered. . . .

The door sprang open. "Paige."

They grabbed quickly for the quilt, dragging it
up over themselves. Paige sat up, her hand smooth-
ing back her hair.

"Lily, you startled us, what's wrong?"

"What is it, kid, don't you know about knocking?" Jason said, staring at the ceiling.

Paige quickly got out of bed and took Lily back
to her room. She tucked her in and sat down
beside her on the mattress.

"What was it, sweetheart, you have a
nightmare?"

She shook her head. "Uh, uh. But I was scared
maybe you would."

"You were, why?"

"I heard you scream last night. So tonight I
was listening real hard, and I thought I should
come see—"

Paige thought about it, then remembered. "I
guess I did have a nightmare last night."

"What was it about?" Lily asked, her huge blue eyes luminous in the semidarkness.

"I nearly forgot about having the dream, let alone what it was about. You know how those things are. It's often out of your mind the moment you wake."

"You forgot the whole thing?"

Paige nodded.

"I bet the dream was about Daddy."

"*Your* daddy?" Paige asked.

"No, silly. Yours."

Paige stared at her, studied her, thinking maybe Lily was teasing her. But even with the way the darkness played tricks on faces, distorting and confusing expressions, Paige was sure she saw concern on Lily's face.

"Why in the world would you think that?"

She shrugged. "Because you hate his guts, that's why."

"That's not true, Lily, not really. Do I care about him? No. After all, he did desert me and my mother. I suppose it's possible I'm still angry at him for running out, but how can you really hate someone you can't even remember?"

Jason tried to get Paige back in the mood when she returned to bed ten minutes later, but any desire she had worked up, suddenly fell flat. And though he didn't say so—by the look on his face, there was no need to—Jason was clearly annoyed at Lily for breaking the moment, and at Paige for allowing it to happen.

Chapter Eight

Jason hadn't left her a note on the pillow in the morning as he often did, particularly when he had gone to sleep angry. Well, Paige hoped he had been able to sleep well, because she hadn't—she'd tossed and turned most of the night, thinking of Lily and their conversation about Paige's father, which she still found rather disturbing.

Once she got Lily off to school, she phoned Jason's office, but he wasn't in yet. Instead she called Brooke and the conversation led immediately to Lily.

"So, do something about it," Brooke said.

"Like what? I just wish he weren't so critical of her. He forgets she's a child."

"Maybe their personalities just don't mesh. Those things happen with people."

"They don't just happen. He's being childish and stubborn, it's so not like him."

"Okay, so maybe he's acting out. Doesn't he get the occasional right, too?"

"Meaning what, that it's usually me?"

"Oh my, did I say that?"

"Why is it you always side with him?"

"Look, Paige, not that you're going to pay attention to what I say, but if I had a fellow who was crazy in love with me like Jason is with you, I'd stroke his balls night and day."

"What you must mean is bust 'em, like you do Gary's. And I suppose Gary doesn't love you?"

"Sure he does. The difference is, I come a distant second after medicine."

"Why must you say things like that?"

"Because they're true. So he's not out there fucking my competition—but trust me, he would if he could. It doesn't make the competition any less threatening. In fact, I'd rather go against a woman any day . . . with that, I know what I'm doing."

"I'll say."

"Meow . . ."

"Not at all, I'm basing my comments on observations. I've seen guys step all over their own feet in response to your come-ons. What can I say—I'm impressed."

A sigh. "Look, Paige, why don't you simply get rid of the kid?"

"How can you be so cold? She's a child, Brooke, one who's had a miserable existence so far. Would you like me to simply boot her out the door?"

"That's the way she came in, isn't it?"

"You're lucky I don't take you seriously."

"What about your relationship with Jason, how seriously do you take that?"

"Not to worry. I'll handle my relationship with Jason with no outside assistance, thank you. He may not be delighted Lily's living here, but he isn't a cold fish like some people I run across—he sees there's no other place for her at this moment. In fact, he's agreed to appeal her mother's case, to try to free her."

"Swell. Be sure to let me know where the nice lady takes up residence once the courts set her loose. If it's in my neighborhood, I'll buy me a shotgun."

"I hate you. I'll see you Friday night?"

"More likely Saturday morning."

At first Paige was ticked off by the conversation, but after thinking it through she realized it was just Brooke's way: passionate, sometimes brutally so, certainly no inhibitions, willing to say or do whatever entered her head. But through Paige's difficult miscarriage last year, the depression following it, then the attack more recently, Brooke had been there for her.

And she had to concede Brooke was right on a few points as well: with all the effort Paige was putting out for Lily, she was guilty of neglecting Jason. He was trying his best to get along with Lily, doing it primarily for Paige's benefit, too. Okay, he was unduly critical of her, but that didn't mean he was unfeeling. Not everyone related so easily to a child like Lily . . . But she surely did. . . .

She strained her mind, tried to dig back into some forgotten cranny to find a face for her own father. But all she could come up with was that damn kid who mugged her in Manhattan—annoyed, she pushed the face with the mustache and the bad teeth from her mind.

*   *   *

Paige picked up Lily right after school and took her along to her obstetric appointment—Lily waited in Dr. Barry's reception room while Paige went into the examining room. The examination complete, Paige changed back to her street clothes, then went into the doctor's office where he'd been waiting. For the second time within a seven-day period, her blood pressure had lowered.

"So what is this now, you want some kind of a note to bring to your husband?" he asked smiling.

"Well, not exactly a note, just mark down my pressure reading on one of your letterhead note-pads so Jason can see the good news straight from you."

"Not taking your word these days, huh?"

"Well, as I explained, not when it concerns the wisdom of letting Lily stay on with us. But she is good for me. I mean, what more proof could he ask for?"

"Look, no question, you're calmer, your blood pressure is definitely lower, in fact, the systolic reading is normal. You seem much less apprehensive than in past visits. So if this little girl is in any way responsible for these changes, then I say, hooray for her. However, not to get my head chopped off, may I suggest you pay a little extra attention to your husband?"

"Excuse me?"

"It happens a lot when a new baby comes. The woman gets caught up with caring for the newborn, maybe to the exclusion of her husband. And though I'm hardly a marriage specialist, from what you've described to me, this may well be part of the problem."

"It's funny you should say so, I was thinking pretty much the same thing earlier. But jealousy . . . Jason?"

"It hadn't occurred to you?"

"Well, no, not exactly, at least I hadn't thought of it that way. But maybe I should."

He wrote out Paige's blood pressure and handed her the paper. "Oh, and by the way, she *is* a little beauty."

Paige took the paper and tucked it into her purse. "Who?"

"Lily, of course."

"You saw her?"

He sat back in his chair. "I surely did. When you were changing back to your clothes, I had a visitor. She actually took the initiative to knock at my office door."

Paige's mouth dropped, then curved up into a smile. "Really, what did she say?"

"She introduced herself, asked a couple of questions about you, the baby. She sounded genuinely concerned, certainly looking forward to the birth."

"The doctor mentioned you spoke to him," Paige said on the drive home.

Lily looked at her. "Are you mad?"

"No, just curious. What exactly was it you wanted to know?"

"If the baby was healthy."

"And?"

"It is."

"What else?"

"How big it is. I mean if something happened now, if you had to have it early."

"I see. Well, did the doctor tell you?"

"He did better than that, he showed me a picture of him."

"*Him?*"

"The baby."

"My sonogram?"

"I guess . . ."

"You could see it was a boy? Jason and I saw those pictures, we couldn't tell."

"Oh, I couldn't either, but the paper clipped to it said so."

Paige's open palm went to her chest and held fast. "The report, you read it?"

She nodded. "It said Baby Boy Bennett right there on the first line. Didn't you know?"

Paige couldn't very well be angry at her. After all, she hadn't known. So first things first—Paige swore Lily to immediate secrecy so she'd have a chance to tell Jason that night herself, then she sat back and digested the news. A boy, a baby boy, wouldn't Jason be thrilled! Though he hadn't actually come out and said so, their little name game had made it abundantly clear: she would have had to be deaf and blind not to know that what he really wanted was a boy.

Paige purposely gave Lily dinner early that night, then sent her upstairs to do homework. If a little coddling was what Jason needed, she'd give it to him in triple doses: candlelight dinner, the good china, cloth napkins, she even hunted through her closet and found the ankle-length silk paisley dressing gown he particularly liked. . . . But it wasn't until she felt herself being shaken gently awake that she realized she'd fallen asleep on the sofa, probably for quite a while.

"Jason, what time is it?"

He looked at her rumpled gown. "Ten-thirty."

She sat up, still groggy. "Where were you?"

"The office. I stayed late."

"I made dinner," she said, standing and heading for the stove. "Oh, gosh, it must be—" She opened the oven door—it was cool and empty. She went to the refrigerator and looked inside—apparently Lily had taken the chicken out and wrapped it. "Looks like Lily rescued it in time. I can heat it, it'll only take—"

"Forget it, I ate."

She nodded, closed the refrigerator.

She gestured to the table—the full place settings, candlesticks. "Pretty fancy plans you blew, Bennett."

"Look, if this is a prelude to your bitching, I don't—"

"I'm not—"

"Good." Taking his briefcase, he headed upstairs. She followed. "Jason?"

"Yeah?"

"What about Craig?"

"What?"

"You know, for a boy's name."

"Okay, I guess. Look, can we put this off?"

"I just thought—"

"Damnit, Paige, I'm not in the mood!"

She didn't go up to bed till much later. When she did, he was already asleep or at least pretending to be. She changed out of the silk gown into flannel PJs, then slid in quietly beside him.

She had tried to tell him about it being a boy, but he had shut her right off. In fact, the baby seemed to be the furthest thing from his mind. None of it seemed to make sense: trying so hard to conceive, living through the sadness and disappointment of a miscarriage. . . . Somehow they had gotten past that. But now with her due in a matter of a couple months, they ought to be euphoric.

Instead, all they could do was bicker.

He hadn't wanted to, in fact he had promised himself he wouldn't go near her apartment alone again, but all good intentions by the board, there he was at five o'clock standing in the lobby of Brooke's building, ringing her doorbell. Secretly he'd hoped he would hear Gary's voice come through the intercom, and that would be that. A quick unexpected visit from a friend. But as it was, Gary was on emergency room duty at the hospital and not expected home until midnight.

This time they hadn't bothered with drinks.

Hillary had asked that Paige drop Lily off at the house and then leave immediately, eliminating even that small link of having Paige waiting in the adjoining room. Whatever relationship Lily would establish with her therapist, it would be a relationship totally apart from what she had with Paige.

Hillary had set up the large corner room downstairs, the one that for as long as she could remember was Mother's sewing room—and with the exception of the venetian blinds, carpeting, and a three- by five-foot mirror secured to one wall, she removed everything.

Now, after spending all day yesterday fixing it and refurbishing it, it had a desk, a file cabinet—the lower file drawer containing family personal papers—three chairs, a chaise lounge, a foam rubber mattress, two blankets, and a card table, dusted, washed, polished, and taken downstairs from the attic.

Newly purchased—thanks to Otis watching Father while she went last evening to the mall—was a chalk board, an easel with paints, papers, crayons, scissors, swatches of material, a fully furnished dollhouse, a metal box with latch, and two sturdy cardboard boxes filled with puzzles, cars, trucks, animals, a wooden hammer, building toys, and a family of six hand puppets. In Hillary's top desk drawer was hidden a tape recorder which would unobtrusively tape their sessions, and following them, of course, she'd record her comments and observations.

Hillary would be Lily's silent spectator, her confidant, her teacher, her conscience, her sounding board, perhaps even her friend. She would be anything and everything Lily needed her to be. In this room, there was nothing Lily couldn't say or do or act out—that is, except inflict physical pain on herself or Hillary.

In return, the patient had to put herself in Hillary's hands so together they could explore the dark corners of her mind. . . . Hillary had always wanted to have a paper published on one of her cases. Maybe this case would be the one.

*   *   *

Jason had put the wheels in progress the day before. He had filed an appearance in the Laurel Canyon County Court, putting his name as Anna's attorney of record, then notified the prison administration in Albany that Doctor M.C. Wendell would be doing a psychological workup on the prisoner.

Most interesting was what finally dawned on him in the second reading of the transcript: Anna Parks had not had a proper voir dire. Neither the court nor her young public defender had bothered to formally question her understanding of the proceedings or explain to her the consequences of her guilty plea. With this error existing, Jason's chances of having Anna's plea vacated had shot up dramatically. If not in the trial court, then surely on appeal.

His biggest problem now was Anna. What good would any of it be if when the time came, she refused to change her plea to not guilty?

Hillary had taken a full fifteen minutes to introduce herself to Lily and explain her basic rules of therapy. Then she slipped her hand in her desk drawer and pressed the record button on the tape. Finally she sat back in her chair, thoughtfully trying to put herself inside the child's mind: would this strange adult really sit by and let her run the show? Or would she be like other intrusive adults, immediately prying, steering, and offering opinions and value judgments without so much as being asked?

Usually children began by going to the toy box, finding something to occupy their hands and minds. They weren't ready to open up, and anything was better than sitting and staring at some elusive adult. But Lily hadn't gone for the toys—at least not yet, and when the creaking sound came through the ceiling from upstairs, she had no difficulty in asking, "Who's the old man up there?"

"How did you know there was an old man?"

"When Paige and I drove up, he was looking out the window."

"I see. Well, that's my father."

"You keep him locked upstairs?"

"No, why would you think so?"

Lily shrugged, then put her head back on the easy chair, resting it, and closed her eyes. She didn't open them until four o'clock—as though an alarm had gone off in her head—when the session was to end. She stood up, went to the door, then with her hand cupped around the doorknob, she looked at Hillary.

"Can I ask you something?"

"Of course, ask anything."

"You're a fuckin' ugly cunt, did you know that?"

Hillary caught her breath—this was a test, only a test.

Though it was less than a mile walking distance to home, this time Paige picked Lily up.

"How was it?" she asked driving away from the house.

"Good."

"What do you think of Dr. Egan?"

"She's nice."

"See, told you so."

"Where're we going?"

"I thought Ruthanne's. Mind?"

"Uh, uh. Is Roger home?"

"Hmmm. I think you like him as much as he likes you."

"Does he really?"

"Ruthanne says so."

"I think she's probably wrong."

"Why do you say that?"

"Because people don't like me much."

"It's funny, I don't get that impression at all. In fact, I think most people take to you rather quickly."

"Not Jason."

"Jason is just one person. I can name three others who think you're great—Ruthanne, Roger, and Dr. Barry. And though I haven't spoken to Hillary, your teacher, or any of your classmates, I imagine many of them do, too."

Silence.

"Speaking of classmates, Lily, whatever happened with that girl you told me about, what was her name?"

"Sandy. Oh her, she's kind of quiet. The other kids say she never used to be so quiet, only since she went nuts like that, you know, cutting off her braid and all."

"Did you find out why she did it?"

"She won't talk about it."

"Well, there's got to be some reason, and if it were up to me I'd insist she tell me—better to get it out in the open."

Lily shrugged. "Dr. Egan doesn't believe in pushing."

"Really? Well, she's probably right. I doubt I'd have the patience or temperament to be a good therapist."

Silence.

"I let her play first base today."

"Who?"

"Sandy. I felt bad for her."

"Were you team captain?"

"No, but Trish was, she let me assign."

"Really, what position did you take?"

"Pitcher."

Paige smiled. "Of course, I should have guessed."

It was encouraging to hear that Lily was obviously getting along well with her classmates. In fact, it sounded like she was quite popular. From what Paige could observe, Lily's biggest failing was her lack of self-esteem. It would take time and love to nurse it to strength.

Though it was Paige's intention to tell Jason about the baby being a boy, she didn't want to do it with the bad feelings still between them. So that night she tried to set another mood, this one falling flat at about ten when Paige could wait no longer and dished herself a plate of macaroni and cheese and ate it along with a chunk of crusty Italian bread. Jason walked in at about eleven.

"Where were you?" she asked as she deposited her empty plate into the sink.

"Clubbing."

She stared at him.

"Where do you think I've been?"

"You could have called and told me you'd be late."

"I thought we went through this before the

move here. Wasn't it you I was telling about that long drive?"

She turned away. "Did you eat?"

"I picked up a sandwich on the way."

She sighed, covered the casserole with foil, and slid it into the refrigerator.

"What about you?" he said.

"I ate. I couldn't wait."

"Where's the kid?"

"Sleeping." Paige went to her purse, took out the doctor's note. "I thought you might like to see this."

"What is it?"

"My blood pressure. It went down again."

He nodded, tossed the paper on the counter.

"That's it?"

"What do you want, it framed? Hey, not such a bad idea, why not show it off?" He opened a kitchen drawer and fumbled around. He brought out a hammer and nail, then picking up the paper, went to the wall and nailed it up. She went over to him, cupped her hand over his upper arm. "What's wrong, Jason?"

"Wrong, nothing's wrong, what gives you that idea? I hung up the paper, not a big deal."

"Are you drunk?"

He turned, breathed in her face. "How's that, do I pass?"

Silence. She swallowed what felt like an inflating ball in her throat.

"Look," he said finally, "I'm going to need you to tell Lily about my efforts on her mother's behalf."

"I thought you didn't want to get her hopes up."

"I don't, but I might not have a choice. So far the mother doesn't want my representation. I've begun without her knowledge, but she ultimately has to give me authority to represent her. By the time I get to court, I want her ready to change her plea."

"You want Lily to go see her?"

"If necessary."

"I hate having her go to the prison."

He sighed. "Maybe it won't be necessary, maybe she can give me a message, a letter to give her mother. The bottom line is, I want Anna to realize how important it is that she fight."

"Doesn't she know that? What is it with that woman? Sometimes I wonder if we're doing the right thing for Lily."

Jason held his hand up like a stop signal, then headed upstairs. "If we're not, I don't even want to know about it."

How in the world was it possible that her blood pressure was down? Right now she felt tense enough to explode. She went to the cabinet and took down a bag of Hershey Kisses.

It was the next night, Thursday, and Jason had come home at seven, his disposition and attitude noticeably improved. Though Paige had tried countless times in the past couple of days to get him to open up, each time he blew it off as nothing.

After dinner he sent Paige to the sofa with a bunch of magazines and told her to relax while he and Lily did the dishes. It was apparently the way he was choosing to say, "I'm sorry," and though she would go along with it, it wasn't quite over yet. Not until she knew what had gotten into him. But for now, it would have to do—she wasn't willing to chance reversing his mood. When the telephone rang, Jason picked up the receiver, said hello, then started to hand it to her.

"Who?" she whispered.

"Brooke."

"I thought maybe it was a salesman."

He put the receiver back to his ear. "I'm being harassed on this end for my antisocial behavior."

Laughter seeping through the receiver.

"So, I hear we're going to have the pleasure of your company this weekend." Some hesitation, then: "Paige mention we were thinking of naming the baby Brooke?" Apparent glee from Brooke's end, then: "Yeah, nothing certain, of course. Here, let me give you over to her for the particulars."

Though Paige had shaken her head in an effort to stop him from discussing baby names, it had done no good. He had seemed suddenly discombobulated as though he had picked up a script and wasn't about to tamper with it. Now apparently eager to get rid of the phone and get back to the dishes, she took it from him.

"Brooke, I'm beginning to think you make my husband nervous," Paige said, smiling at Jason as she teased. Back into the phone: "Warning you now, we don't want to hear of any plan changes."

"Well, there is a very minor one, hopefully one you'll consider positive."

"Okay, I'm listening."

"We'll be coming tomorrow night versus Saturday morning, that is assuming you people have no prior commitments."

"If we had any, we'd gladly change them. What's gotten hold of you, don't you know how much we miss you two?" Then mouthing to Jason, "They're coming tomorrow."

He nodded, then went back to the dishes.

Brooke laughed. "I like that kind of enthusiasm, it's nice to be appreciated. Jason feel that way, too?"

"Need you ask?"

"Tell me more about a little baby girl named Brooke."

"Oh, it's just one of the names on that long 'possibility' list."

Lily was listening quietly to Paige's end of the conversation and rinsing the last glass when she said to Jason in a hushed voice, "Brooke's sure a dumb name."

He picked up the glass, dried it, then placed it upside down on the cabinet shelf.

"Yeah, think so?"

"Know so. Other kids will laugh."

"Between you and me, I'm not big on it either. However, I doubt anyone would laugh at it. I think it's a pretty respectable name in most circles."

"For a girl."

"Naturally. What do you think, we'd mean it for a boy?"

"Why would you care about a girl's name?"

"Why wouldn't I care?"

She smiled a tight smile, then shrugged. "I guess because Paige isn't having one."

*　　　*　　　*

Paige was still on the phone when she saw Lily rush upstairs and Jason rush to her, his arms folded at his chest. Two blood vessels on his neck were as taut as fiddle strings. "Jason ... I've got to go, Brooke," she said into the receiver. "Yes, now ... see you tomorrow." She put down the phone, then to Jason: "I don't like that look at all, what is it?"

"Don't you know?"

She shook her head.

"Lily just gave me the good news. A boy, huh?"

She drew in her breath. Oh God, of all ways for him to learn of it ...

"Well?"

"I wanted to tell you, I was about to ... In fact, tonight."

"I see." He ran his hand through his hair, took a few steps away from her, then circled back. "So if I'm not being too intrusive, when did you two girls learn of this?"

"It's just that things have been so unbelievably messed up ... I was waiting until—"

"When did you know?"

A deep sigh. Why was this coming out to make her sound so deceitful? It wasn't that at all. "Tuesday," she said finally. "I learned after I left the doctor's office Tuesday."

"After?"

"Lily told me. She's the one who saw the report. Accidentally."

He shook his head in confusion. "Report, what report?"

"Attached to my sonogram."

"She was reading your medical records?"

"She didn't, I mean, the doctor showed it to her—"

"Christ, will you tell me what's going on here! The doctor discussed your sonogram with Lily, an eleven-year-old kid who has nothing at all to do with this family?"

"Wait, stop! Give me a minute to explain, and stop interrogating me as though she or I did something underhanded. Dr. Barry showed her a picture of the baby because she asked questions pertaining to the baby's size—it was all quite innocent. She's simply interested, concerned about the baby's welfare."

The worst part of all of this was the ridiculous anger. Anger when he and Paige should have been out there celebrating. Christ, a boy! Though he wouldn't have complained either way, he'd be lying to say he hadn't always pictured his firstborn a son. And here he was, actually about to have one. So why was it so hard to squash these bad feelings, and concentrate only on the important?

But just how trivial was it that Paige hadn't told him right away, as soon as she'd *accidentally* found it out herself? Instead he had to learn it from a strange kid who'd come into their lives, a kid he didn't even much like.

Chapter Nine

"You're rich," Lily said as she sat on Paige's bed watching her brush her hair.

"What makes you say so?"

"You own two houses, right? One here and one right in the middle of New York City."

"Right, but that doesn't mean—"

"That's rich. Rich as I've ever seen."

Paige thought about it. "I guess in a way it is rich. . . . Certainly I have more money and clothes and things than I ever thought I'd have. I'm lucky in many respects. I have a career I like, Jason . . . of course, soon to have a baby and—"

"That's okay, you don't have to say me."

Paige reached out, but Lily quickly slid herself to the floor. "But I want to—" Paige said.

"It'd be a lie though 'cause you don't really have me."

Paige sat there a moment looking at the back of Lily's head and seeing bits of herself at that age. "When I was little, I used to think I was adopted," she said. "Well, maybe not really think it, just wish it. I didn't look much like my mother, didn't act it either."

"I bet you were the good princess, she was the wicked one."

"So, I guess you must have been in one of those fairy tales yourself."

She turned herself around, facing Paige. "Except I was the wicked princess."

"Oh, come on, I find that hard to believe."

"That's only because you're one of the good ones."

"You know what, Lily, I think a lot of kids have those daydreams, wishing or imagining they were someone other than who they are. Though I've never thought about it much, I'm sure there were good things about my mother, too, things I didn't notice because I was too busy noticing the bad. No one is all good, or all bad."

"What about your girlfriend from New York, the one coming to visit."

"Lily, do you understand what I'm trying to say?"

She nodded. "I guess, but I don't want to talk about my mother. I want to talk about your friend."

Paige sighed, reached down and ruffled her hair.

"Brooke? Well, let's see . . . she's beautiful, glamorous in fact."

"Like you?"

"Me?"

"Yeah."

"But I'm not—"

"You are, too."

Paige laughed. "Anyone ever tell you, you're marvelous for a lady's ego?"

"I'm not just saying it to make you like me. You *are* beautiful. Doesn't Jason tell you that?"

"Well, yes, I mean, no." She laughed, sighed, then leaned forward and ran the hairbrush through the child's long silky hair.

"Tell me more about Brooke."

"More?" Paige pulled herself up straight. "Okay, let's see, she dislikes children."

"Really?"

"So she tells me, and I have no reason to believe otherwise; according to her, she's not planning to have any."

"Is she mean?"

"Not at all. Some people just aren't the parenting kind. And I suppose it's better they admit it beforehand rather then go ahead, have a child, then find out they don't have the patience and . . . Well, you pretty much get the point."

"Beat on them, is that what you mean?"

She nodded. "I guess something like that. Lily, did your daddy beat on you?"

"Do I have to talk about it?"

"No, of course you don't. But I just want to remind you that if you should want to talk, I'm here to listen. And Dr. Egan, too. Take advantage of that, sweetheart. It's so much better to get feelings out, talk about them, rather than let them slip into some dark place where you lose control over them."

"Is that what you did, Paige?"

A pause, then: "If you'd have asked me that a month ago, even a few weeks ago, I would have said, no way. But maybe I did do some of that . . ."

"When you were little?"

"I think."

A few minutes' pause while Paige changed into another shirt to go with her black and white striped pants, then: "Lily, while we're talking about this . . ." Lily looked up at her—a stare so wide and clear, it seemed as though it were reaching from her soul. "Sweetheart, what would you say if you learned your mother had a chance to come home?"

Lily swallowed hard, wet her lips. "Does she?" she asked, in a voice Paige could barely hear.

"Well, not for certain. You know Jason's a lawyer, right?"

She nodded.

"Well, he's working on trying to get her home."

"How can he?"

"Well, it's called postconviction relief. He wants to make a motion to change her plea and remove her sentence." Paige spotted the confusion and tried again. "The thing is, your mother never had a real trial . . . she just pled guilty and let them lock her away."

"She shouldn't have done that?"

"Well, she had a side to tell, too, and she should have stood up and told it. That's called a defense and that's how the legal system works. Seldom is something all right or all wrong, there are circumstances that apply that make each situation unique. Think of it, Lily, she didn't suddenly wake up one morning and decide to kill your dad. It happened after years of abuse, tears, bruises, broken bones. Surely you would know the story even better than I."

"Then she was right to kill him?"

"It's not a matter of right. There's such a thing as self-defense, and Jason thinks what your mother did could be considered that. But first he has to convince the judge to let her start over again, that's because the first time around she wasn't mentally able to defend herself."

"Does that mean she was crazy?"

"It means she was in shock, not in full control of her senses when she pled guilty to the crime. And if Jason can prove it, then again, prove the murder was self-defense ... Lily, your mother could go free or at least get a much lighter sentence. Now, it's not for certain, and I don't want you to think it is ... but if there were a possibility of that happening, what would you think?"

"I guess it'd be good. Real good."

Paige smiled, then hugged her.

"How about if you write her a letter, saying so. You see, Lily, one of the difficulties with your mother is, she's her own worst judge and jury. She's not willing to forgive herself and fight for her freedom. So it's up to you to convince her that you love her and need her to come back home to be with you."

Brooke and Gary arrived at six—twenty minutes before Jason. After the rounds of hugs and kisses, accompanied by absurd screams and groans and the usual silly jokes about pregnant women, Paige introduced Lily, giving her due credit for the colorful and tasty platter of canapés arranged on the coffee table.

Gary—tall, sandy blond hair, and fine-featured—was already at the buffet, pouring himself white Chardonnay to accompany the little plate of canapés he had made up for himself.

"She's a magnificent cook and she's gorgeous to boot. How old you say you are, young lady, eleven?" He turned, his blue eyes on Lily. "Hey, I don't suppose you'd consider a solid job back in the city."

"Better pass it up, honey, bad deal," Brooke said as she poured herself wine into a long-stemmed glass. "The big talker here works for close to minimum wage himself."

Gary winked at Lily. "Ah, that's only what I tell *her*, and for her own good I might add. Actually the woman's loony, got this mental disorder that makes her hyperventilate whenever she gets near anything green and foldable."

"Lucky I need not count on him to cure any of my disorders—sooner I should scribble out a last will and testament. Wait," she held up her finger, "isn't *he* the one who got the record for lowest scores on the medical boards or was that one of his asshole buddies?"

Paige stood up. "Lily, why don't you go upstairs and start that letter we talked about." Lily left and Paige crossed her arms at her chest, looked from one to the other. "Will you two get it under control? You just got here and already you're at it."

Brooke gestured to the stairs.

"Well, it's not like the princess isn't used to a little good-natured sparring."

"Good-natured by whose standards? Besides, I don't want Lily treated like one of your stage props. So for this weekend, the object of the game is to pretend to get along with your chosen partner. The one who manages best—that is, without breaking into hives or some other horrendous affliction—wins."

Clapping from the doorway. "Bravo, that was marvelous. So marvelous I think I'll buy into the concept. Fighting's strictly off-limits for the weekend, those the rules?"

Paige looked at Jason. "Have you been drinking?"

"Nothing you should worry about." He lifted a brown paper bag, put his hand in, and pulled out a huge red tomato. "This, my friends, is what's called a home-grown tomato," he said displaying it.

"Whose home we talking about?" Gary asked.

"Doesn't matter. Wait'll you taste the pasta sauce I'm gonna make with it tomorrow."

"Come, come," Brooke said, holding out her arms. "First things first, where's my hug?"

Despite the late hour they'd gotten to bed, Gary, Jason, and Lily got up early the next morning, then thought nothing of waking the others. A little exercise, followed by breakfast at the diner was voted in. So while Gary and Paige walked along the graveled road, talking, Jason, Brooke, and Lily ran along the path through the woods down to the river.

"Meet you two guys at the Pathfinder in let's say, thirty minutes," Jason said.

Jason and Brooke stopped twenty minutes later as they made their third pass of the river. Lily hung back at the weeping willow, gripping both hands to a low tree branch and swinging from it. Jason, feeling the awkwardness of being alone with Brooke, stooped at the bank flipping pebbles through the water while Brooke studied the big oak tree in front of her. Suddenly she began to climb up, branch to branch till she reached a long sturdy one about twenty feet off the ground. She let go of the tree and spread her arms wide—the bottom of her knit shirt lifting high enough to bare her midriff.

"Would you look at this?"

He turned, looked. "Hey, watch yourself, sit down, you're pretty high up."

"Don't fret, I'm fine," she said, lifting her chin, stretching her long neck, and breathing in deeply. Finally, one arm leaning on the tree for support, she sat.

"What a magnificent view, I must do a painting from here."

"How's the art going?"

"Good. I'm making some money, enough so we don't have to rely strictly on Gary's meager wages. I hate not being able to afford everything I want, one of those little quirks of mine."

"Another couple of years, and Gary'll be raking it in faster than you can spend it."

"I suppose I wouldn't mind that. Meanwhile, it's just a lot of long, inconvenient hours for very little payback." She turned toward the willow tree and gestured with a nod. "How's our little princess working out?"

"It's not family bliss if that's what you mean."

"I tried my best to talk to Paige. But—"

"No, I don't imagine any talking to her about it would work at this point. She's already way too attached to her. What a mistake to come up here."

"Well, it's hard to say. Remember, Paige wasn't in the best of shape when she left the city. She couldn't step fifty feet out of the apartment without feeling threatened by someone or something. Either real or imaginary."

"Yeah, I suppose it was pretty bad for a while there, I just wish . . . Will you look at this—" He took a step toward the water's edge, then carefully reached in.

"What is it?"

"Wait." With both hands, he lifted out a turtle then held it up. "Check out the size of this thing!" He turned toward the willow tree and shouted. "Hey, Lily, quick, get on over here."

Lily came running out of the woods with Brooke and Jason following behind.

"Wait'll you guys see what Jason found!" she shouted.

The turtle he was carrying was the largest Paige had ever seen—the heavy greenish brown shell looked to be about eight, maybe nine inches in diameter.

"Will it snap, Jason?" she asked, studying the creature's eyes, shaded well by thick-skinned lids.

"Only if you put a finger near its mouth. Lily, go to the cellar, there's a steel washtub there. Get it. It ought to be big enough to hold this thing, at least temporarily." When Lily came running back with the tub, Jason put the turtle inside.

"Where're you going to keep it?" Lily asked.

"Well, I know where *you're* not going to keep it, anywhere in the house."

"*Me*, he's mine?"

"You've got to take care of it, that means feeding it, cleaning out the container." He pointed to the tub. "He'll need something bigger than that, maybe after breakfast—"

"I never had a pet, never ever!" She leapt forward and without thinking, threw her arms around Jason, then realizing what she was doing, stepped back. "Thanks a lot, Jason," she said, then began a dash toward the house.

"What, where're you going, Lily?" Paige called. "We're just about to go . . ."

"Right back, one second. Water, a turtle needs to have water!"

Jason and Lily decided on a hard plastic two-sectioned sandbox with about an eight-foot diameter and a twelve-inch wall. And since it was getting cold outdoors—fresh water would freeze—Paige agreed to let it stay in the basement. With the washer and dryer conveniently in the kitchen, Paige had little occasion to visit downstairs.

"You will keep it clean though?" she asked Lily.

"I promise."

When they got back from town, Lily filled the sections with sand and water, then tossed in lettuce, raw spinach, broccoli, rocks, sticks, and pebbles. Still, she decided to take the turtle outdoors.

"Most kids like dogs and cats," Brooke said, gathering up her painting supplies.

"And most artists are willing to keep their feet on the ground," Paige said.

"Oh that, come on out there with me. You'll see, it's not all that dangerous."

"I can't. I'm beat. I'm no longer one of those party girls who takes three-A.M.ers in stride." She patted her belly and smiled. "I've got some very valuable cargo here, and it's demanding immediate rest." She started up the stairs, then turned: "Still, Brooke, it worries me, you climbing so high in a tree with all that stuff to carry. Maybe someone—" She looked to Gary, then finally to Jason. "Would you?"

"You nap," Jason said, "I'll go down there with her, set her up in business."

"I have a couple of calls to make to the hospital," Gary said.

"You promised you wouldn't—" Brooke began.

"Hush," Paige said. "Remember the rules, no picking, no fighting, no bitching."

It happened when Jason climbed up the tree to hand the canvas to Brooke—she took it, carefully stood it against the tree trunk, then leaned forward, her cool hand startling him as it slid smoothly and expertly beneath his jeans. And the next thing he knew he was kissing her, touching her . . . But it went on only moments when he suddenly stopped, pulled free, and jumped to the ground.

He backed up a few steps, looked at her sitting there: her shirt open exposing a dark mole between small naked breasts and pink erect nipples. He shook his head. "I can't."

"Why the hell not?"

"I'd die if I lost her, Brooke, I mean it."

"But who's telling? Certainly you don't think I—"

A pause, then: "Don't you get it—it's me; I can't keep lying like this. . . . She trusts me, and suddenly I can barely stand to look at her. This woman's my whole fucking world, and she's carrying my kid inside her. And I'm afraid if I really look at her, she'll be able to see right through me."

"Not to worry, sounds to me like a simple case of what's called, 'pangs of conscience.' And here I thought that particular malady went out in the fifties with DA haircuts and white buckskin shoes. You're being a total nitwit. Here, let me show you how much of one." With that, she took off her shirt, dropped it to the ground, then slowly pushed herself from the limb. . . . "Better catch."

Off guard, he caught her but only enough to break her fall. Together they collapsed to the ground, she landing on him. She began tickling him and fondling him, but he pushed her away and stood up. Finally, he bent forward, picked up her shirt and tossed it to her.

She sat up, took a deep breath, put on her shirt, then as though she wasn't sure what to do next, ran her hand through her hair. He hung his fingers in his jeans pockets, looked down at his sneaker digging furiously into the dirt. Why did he suddenly feel like a dumb-assed adolescent, up to his ears in deep shit?

"Let's not get overly hung up about this, make it into more than it was," Brooke said finally. "If it makes it easier on you, put the blame on me."

"Look, I'm not looking to put blame . . . How about we try to pretend it never happened?"

She nodded, then climbed up to her spot on the branch. He lifted the pallette and box containing chalk, oils, charcoal, brushes, and cloths onto the joints of the oak branches, balancing it there for her. Quickly, he climbed to the ground.

Brooke looked at her watch. "Tell Paige I'll be back by three, three-thirty tops."

He still felt dazed when he headed back. If not, he surely would have spotted Lily sitting up in the willow, watching.

They had given Lily dinner early and it was eight o'clock when Jason's sauce was complete.

"Here, try a little," he said, holding the steaming spoon out to Gary.

Gary finished pouring the red wine, then tasted the sauce.

"It's good, damnit, it really is as good as you say. Why didn't you ever make it for us before?"

"He did, numskull, twice. Both times you were called to the hospital on an emergency," Brooke said.

"Uh, uh, we will have no negatives," Paige scolded, pouring herself a club soda and thinking how sensational Brooke looked in those black leggings and red filmy top with wide belt that cinched her nineteen-inch waist. Paige couldn't remember ever having a nineteen-inch waist—at least not past age twelve.

"Well, in any event, give Brooke the recipe."

"There is no recipe," Paige said picking up on the conversation.

"What does that mean?"

"You know," she said passing the plates of angel-hair pasta to Jason for sauce. "A little of this, a little of that."

"I see you got her conned good, Jay old boy. Look, if you're that protective of the ingredients, better get it copyrighted."

"Well, I suppose I could measure it out, write it down."

"Why didn't you ever say that to me?" Paige asked as she took the two ready plates from Jason and handed them to Gary and Brooke.

"Good," Gary said as he ground more pepper over the steaming dish. "When you do, give a copy to Brooke."

"Why so quiet?" Paige asked Brooke as she took a chunk of warm garlic bread, then passed the basket.

"Nothing, just appreciating the wine. I can't detect—what is it?"

"Chianti," Gary said. "May I remind you, dear, you're the one who picked it out of the wine cabinet."

Lily came upstairs from the basement. "It gets out," she said.

"What?" Paige asked.

"The turtle, it can climb over the top of the pool."

"Improvise," Jason said.

"What does that mean?"

"Figure a way it won't happen. In other words, set up something to stop it, a barrier, whatever. Meanwhile it's dinnertime—and as I recall, you ate, now it's our turn."

"Brrrr, if looks could kill," Brooke said as Lily disappeared again downstairs.

*   *   *

"Do you notice anything odd about Brooke's behavior?" Paige asked once she and Jason got into bed.

"Not really, why?"

"I don't know, she seems moody, preoccupied, not herself."

"Maybe it's to do with Gary."

"Maybe. But it doesn't seem, I mean, considering how those two normally behave, I think they're doing remarkably well." She nuzzled her lips into the back of his neck. "And considering our past week, so are we. Don't you think? I know it was unforgivable me not telling you about the baby, but I swear I didn't plan it that way, Jason. So much bad feeling was circulating, I was looking for the right moment, the perfect way to say it . . . Then suddenly before I knew it, two days had passed and . . ."

"Let's not talk about it."

"Then you forgive me?"

"Have you told anyone else?"

"No, of course not. But I suppose, now we can . . . You are happy about it, aren't you?"

"How can you ask that? When my anger lets up, I think about it—about you right now carrying our son . . . I can't describe the excitement, the exhilaration." He looked deep into her eyes, reached out, and ran the back of his knuckles down her cheek, then let his hand and eyes drop away.

"But the anger comes back, is that it?"

"It'll pass. I've never been able to stay angry at you for long."

"What about Lily?"

Silence.

"She really loves that turtle."

"Yeah, so it seems."

"Why so negative? She's clearly nuts about it, and is so appreciative of you giving it to her."

"Okay, okay."

"Sorry, I didn't mean to push. In fact, other than Brooke being a little off-kilter, the weekend is going wonderfully. Particularly with you and Lily and this whole turtle thing ... Maybe I'm wrong, but it feels like you two have called a truce." She ran her tongue inside his ear. "Jason, notice me watching you this evening? I was thinking—"

"It's nearly three, Paige. I'm tired."

"Apple picking? It's supposed to rain."

"Not until tonight. Come on, it'll be fun, Jason," Paige said. "The orchards are spectacular this time of year. Listen, I don't hear Gary complaining."

"That's only because I haven't had time. When did it come up for a vote and where was I at the time?"

"Probably your mind was too drawn into spreading that quarter of a pound of chive cheese on that bagel you're about to devour," Brooke said. "Jason, why don't you tell me more about you naming a sweet baby girl Brooke."

Paige looked at Jason.

"Cancel it," he said shrugging. "Looks like we're definitely having a boy."

"Hey, you're kidding? Great!" Gary said.

"Wait, I thought we were determined not to

know the sex, to wait—" Brooke looked at Paige, then Jason. "Uh, uh, what's going on?"

"Nothing," Paige said. "Last doctor appointment, we found out accidentally."

"Okay, the doctor's appointment was Tuesday, I remember you telling me, Paige—"

"Right."

She turned to Jason. "Well, then why did you only yesterday tell me about—" She stopped, then, "Oops, shut up time."

"About this apple picking fancy of you girls," Gary said to cover the moment. "How long you figure it'll take? We need to start back no later than four."

"Not a problem," Paige said. "It'll take less than an hour to fill two baskets."

"I can see rotting apples still in the refrigerator come February," Gary said.

"Oh yeah, before I forget," Paige said, tapping Brooke's shoulder, "show me the painting."

"Which one?"

"You know, the one from the tree."

"Oh, that one. You'll have to wait, you know how I am about showing work not finished."

"So when will it be?"

She shrugged.

"Why don't you stay another couple days, finish it," Gary suggested. "You can hitch a ride back to the city with Jason let's say, Wednesday morning. That way you'll have two days free to paint, shoot the shit with Paige."

"She's got a commission to do," Paige said.

"It was canceled, right, hon?"

Brooke shrugged. "Yes, but I don't know if it's a good time. I really ought to get back."

"If you're thinking of me, forget it," Gary said. "I'm on duty till 3 A.M. both tomorrow and Tuesday."

"Okay," Paige said. "So what's the problem?"

"No, well nothing. What about Jason, he doesn't even need to go near Park Avenue in the mornings—"

"He'll drop you at the bus or subway. Why are you being so . . . Jason, will you tell her it's not a problem . . . Yoo hoo, Jason Bennett, are you here with us?"

"Oh yeah, sure . . . No, right, not a problem."

"Okay, then it's settled, you're staying."

Brooke gave one of those what-can-I-do shrugs, apparently catching the interest of Lily, whose eyes were now fixed on her. Paige leaned over, tapped Lily's shoulder.

"Young lady, you are staring something fierce. What is it, sweetheart?"

Brooke looked up, uneasy as she met the child's stare. Finally, Lily turned her attention to Paige.

"I was thinking, is all . . ."

"Oh, what about?"

"Apple picking. When we go, could I get a pumpkin?"

"You didn't seem thrilled about Brooke staying," Paige said that night as they got into bed. Gary had left about six, in plenty of time to miss the rainstorm that had come in from New Jersey. Now, Jason lay down, his back to her, and she beside him, facing his back.

"I didn't mean it to sound that way," he said. "If she wants to stay longer, hey great."

"Are you upset with her?"

"Christ, Paige, must you dissect my every reaction? I guess I thought maybe you pushed a little hard."

"Did I? I just thought she was hesitating because . . . Do you really think I pressured her?"

"Forget it. She agreed to stay which means if she had second thoughts, she got rid of them."

"Do you think she's angry at me?"

"Why would she be?"

"I don't know, she just seems . . . I don't know, standoffish."

"You're imagining things." A long silence, then: "Paige?"

"Yeah, I'm here."

"You're the most important thing in my life—you know that, right?"

"I guess I count on that, maybe more than I have a right to. So now will you talk about it?"

"What?"

"What was happening with you last week?"

Silence.

"Jason, I need to know."

"Just pressure, you know how sometimes things build up."

"And that's all it was?"

"You need more?"

She smiled and cuddled closer into his back. Suddenly the baby delivered a wallop.

"Oh, oh, someone is up and ready for playtime. Feel him, Jason?"

"Are you kidding? It feels like an elephant stomping. Very much like the way you take those stairs in the hall." She swatted him playfully, they laughed, and he turned around and held her close to him.

As she began to fall off to sleep, she said, "Jason, did you notice how Lily carved her pumpkin's face?"

"Not really, why?"

"It was different, is all. Nice—instead of the usual menacing face, she carved a smile."

She had only been sleeping twenty minutes when thunder crashed the sky and she shot up in bed. Jason, who had not yet fallen off, sat up, took hold of her arms which were thrashing about and steadied them.

"It's okay, honey, relax, just a little thunder out there."

She looked at him, then her senses clearing, took a deep breath.

"Another dream?"

She nodded.

"That same guy?"

Again she nodded, then: "No. It looked like him, but I don't think it was."

The next morning Lily insisted she leave for school early, wanting to have extra time in the schoolyard to brag about her turtle, who she had named Wally. By the time Brooke woke, Paige was on her third cup of decaf and her second English muffin. Paige poured her coffee.

"How about a muffin to go with it?"

"Nothing."

"You're sure, I have OJ, cereal, eggs?"

Brooke shook her head, then looked out the window—it was still wet and dismal.

"Not to worry," Paige said, "the forecast promises sun, give it a few more hours."

"Okay."

"Come on, tell me," Paige said finally.

"Have we something particular in mind?"

"You seem not as effervescent as usual."

"Come on, even us bubbly gals need a reprieve."

"Are you upset with me, something I said, did?"

Brooke was quiet a long moment, then, "Want me to be truly brutal with you?"

"Of course."

"I think that girl Lily is a mistake."

"Oh? For whom—you or me?"

"You and Jason as a couple."

Paige sighed, shook her head. "My, my, coming from the marriage authority herself."

"I'm not pretending my marriage is perfect, I'm just saying that your marriage, the one that always looked so good from my perspective, suddenly seems murky. I mean, you two should have it all going for you—communication, successful careers, even a baby coming, a baby you've both wanted for such a long time—And what's this about you knowing it was a boy and not telling Jason?"

"It was an accident. I found out unintentionally."

"All right, I suppose that can happen. But why didn't you tell him right away?"

"I tried to . . . There was a lot going on."

"Dare I assume it had to do with Princess Lily?"

"Damnit, stop it! You sound just like Jason now . . . blaming her for everything!"

*   *   *

That afternoon, Ruthanne had a couple of strong labor pains, so strong she telephoned Paige. Paige hurried there, but by the time she arrived at Ruthanne's, the pains had dissipated. She looked at the clock—Lily was still at school and Brooke was still out painting—she had been outdoors since late morning, asking Paige not to bother her with lunch. Paige now fixed tea for Ruthanne and sat her down.

"Should I call the doctor?" Paige said. "Or maybe Charlie?"

"No, let's wait a while, I think it's false labor. I didn't mean to bother—"

"Don't be silly, you can expect a much bigger panic from me. Remember this is my first."

"I do forget . . . when I see you with Lily, well, you're so much like mother and daughter."

Paige smiled. "I know, I feel that way, too, though I'm not supposed to."

"Says who?"

"My girlfriend, the one up from the city. And, of course, Jason. Do I need more?"

"They'll come around. Sorry, maybe I shouldn't be saying that. What with all that business coming up in court—"

"I told Lily about it."

"Really, was she excited?"

"Well, yes. Not as excited as I thought she'd be, though."

"Maybe it has to do with how she feels about you. It's clear she loves you. I doubt she wants to leave."

"And I love her, too, but still I'm not her mother. The thing is, Lily's carrying around a lot of anger, and it seems some of it is directed at Anna Parks."

"Because she didn't throw the husband out sooner?"

"I'm sure her mother's reluctance to act, to be the strong, reliable parent plays a large part in it. Also the horror of the murder itself. God, can you imagine how terrifying it must have been to witness one parent killing another, and to do it in such a ghastly way? But I really do think she's starting to ease up on Anna, forgive her."

Ruthanne shrugged. "Who knows what goes on in a kid's mind? Here I am the mother of a nine-year-old, and still have no idea of what lurks and simmers inside those heads." She patted her big belly. "And as far as delivering this baby—it's been so many years between—I feel as nervous as a first-time mother."

Paige smiled. "What made you wait so long?"

"Oh, we didn't plan it that way, try as we did once Roger hit two years old, I just couldn't conceive again. The doctor wanted Charlie to come in for fertility tests, that sort of thing, but he flat-out refused. He said, if the Lord wanted us to have more kids, he'd see to it that we did. The fact is, we pretty much gave up, decided to count our blessings for the one. And then what do you know? Boom, it turns out, we're to be blessed twice."

"Do you know the baby's sex?"

"Uh, uh. We refused tests."

"Why?"

She gestured to her stomach. "We don't need pictures to know there's a baby in here."

"What about checking to see if it's normal?"

"And if it weren't, would we refuse it? Uh, uh, we're not fussy, we'll take what we get."

Lily was near hysterics when Paige took the phone receiver from Ruthanne.

"Calm down and tell me what happened."

"It's Brooke. When I came home, I took the turtle out to the woods to play. And that's when I saw her on the ground. I tried to help her get up, but she just screams and screams . . ."

"I'll be right home, you wait for me at the house." She looked at Ruthanne. "It's my girl-friend. She's hurt. Will you do me a favor, call an ambulance?"

She had already taken the phone from her. "Of course."

Paige was out of breath by the time Lily led her to Brooke whose lower right leg was swollen and turned at an odd angle. A thick tree branch was lying on the ground beside her.

"You go back to the house, Lily," Paige in-structed. "Wait for the ambulance to come. As soon as it does, lead them here."

Lily ran off, and Paige got down on the ground, running her fingers across Brooke's cheeks and forehead, pushing her damp hair away from her face. "Does it hurt?"

"It kills. Stop that crying, you're splashing all over."

"How did it happen?"

"I don't know, the branch seemed suddenly weak, like it wouldn't hold my weight. Before I could get off it, grab onto something solid, it cracked right under me. Paige, call Gary."

"Oh, God . . . when did this happen, how long have you been lying here?"

"Call Gary."

"I promise, as soon as we get to the hospital."

"How could I be this stupid and clumsy? I should have spotted right off it was so weak. Losing so much time this morning, I was just too eager to get settled in and paint."

"Probably rushing it because of me, right? I'll never forgive myself for fighting with you, then letting you climb up this damned tree . . . Thank goodness for Lily, what if she hadn't come along and finally found you when she had?"

Though Gary spoke with the orthopedic surgeon at Poughkeepsie Medical Center and concurred that Brooke should not travel until the following day, Brooke insisted once the break was set that she return to the city. And it was Jason who, at about ten o'clock that night, with Paige's help tucked Brooke into the back of the Pathfinder with a dozen pillows and blankets.

"Tell me if the bumps get to be too much," Jason said as he pulled out of the hospital emergency parking area, leaving Paige to drive back to the house with the Volvo.

"The doctor gave me a shot of Percodan, that ought to do it. What about Gary—"

"He'll be at the apartment waiting when we get there. I still don't get it, why you couldn't have held off until tomorrow, if not at the hospital, then come back to the house, stay overnight? At least you would have been in better condition."

"I need to get back . . ." She paused but he

sensed there was something else. "Jason, about the other day in the woods—"

"I told you, forget it. That's what I'm trying to do, and that's what you ought to do, too."

A long silence followed except for the muffled sounds of cars on the road, then: "Brooke, you're pretty agile, strong, too. I mean, how the hell did you fall out of that tree?"

"I don't know. The branch was so damn solid yesterday, but then again it did pour last night. There was thunder and lightning, the wind was strong, it woke me a couple of times in the middle of the night. I guess it cracked the branch in a place I couldn't see."

Jason left it at that and Brooke soon drifted off to sleep. Despite the perfectly rational explanation, an uneasiness nagged at him, and all the way to Manhattan he couldn't shake it.

Chapter Ten

This time, coming directly from school, Lily arrived early for her appointment. Hillary greeted her, then seated her in the therapy room as she hurried off to do one last laundry changeover in the basement. When she returned, Lily was gone. After searching through the entire downstairs, she discovered her upstairs in her father's bedroom, admiring his old pipe rack. Father was propped up, staring at Lily.

"What are you doing here, Lily?" Hillary asked.

"The buzzer rang—you weren't around so I answered it."

"I see. Well, thank you for your thoughtfulness, but Father doesn't like strangers visiting unannounced. So next time, if you'll be kind enough to tell me, I'll handle it."

Lily nodded, then gestured to Mr. Egan. "I think he wants to smoke."

"I doubt that, he gave up smoking quite some time ago. I think what he wants is help with his newspaper. She reached over, turned the newspaper to the sports section, then adjusted it for easy reading on the over-the-bed hospital stand.

Hillary switched off the buzzer, then propped the old man's pillows, and kissed his cheek.

"Forgive the intrusion, Father ... When I come back, I'll bring tea and toast."

She smiled at Lily. "Now how about you and I go downstairs and begin?"

Hillary slipped into her chair, cracked open the top desk drawer, with a finger activating the recorder, then closed the drawer. Though there was always the possibility that Lily would say nothing of consequence throughout the entire session, as evidenced by their last meeting, it was important to be prepared. And it took only fifteen minutes of Lily staring at the dollhouse, the various rooms in it, for her to initiate conversation.

"Once Mommy and Daddy had a fight over what she served him for dinner," Lily said.

"Really? Would you like to tell me about it?"

"Not much to tell ... Daddy asked Mommy to make spaghetti and meatballs. When dinnertime came, she put plain old spaghetti and sauce on his plate. And was he mad!"

"What did he do to show his anger?"

"He dumped the hot sauce over her head."

A few moments of silence, then: "How old were you then, Lily?"

"About five, maybe six."

"It must have been frightening to see that happen."

She shrugged.

"Can you remember what thoughts went through your mind when it did?"

She nodded. "I remember wondering, 'Why didn't Mommy make meatballs?' "

Over the next few weeks Paige spoke to Brooke almost daily; the bone break had been a clean one and it was healing nicely, but regardless of how much Paige urged—and Jason's repeated willingness to pick up and deliver her—Brooke refused another visit to the country.

Lily was a subject she and Brooke tried to steer clear of, and just as well: after all, Brooke considered all children bothersome and uncivilized, it was something she readily admitted to. So despite the good motives that surely prompted her criticisms, it was impossible for her to understand the depth of Paige's feelings for the precious little girl who fit so nicely into their household.

But if Jason didn't understand her feelings, he didn't say so. While he moved quietly along on Anne Parks' case, he made a real effort to accept Lily into the family. And it was that effort that made his bond with Paige stronger than it had been in months.

Not that everything was perfect: though they touched and caressed one another, the act of intercourse was something they decided to put aside temporarily. And still there were those nightmares, some she couldn't even remember or remembered only as isolated, unmatched segments. Clearly, Lily's questions—those innocent questions that would pop up from time to time about Paige's childhood—were jarring Paige's memory, forcing her to retrieve bits and pieces of her past that until now she hadn't even known were gone.

Jason and Paige went to Lamaze class and got silly and giggly as they talked and planned and dreamed about their soon-to-be baby boy. But because of Jason's absolute insistence on some privacy in this area, the talks and silliness were usually at night in bed, or somewhere with the two of them alone.

Not that Lily would have been jealous to hear them go on about the baby—even Jason had to admit that Lily's interest and enthusiasm for the coming birth was sincere. In fact, Lily had charmingly nicknamed him My Boy.

And if Jason needed an ally to keep Paige's diet in line while he wasn't there to do it himself, Lily was it. Always going out of her way to prepare healthy but tasty snacks to keep wrapped in foil in the refrigerator waiting for Paige. Always urging Paige to join her in brisk walks through the woods. And as a payoff, not only did Paige's weight gain stabilize at about twenty pounds, but she was in good spirits and according to Dr. Barry in extraordinarily good health.

Lily's Halloween trick-or-treat partner, and then after-school partner in crime, became Roger Beeder. And with Paige and Ruthanne becoming so friendly, it was convenient and nice that the children were pals as well. Twice, Hillary asked Paige to stop by—which she did—so she could question her about Lily's problems adjusting at home. But the remarkable thing was, there were none.

With it all going so smoothly, Paige was taken

by surprise when she received a call a couple of weeks before Thanksgiving from the Briarwood elementary school asking her to come by. Until now, Lily's papers and in-school activities indicated her classwork was fine. And Paige said so to the two female teachers and male principal who were now sitting across from her.

"It's not her academic performance that is in question," Miss Harris, the chubby, gray-haired homeroom teacher said.

"Well, then what?"

"Well, for one, there've been missing articles from the students' lockers."

"What kind of articles?"

Miss Harris looked down at her list.

"A navy blue sweatshirt, a notepad, a pink plastic change purse, two bangle bracelets, a black elastic hip belt, white sneakers. Nothing that expensive, but still—"

"Wait, stop. First let me say, Lily doesn't need one item you mentioned. In fact, before she started school, I took her to the mall shopping and pretty much gave her carte blanche at the clothing store. Which she handled quite nicely. Oh, we picked up some lovely things, I suppose the sort of things most girls her age would pick if they had the chance. The thing is, a girl with a gold charm bracelet doesn't need a bangle nor does she need a plastic change purse when she already has one that's leather."

"Being a teacher yourself, I'm sure you're aware that neediness is not always the cause for stealing," Miss Harris said.

Paige put out her hands like palms spread on windowglass.

"Okay, you've got me on that point. You're right of course." She smiled and shook her head—she could feel her cheeks warming. "Now I see how this mother tiger instinct works. It's true Lily's not mine, but caring about her as I do, I sometimes forget that. Tell me—why Lily? Why not accuse one of the other students?"

"Before Lily came, we hadn't any incidence of stealing."

"I see. 'New one out' kind of thing?"

Mr. Marcel who until then had been sitting back, his slim legs crossed effeminately, sat forward.

"It's not quite as simple a statement as it might seem, Mrs. Bennett," he said in a well-modulated voice. "There's not a child in the entire sixth grade who hasn't been here since kindergarten. And while I won't sit here and tell you that any one of them is perfect, I can assure you, there isn't a thief among them."

Paige sighed. "Tell me, Mr. Marcel, how much do you know about Lily?"

"Well, naturally I've read her record—"

"What about the newspaper articles, the gossip?"

"I beg your pardon?"

"Simply, do you know her history—what happened to her father, her mother, how she came to live with me?"

"Well, yes, of course. One couldn't live here and not—"

"Don't you think there's a possibility you're being unfair? You're assuming things based on what background information you've heard about her parents. I intend to go home and ask her about this, but I have to be blunt—even if she were responsible, I resent you zeroing in on her as though she were first on your 'most wanted' list." Paige began to stand, but stopped. "Oh, while I'm here, I'd like to make sure . . . Is there any area where Lily's having difficulty? She did miss an entire year, so if she should need tutoring . . ."

Mrs. Harris cleared her throat. "No, she has no problem keeping up with her classes. In some areas—math for instance—she's actually ahead of the others. Yes, she's very quick."

"I'm pleased. Though I don't suppose that was one of the things you called to tell me."

The physical education teacher sat forward.

"Well, I don't know that you'll want to hear this, but as long as you're here, I think I ought to tell you."

"Please."

"I think the girls in Lily's class are intimidated by her."

Paige drew in her breath. "Excuse me?"

"That's certainly how it seems."

"Who is . . . and why?"

"The girls in her phys. ed. class—at least a good portion of them. The same for girls from her homeroom. And while Miss Harris hasn't noticed it to the degree I have, she did suspect something funny going on. As to why, I haven't got a clue."

"Has she fought with anyone?"

"Not that I've seen," the gym teacher said.

Paige looked at Miss Harris, who folded her arms at her chest and shook her head. Then back to the gym teacher. "Well, then she's made threats . . . is that it?"

"Not that I know of."

"Just what is it that makes you think she scares them?"

"Mostly the other girls kowtow to her, give her her own way. She always gets to pick the team position she wants, no matter what the sport or who I've chosen to captain."

Paige's eyes now went to Miss Harris.

"I've observed some of the same thing. She's often chosen first for fun things, and she's been picked several times to perform a job or activity I know the other girls want."

Paige laughed and shrugged. "I don't know what to say—in my school, they called that popularity."

"No, I don't think it's that at all," the gym teacher said. "It seems quite different."

"How?"

"It just is . . . I'm sure the other girls don't really like her."

"Have they told you that?"

She shook her head.

"Then get me some children to talk to, someone to validate your suspicions. Please."

"Even if you asked them, none would admit—"

Paige stood up and lifted her purse.

"I think this has gone far enough—I'm embarrassed at your lack of professionalism. You're going on hunches, not evidence. When you have something concrete to show me, by all means call."

Lily was walking around the therapy room, examining things, when Hillary came in and sat down. Even before Hillary could begin to record, Lily asked, "Why don't you let the old man loose?"

"Father is quite comfortable in his room."

"Did he tell you that?"

"Well, not exactly. You know he doesn't speak. But I think I know him well enough . . ."

"Well, enough for what?"

"Lily, when you live with people long enough, you get to know about them, sometimes you know what they want without them even having to say it."

"Then why can't you tell when he's gonna shit his pants?"

Rather than steer her away, Hillary had foolishly taken the bait. Lily, not really expecting an answer to her question, turned her attention to the toys. She sat on the floor next to the dolls, picked each one up, roughly manipulated the parts of the body, then tossed each one but the girl doll aside. The girl she laid down gently on the floor and with a swatch of colored material, covered her.

"Is she sleeping?" Hillary asked finally.

"I guess. She's trying to learn to dream."

"I don't understand, why must she learn?"

"Because she's never done it before. It's very sad." She picked up the girl doll and began to pet and caress it in a parodylike performance. "Poor, poor baby, doesn't even know how to dream. What *will* we do with you?"

"Are you saying that baby has never even had an occasional nightmare?"

She nodded. "Just daytime dreams."

"I see. Well, certainly the one nice thing about

daydreams is there are no rules, at least none that you don't set yourself. You get to do whatever you want to do."

"Do you ever have daydreams?"

"Occasionally. But why don't we talk about the baby's daydreams?"

"Did you ever daydream the old man was dead?"

A moment's pause. "No, never."

"I got a good one—did you ever daydream you were sitting at an open window, looking out, and holding a gun. Then every single person who came in the line of fire, got a bullet in his head?"

From Hillary's recorded notes: *Though the patient hadn't really intended to admit as much—that in her daydreams, she wished her own father dead—it happened quite by accident. When Lily realized her blunder, she refused to go on with the playacting, instead choosing to sit silently for the remainder of the session, staring into space.*

It must not go without notice, however, that her question about Hillary's father was meant to harass. Just as were all the inferences about the therapist mistreating her father. The patient apparently perceives the difficulties in caring for an elderly invalid and sees this as her access to control the therapist.

She has a gift in being able to readily recognize a person's flaws and peculiarities, and plays into those weaknesses, managing to shift ground, forcing her opponent to the defensive. It is essential that the therapist be aware of this, not let the patient's jarring comments infiltrate and sabotage therapy.

It is interesting to note from the conversations with the guardian, Paige Bennett, she remains to-

tally unaware of Lily's scheming and manipulations. In fact, she describes the child as helpful, sweet, sensitive, caring, even fun. . . . Proving how adept the patient is at camouflage.

Please make note: a full battery of psychological and IQ tests would be useful. Estimated IQ: in excess of 130.

As always, Hillary ejected the tape from the recorder, labeled the name and date, then put it in the large blank manila envelope in the third drawer of the steel filing cabinet.

He was running late all day so it wasn't until late afternoon when he got to the Bennett house. The little girl who answered the front door and stared at him was tall, skinny, and had two white-blond ponytails. Clyde held a red lantern flashlight in his left hand.

"Who're you?" she asked him finally.

"Name's Clyde." He pointed to his van parked in the driveway. "Klondike Exterminators. Miz Bennett around?"

"That's me."

"Yeah sure it is. Look, she here or not?"

"Not."

He sighed. "Damn . . . See, the thing is, I left an animal trap up in the attic a while back. I need to get it now."

"Really. Any more to that interesting story?"

A pause, then, "You're a real ball buster, aren't you kid?"

"Why, are your balls in pain?"

He looked at her—was she for real? Either way, he decided he'd better let it pass.

"Look, do you think you could maybe let me

in just long enough to get the trap. I'll leave a note for your mom saying I took it. That way you won't get in trouble."

"Oh, *can* you write?"

Clyde could feel his face redden at her put-down, but he didn't answer. She finally opened the storm door and let him in.

"How do you know we still don't need the trap?" she said.

He started up the stairs and she followed.

"If there was a squirrel in this house, it would of been caught by now."

"It was, retard. You see, I'm the squirrel."

He looked back at her just before he entered the narrow stairwell to the attic.

"Actually you look more like a white rat than a squirrel."

"I'll tell my mother you said that."

He pushed open the door and climbed up.

"Yeah? Proving it's the tough part."

He went to the cage, laid down his lantern on the table, then unhooked the door spring from the cage. The girl came in, picked up the lantern, and ran with it to the other side of the attic. She bent down and shoved it under some old lawn furniture.

"Hey you, come back with that thing," he said.

"Uh, uh, want it, find it."

"Shit, I don't have time for baby games." She came back to the table showing her empty hands, and he looked at her thinking he'd like to slam her.

"I wouldn't try that if I were you," she said.

"Probably are a white rat, you sure in hell got those beady little eyes. Real close together, pink, and sick-looking." As he spoke, he went to the other side of the room, knelt down, and reached under a wooden chaise lounge, retrieving his flashlight. He got back to the table, lifted the trap . . .

Pow!

"OW! GET IT THE FUCK OFF!" he yelled, unable to free his hand and stop the pain. . . . The girl reached for the cage, forced back the wire door and held it while he yanked free. Then she let the cage drop to the floor, and the door smashed shut.

He looked at his nearly flattened fingers. "Christ, they're broke, I think they're broke!"

"Try to move them."

"Hurts like someone's holding a flame on 'em. I gotta go!" With his one good hand, he lifted the squirrel cage, then took off, two stairs at a time. Maybe he'd head over to Doc Healy's, have him look at those fingers. How could he have been such an asshole? Still, he'd bet a week's pay that he had released that door spring. . . .

"What about hypnotizing her?" Jason said to W.C. Wendell on the phone. "Get out the whole miserable story."

"I suggested it to Anna, but the idea petrifies her, or at least she says it does."

"So, we do things every day we're scared of. Particularly if it means saving our asses."

"Unfortunately, it doesn't work quite that way. If she's scared, she'll make a lousy subject. We're not Svengalis who suck people unwillingly under our spells. People who don't want to go under, can't. It's that simple."

"Okay, how much does she attest to knowing?"

"Enough. In fact, her memory lapse is apt to work to our benefit. She recalls the argument that took place that afternoon. She recalls her own anger as she prepared his dinner—how instead of it dying down as time passed, it continued to grow until she was feeling a fury beyond anything she'd ever experienced. She remembers lifting the sickle from the toolshed, coming back into the kitchen, and then the sickle flying toward his chest. From there on, it blurs. Next thing she knows, a week or two has elapsed, she's in jail, she's already pled guilty."

"I agree, it sounds good, certainly it sounds like she lost it for that period. Okay, so what pretty phrases can you say for me when I put you on the stand?"

"Exactly what you want. A docile woman goes through years of being suffocated, trampled on, beaten physically and emotionally by a sociopath husband, leaving her with not a teaspoon of dignity. Suddenly in a moment of insane, accumulated rage, her hand raises by its own volition and strikes him dead."

"If you can please tone that down just a little. No poetry." Jason laughed. He was beginning to like this case.

"Lily!" Paige shouted as she set down the two bags of groceries she was carrying.

"I'm down in the cellar with Wally."

Paige smiled. "Ask Turtle if he'll excuse you a moment."

She came running upstairs, threw her arms around Paige, then sat down at the kitchen table.

"What'd the teacher want?"

"Well, it seems there're some things missing—"

"I didn't take any sneakers or sweatshirt or bracelet or anything else, Paige, honest."

"How did you know what the items were?"

"Easy, that's all Miss Harris talks about these days. Most of the kids are getting sick of hearing about it."

"You know, sweetheart, if you did take something not yours, you can tell me. I won't be angry, I swear. But it's important you own up to it."

Lily drew a cross over her heart. "Swear to God, hope to die. Why would I anyhow, Paige? With all the good stuff you bought me, I betcha I'm the luckiest kid in the whole sixth grade. I know Miss Harris thinks I did it, but that's because she doesn't like me."

"I think the problem is, she doesn't really know you—at least, not like I do. She's made some judgments that aren't really fair; sometimes adults do that kind of thing. It doesn't make it right, but as long as you know what you did or didn't do, that's all that counts."

"I never stole, Paige. Not even when I lived in Laurel Canyon and didn't have much of anything. If you don't believe me, you can ask my mother."

"No need to, I believe you. So let's forget about it, okay?"

Paige began to unpack the grocery bags. Without thinking she reached for a chocolate chip cookie, but Lily took a banana off the refrigerator and handed it to her.

"Eat this. Jason says it has potassium. You know, I bet we both like to pig out because when we were little, we couldn't."

Paige sat on a stool and peeled back the banana skin while Lily took over the groceries.

"Oh? You never before mentioned you went hungry."

"Sometimes, when Daddy didn't have cars to fix. Or if it was a fast day."

Paige looked at her—Lily shut the cabinet door and jumped down from the counter.

"Well, once in a while Daddy'd pick out a day for him and me not to eat. He said it cleansed our bodies, took away any badness trying to inch its way inside."

Paige didn't need any affirmations of how sick a man Maynard Parks had been but hearing Lily relate this story was a certain reminder. "And your mother?" she asked.

"Not her. There was no hope for her."

"You didn't believe that, did you?"

Silence.

"Lily?"

"Know what, Paige? I think when I'm big I'll become a psychiatrist. What do you think?"

The phone rang and without waiting for an answer, Lily picked it up, listened, then handed it over to Paige.

"Ruthanne for you."

She took the phone. "Hi, what's up?"

"This is it."

"What is . . . you're kidding? Ohmygosh, what should I do?"

"Not to worry, Charlie's here. The thing is, Roger's giving me a hard time. He was supposed to spend the night at my mother's, but he's gone on strike, he won't budge from the doorway. He insists he wants to be with Lily."

Paige laughed. "That's okay. I've got an extra room so—"

"Are you sure?"

"I'm already making up the bed."

"If I ever hear another bad word about you big city yuppies . . ."

Paige put down the phone, still chuckling. Lily was nudging at her elbow. "What, Paige?"

"The baby's on its way."

"And I bet Roger said he didn't want to be at his grandma's."

"How did you know?"

"I just know him. Oh, almost forgot, Paige. A dirty long-haired boy named Clyde Somebody came by to get a squirrel cage. He said you'd know all about it?"

"Oh, Clyde, of course. So?"

"Nothing much, just that I let him in to get it."

By the time Jason got home at seven, the first snowfall had already begun. Paige met him at the doorway, helped him off with his trench coat, and took a Sears shopping bag and snowy black leather briefcase out of his hands.

She hugged him, then: "Guess what?"

His eyes widened. "Not the baby?"

"No, no, not me, it's Ruthanne. She went into labor late this afternoon."

"She's lucky she made it before the heavy

snow; the roads are getting treacherous. The best thing I ever did was insist on that four-wheeler in the driveway."

"Roger's here. He's staying over. I'm so anxious, I can't wait for Charlie to call with news."

"It could be awhile."

"Maybe not, it's her second. Labor's usually quicker after the first." Paige opened the shopping bag, took out a box and pieces of hardware while Jason went to the stove, lifted the cast-iron lid from the pot and peeked inside. "What's all this, Jason?" she asked.

He turned his head. "A new bolt for the attic door. I want to replace that rusty one."

"And the cement?"

"Plaster. To plug up holes around the house."

"Forget? There weren't any squirrels." He was already about to respond when she said, "Please Jason, don't say—"

"Hey, not me, what do you take me for? All I was going to say was mice. You remember, there *were* mice in the cellar? And speaking of those cute little rodent creatures, what is this bad-looking stuff you and Lily are cooking?"

"We've got to talk about Anna," Jason said after dinner when the kids went down to the cellar to play.

"Why?"

"Because I'm going in on it next week."

"You're not?"

"I am."

"I thought there were some court backlog problems; scheduling was taking longer than expected."

"That was before this afternoon."

"What happened then?"

"I was told very nicely to fuck off. I have two motions on file there, one to vacate sentence, another to change the plea. Today the clerk notified me that the judge won't hear either. According to Kraft, they're too late coming."

"Can he say that?"

"He can say anything."

"Well, then?"

"I had no other option, I filed a writ of habeas corpus."

"What did you say in it?"

"I claimed the jurisdiction is holding Anna Parks illegally."

"But how can that be?"

"The law requires that a defendant pleading guilty be questioned, to be certain he or she's aware of the consequences of such a plea. Since Anna Parks was not formally questioned, she was denied due process. So I'm telling them, bring in the body."

"That's wild. But suppose they ... who are *they*, Jason?"

"The prison warden, the D.A., whoever."

"Okay, suppose they don't bring her in?"

"I subpoenaed Anna. Either way, I get to argue it. If I lose, I've got something to appeal."

"And if you win?"

"Anna enters a not-guilty plea. And I set a date to try it."

"She's ready to do that?"

"She doesn't like it, but she's promised to do it. Lily's letter convinced her, along with my assurance that we won't need Lily to testify—at least, not now at this hearing."

The phone rang and Paige lifted the phone. "Hello."

"Paige . . . Charlie . . ."

"Ruthanne, the baby?"

It took a few minutes—Paige could hear sniffling, then him blowing his nose. Finally, he said, "A girl, a little girl, pretty as a picture. Just like Ruthanne."

After she hung up the phone, Paige went to the top of the stairs and called, "Attention, attention, is there a Mr. Roger Beeder anywhere in this house?"

Roger came running up from the cellar, Lily followed.

"You've got an eight-pound, eleven-ounce baby sister, Roger," Paige said. "And her name is Carolyn."

"Oh, wow," he shouted out, his grin wide. "Can I go see her now?"

"Your dad said, tomorrow. He'll pick you up at nine-thirty, and take you to the hospital."

Roger was hard to contain after that. Later Paige got them both bedded down. Lily—still insistent on having her mattress on the floor—was quieter than usual.

"What's wrong?" Paige asked.

"Roger didn't want to finish our game."

"Which game was that?"

"Just a game with the turtle. We were playing it when you called us upstairs."

"Oh. Well, I imagine he was too excited after the news. You'll play it another time. Come on, give me a hug. No, no, not skimpy like that, a big one."

Later in bed, Paige turned to Jason. "I think she's jealous."

"Who?"

"Lily, of course. You know, Roger having a new little sister."

"You'll be having a baby."

"It's not quite the same thing, is it? I mean, sure, she goes around calling him My Boy—because she likes to think of him that way—but the reality is, he won't be her brother. And soon, before you know it, she might not even be living with us."

"Well, we're hoping she'll be with her mother . . . Aren't we?"

"Yes, of course. It's just that I'll miss her."

Five minutes later—Jason was busy jotting notes on a legal pad. "Jason?"

". . . Yeah, what?"

"I stole a box of Fanny Farmer chocolates."

He stopped and looked at her. "You did what?"

"Not now, silly, when I was a kid."

"Oh. Well, so what about it?"

"Nothing. It's just something I remembered." And as Jason said, so what about it? Didn't most kids steal an item at one time or another? Why did those teachers need to believe Lily was responsible for the thefts, and then make it as though they were dealing with big-time crime? Surely they knew stealing was not uncommon with kids. . . .

She put her hand to her stomach, thinking that soon little Joshua—the name they had finally decided on—would be born; it would be up to her and Jason to teach him about right and wrong, see to it he was properly socialized. A sweet innocent child one moment, and you look away a moment too long to find a budding criminal sitting across from you at the breakfast table. Definitely frightening.

Paige turned over in bed, one arm hugging her pillow. Perhaps the most annoying part of that circus today was that Lily wasn't even their thief. And with respect to the brass of that phys. ed. teacher: her allegation was just plain silly. Lily had a knack with kids, Paige had seen it in full operation Lily's first day at school. And she had certainly seen it with Roger.

After breakfast, Lily and Roger went outside in the snow to wait for Charlie Beeder. It had stopped snowing sometime in the night, and now there were about eight inches on the ground and a bright sun shining overhead.

"Going to go see Ruthanne today?" Jason asked, coming up from the cellar.

"Charlie says she'll be home tomorrow. So I thought I'd wait. I want to go to the mall, though, pick up something nice for the baby. Want to come along?"

"How are the roads?"

"According to Charlie, plowed early this morning. Does that mean you're not coming?"

"Well, I've got those repair jobs I want done. Besides, there's something else I had in mind for now." He looked out the window at Lily, by herself building a snowman, then grabbed his woolen jacket, gloves, and hat and headed outdoors.

"Like it?" she asked Jason, seeing him on the porch.

He sat on the step, lifted a clump of snow from the ground, and began manipulating it into a snowball.

"It's okay. That is, okay for a snowman."

"What's so bad about a snowman?"

"Hey, nothing. Just that when I was a kid, I made bigger and better things. Like for instance, a fort."

"A real one you could crawl inside?"

"It was no one-wall rinky-dink affair, if that's what you're picturing—it was a bonafide igloo. I mean, no question someone could actually have lived there."

She stood there, staring at him.

He threw his snowball and it landed at the snowman's head, pushing it to one side.

"I mean, if you're curious how to build it—" He shrugged.

"Will you show me how, Jason?"

He looked at his watch. "How about I meet you down at the river in let's say, twenty minutes?"

"Why there?"

"It's colder, and we'll need some ready water to ice it over."

The turtle was all tucked in its shell—it was the third time Jason had been down in the cellar in two weeks and seen it that way. After finding the wire cutters, the roll of wire, and gathering squares of cardboard from a dozen boxes to serve as a mold, and then later as insulation for the igloo, he stopped at the sandbox and knelt down: there was plenty of fresh food and water, and Lily was keeping the big plastic tank relatively clean. He touched the turtle's head—it opened its eyes and pushed its head out, then drew it back, the rest of it holding fast and tight inside the thick shell.

As though it were scared to pull out. Was it possible Lily was scaring the turtle? Jason shrugged, then headed with his supplies to the river.

It was much later in the afternoon—Paige was back from shopping and in their bedroom showing Lily the automatic musical swing she had bought for the Beeder baby. Jason was in the attic—he noticed the squirrel trap gone and a big, red plastic lantern on the table instead. He unscrewed the rusty bolt from the outside door and while he was doing it, he could hear the voices coming from the bedroom.

He went to the corner where the sound seemed to be coming from and spotted the dime-sized hole. He lay down and looked through it: Paige was sitting on the bed.

"Like it?" Paige was asking Lily.

"Can we get one for My Boy?"

"Of course we can, you be sure to tell Jason to pick one up when I'm in the hospital. So now tell me about your day."

"Jason and I made an igloo, like the kind real Eskimos use."

"Really? Can I see it?"

"Sure, if you're good," Lily teased.

Jason pulled back, sat up, sweat suddenly

beading along his forehead. All the time she was upstairs in this attic, she was able to hear everything he and Paige talked about. And the bed, she had a bird's-eye view ... It wasn't the kid's fault the hole was there, was it? *Come on, Jason, who the fuck you trying to convince here?* Damnit, why hadn't he ever noticed it from downstairs?

He thought back to what Anna Parks had said that first time—if Lily hadn't wanted them to find her, they wouldn't have. That clear, that simple. Was she right about it?

There were acorns in the reception area downstairs; that was the first clue something, someone was in the house. And that made perfect sense—she ate squirrels, right? So did that mean she ate acorns, too? Not likely, and she surely didn't use them to lure any squirrels into a wire cage, not with about six million acorns scattered along the grounds. Funny, he had never really thought about it before....

Could the acorns have been there to lure him and Paige?

Chapter Eleven

According to Ruthanne, her labor was a piece of cake—forty-five minutes; they barely made it to the delivery room. However easy the labor, Paige insisted Ruthanne tell her about it. Paige had read every book available on childbirth so she certainly had a good idea of what to expect. But she found it interesting, if not a little unnerving, that every new mother had a different version to relate.

Though Lily didn't show as much interest in Baby Carolyn as Paige would have expected, her interest shot up dramatically when Ruthanne opened up her pink furry robe and released her nursing bra, putting the beautiful dark-haired baby to her breast. Lily sat in a chair across from Ruthanne and stared while Roger lost interest quickly and went to the kitchen for cookies.

"Lily, why don't you go along, too," Paige said, but Ruthanne hushed her.

"No, no, it's okay, it doesn't make me a bit uncomfortable."

Finally the baby took her last burp and closed

her eyes, her tiny fists clenching onto her mother's shirt. Paige scooted Roger and Lily out of the room.

"Go on, you two, let Carolyn sleep."

Paige took the baby from Ruthanne, rocked her for a few minutes, then placed her in the cradle, and after several minutes more admiring the infant, she went to the sofa and poured tea from the thermal pot on the coffee table. She handed a cup to Ruthanne.

"Can I get you something to eat with it?"

Ruthanne shook her head.

Paige sat and gestured to the cradle. "She's so beautiful. I'm so happy for you, so excited."

"Soon it'll be you, my friend."

"I keep telling myself that, and the reality of it nearly bowls me over. I mean, when you really take out time to consider it—being so entirely accountable for a new life—it's downright awesome. Am I overdoing it or what?"

"Gee, I thought that was expected of new mothers."

"Perhaps it's set off by the hormones. What I really want to know is, why, when I was a kid, did I feel adult, and now suddenly I feel no more than twelve years old?"

"I know what you're saying. When Roger started calling me Mommy, I was sure he was calling my mother. Then when his friends began calling me Mrs. Beeder, oh Lord!"

Paige laughed. "Listen, I ought to leave. What was it they tell you at Lamaze—baby's nap time is mother's nap time?"

"That only works with first children. But Charlie's around today, so I'll get all the sleep I want. Stay a few more minutes," Ruthanne said, placing her hand over Paige's.

"By the way, if I haven't said it two dozen times already, let me say for the record, you look radiant."

Ruthanne put her hand to the waist of her robe. "Twenty extra pounds of fat still, yet if I could, I wouldn't change a thing. Even Roger, not a bit of anger or jealousy directed at his sister. Now you tell me, how did I get so lucky?"

Lily took a pencil and dug the point into the doll's leg.

"Ouch, that hurts," Hillary said.

Lily looked up at her and smiled.

"Are you angry at her?"

"No."

"Then why hurt her?"

"I like how it makes me feel."

"How is that?"

"I don't know, warm I guess."

Hillary picked up the doll, rocked it.

"What about *her* feelings?"

"She likes to be hurt."

"What makes you say so?"

Lily pointed to the pursed red lips. "Look at that, still a smile."

"It doesn't look like a smile to me. Why do you suppose we see it differently?"

"Maybe because you suck cock and I don't."

Perfect, Hillary, didn't let her catch you—not even a blink of an eye . . . Now, pursue it.

Anna Parks sat stiffly in the first row of seats of the Laurel Canyon Courthouse, two husky guards like bookends on either side of her; the court stenographer, requested by Jason, sat off to the edge of the room. In the second row sat the psychiatrist, M.C. Wendell—silver gray wisps spread effectively through thick, dark sideburns. Judge Kraft, sitting high on the bench, was a puny, bespectacled man with a deep resounding voice that overcompensated for his unimpressive appearance.

The public defender, Sam Bender, who'd handled Anna's original defense—Jason had subpoenaed him as well as the one county D.A. who was now handling today's motion— was sitting in the rear of the small, nearly empty courtroom, his eyes low and his head nodding as though he were negotiating with the gods not to call on him to testify. And if Judge Kraft or the rest of the tightly knit courthouse staff had their way, he wouldn't need to.

"Mr. Bennett, you forget, I was in the courtroom," the judge said. "I know what transpired here. So as valiant as your argument may be, I'm afraid it simply doesn't hold. Writ hereby denied. Next case," he said looking toward the clerk.

"But I have witnesses . . ."

"This is a motion session—I have no intention of hearing witnesses. Clerk, next case please—"

"My client has an absolute right to present evidence. Section Nine, Article One of the Constitution states the privilege of the writ of habeas corpus shall not be suspended except in times of rebellion or invasion. We needn't be concerned on those counts—at least, not today. In fact, in the history of the United States, Your Honor,

only one man—Abraham Lincoln—ever suspended—"

"Mr. Bennett, I do not need a history lesson!
Nor do I need your sarcastic wit. My intention
is not to suspend the habeas corpus, but you
have been adequately heard. Now, I am simply
trying to shorten what has become tedious, over-
long proceedings. I repeat, writ denied."

"Is that a final ruling?"

"Were you expecting finale music?"

"In that case," Jason looked at the court reporter, "I'll make an offer of proof as to what
my witnesses would have testified had they gotten the chance."

"There's no need—"

"Your Honor, I simply want to make a record."

"Leave my courtroom!"

Jason stood fast. "The district attorney, Mr.
Delaney, would admit that there was no voir
dire done in this action—neither the Honorable
Judge Kraft, nor he, nor the public defender
asked the defendant questions relating to the
plea, much less if she understood the consequences of it—"

The judge summoned the bailiff to the bench.
"Get this man out of here," he said.

The bailiff went over to Jason, and Jason held
out his arm, preventing him from coming
closer. . . . "I would further call the eminent psychiatrist, M.C. Wendell, to testify that based on
examination of medical records, a thorough psychiatric evaluation, along with his expertise, my
client was not only incompetent at the time of
the crime, but was in no way able to make a
rational decision at her arraignment."

"Mr. Bennett!" the judge shouted. "As knowledgeable as you seem, can I assume you've heard of contempt of court?"

"And finally, Sam Bender, my client's public defender, would testify that he graduated from law school in June of last year, less than six months before he was assigned to this case. And that this was just his *fifth* case since passing the New York State Bar, the other four cases being no more serious than a drunk-driving citation. Attorney Bender barely knew what a voir dire was, much less did he have ability to counsel a client in a capital case! Personally, I don't—"

Judge Kraft stood up, his face a purple spiderweb of twitching veins. He pounded his gavel and shouted, "Shut up!" And Jason finally did— the courtroom at once holding its breath.

The judge took a long look at Delaney, the D.A., then: "Is this true about there being no voir dire?" he asked finally.

Delaney nodded, then stood. "Yes, Your Honor, it is."

"How did that happen?"

Silence, a shrug.

"And is it true that when this case was heard, the public defender was only six months out of law school?"

"I don't know . . ." He looked back and gestured. "He's here . . ."

"Mr. Bender?" the judge said.

"Yes, Your Honor, it is true," came a voice that was only heard because of the heavy silence.

The judge sat down, took a deep breath.

"The guilty plea is hereby vacated. Clerk, set up another arraignment date for next week."

Jason, who had sat, now shot up. "Your Honor, what about bail?"

"Under no circumstances will there be bail set! And while the constitution provides that I consider it next week at the arraignment, I wouldn't count on your client getting it, Mr. Bennett!" He banged his gavel, avoiding the eyes on him. "All recess for twenty minutes."

"Should I tell Lily about it?" Paige said, needing to push hard to get excitement in her voice.

Jason had left the courtroom, gotten into the phone booth, and dialed home, only vaguely aware of the eyes still on him. He had done good though, he knew that.

"Better not," he said finally to Paige, then wondered who he was protecting anyhow. Just how much did Lily or for that matter, Paige, want Anna let out? As was often the case these days, he felt like an outsider in a conspiracy being played out around him.

Jason believed that once Lily wrote the letter to her mother asking that she cooperate so that she might free herself, she hadn't given Anna another thought. Was Anna aware of that, too? Certainly her heart wasn't in any of the proceedings, not even the outrageous performance that nearly got Jason tossed in jail today. But since Lily's letter, Anna's cooperation was definitely there.

And with luck a trial would be set up within a month or six weeks . . . after checking with the court calendar he knew, pushing every key he could push, he could manage that. Actually it was better timing than he had anticipated. Intending to try the case himself, he'd need at least that time to prepare.

By the time they returned to Manhattan with their son, the trial would have already happened, and Anna would either get off altogether or get a lighter sentence. In one case, Lily would be able to go home with her mother; in the other, alternative arrangements would need to be made.

Though he was trying his best to get along with the kid, his bad feelings about her hadn't gone away. If anything, they'd grown. But Paige was in her eighth month, and he had no intention of fighting her now. He didn't want to see her blood pressure fly again. Or worse still, create distance between them when it was so important they be close.

He thought about the hole in the attic Lily had listened through, watched them through, knowing that if he confronted Paige with it, she'd jump right to Lily's defense.

A week later, Hillary Egan recorded the following notes. *The patient has no clear base from which to distinguish between right and wrong. Although she is extraordinarily bright and has caught on quickly to what people want of her, she has no inner guidelines with which to assist her in her relationship with the world.*

On order: Wechsler Intelligence Scale for Children-Revised, Rorschach Ink Blot Test, Blackey Pictures, Children's Apperception Test.

It happened about two weeks later—a Lamaze night and Roger had invited Lily over for the

evening while the house would be empty. But
Lily refused, saying she'd rather stay alone and
play with her turtle. Paige went partway down
the steps, and sat down.

"Okay, what's wrong?"

"Nothing."

"Since when don't you like to be with Roger?"

She shrugged. "Everything's the baby. Carolyn
this, Carolyn that, I get so sick of it."

"Soon we'll have one of those babies around,
too."

"My Boy will be different."

Paige smiled. "Oh yeah, why's that?"

"Just that he will be; he's going to do smart,
excellent things. Not like stupid little Carolyn
who doesn't even look at you when you try to
talk to her."

"Lily! Carolyn is a sweet, darling baby. Infants
don't pay much attention at first, but that soon
changes. In any event, I don't want to hear you
talk like that again."

Quiet, then: "I still say, My Boy will be more
special."

Paige walked downstairs, kneeled next to Lily,
and hugged her.

"What am I going to do with you? Well, I do
have one idea."

Lily pulled away. "What?"

"How about you being my Lamaze partner
tonight."

"Do you mean it?"

"I do."

"What about Jason?"

"He phoned earlier, said he wouldn't be able
to get there until ten, which is pretty near the

end of class. I'll call back and tell him not to
bother at all, to head straight home. I'm sure
he'll be relieved. But it does mean I'll need a
partner for this evening."

Lily scooted upstairs to get ready. Paige looked
at the turtle, and then at all the toys Lily had
placed strategically around the big box. She
tapped Wally's shell.

"Come on out, you sleepy head, get up and
play."

Okay, so Roger wasn't jealous. Lily was.

Everyone thought it was adorable, particularly
Paige . . . seven adult couples and yet Lily came
up with the best questions for Dr. Barry's nurse,
Lenore, who was running the class. Paige was
lying on her back, pillows wedged at her sides
and her feet on Lily's lap, having them lovingly
massaged while she practiced her breathing and
focused on a short cactus plant on the win-
dowsill.

"What happens if she breathes too fast?" Lily
asked.

"The blood would likely rush to her head,
causing light-headedness. Perhaps hyperventila-
tion. Come on, ladies, let's practice the deep
breathing . . . inhale, hold—one, two, three—
exhale."

"You've got to be careful and do the right
things," Lily said on the way home.

"Why is it I think if I close my eyes tight, I'll
find Jason sitting beside me?"

"It's just that some mothers are dumb."

"Oh no, are we into insults here?" Paige said,
as though she were wounded.

"Not you."

A quick glance at Lily, but the darkness made it impossible for Paige to make out her expression. Still, Paige detected seriousness in her voice, not teasing.

"Well, would you like to elaborate?" she said finally.

"Mommy lost a baby once."

A deep intake of breath, then: "Oh, Lily, how awful. I'm so sorry."

Silence.

"How old were you then?"

"I think three, maybe four."

Paige shook her head. "It must have been painful for you . . . and your mother. It's certainly not an easy thing to go through. I know, Lily, it happened to me."

She looked at her. "It did?"

Paige nodded, thinking of the blaming remark Lily had aimed at her mother.

"It just happened," she said. "Everything was going along fine, then one day the pains started . . . I was only in my third month, way too early for the fetus to survive. Sometimes terrible things happen, and it's really no one's fault."

"Maybe it wasn't your fault, but it *was* her fault."

Had Paige spotted a little anger in her voice, too? "How?" she asked finally.

"She wouldn't eat; she used to make me eat her food so Daddy wouldn't know."

"Maybe it's not exactly as you remember it. You were so young."

"Oh, no, I remember."

Did Anna really do that or was it just some

painfully tangled memory of a four-year-old? Certainly she herself had been noticing more and more that her memories weren't so reliable. In fact, earlier during class she had a recollection of her mother sitting beside her, stroking her feet like Lily had been doing. She wasn't sure why she was doing it, but it was a good feeling, comforting.

Not having many of those memories of Mother, she wondered why she hadn't had this one sooner.

Though Jason hated to think of Lily as his replacement at Lamaze, he wasn't sorry she was keeping Paige company tonight. Reaching the Briarwood town line at almost nine-thirty, the last thing he would have wanted to face was another twenty miles of driving.

He noticed the cellar light on from outside, so as soon as he opened the front door he headed to the back stairwell. But it was one of the smaller downstairs connections lit ... Sighing, he headed down to the overhead bulb and just as he was about to pull the string, he noticed the cardboard box tucked under the table.

It was just simple curiosity that pulled him to it and made him lift off the cover: two jack-knives, a can opener, books of matches, a bag of acorns, pieces of moldy bread in plastic wrap, pine cones, rotted berries ... and what looked to be a squirrel's tail.

Lily's goods. Apparently the attic hadn't been her only home. . . .

He closed the cover and on his way back to

the light, he stopped at the turtle's box and stooped down.

"Hey, Wally, what's your problem, huh, some kind of energy deficiency? Tired blood? He picked the turtle up, examined it from all angles—its long neck stretched way out, stayed out. Jason flicked the edges of the shell with his fingertips, at where his legs—"Come on, pull them suckers out and—"

What had she done? The turtle had no fucking legs!

He was sitting on the floor in the cellar a half hour before he heard them come home. He got up, went to the bottom of the stairs, and called to them. Paige came to the top landing.

"What're you doing down there?"

"Where's Lily?"

"Here in the kitchen. We thought we'd have a snack before—"

"I want to see her."

"Jason, can't it wait? It's late, she has school tomorrow."

"Now."

Paige stepped aside, making room for Lily.

"Come down here," Jason said.

Lily looked at Paige, then started down. Paige began to follow. "Can I be let in on this, too?"

"Sorry," Jason said. "This is between me and Lily."

Paige stepped back.

"And if you could close the door—"

Paige shrugged, then stepped back and closed the door to the kitchen.

Jason led Lily to the box, then: "Well, I assume you know why you're here?"

She shook her head.

"Don't lie. I'm not Paige."

Silence.

"Why did you do it?"

"You were the one who told me to."

"What?"

"Wally climbed over the tank wall, you said to do something to stop it. So I did."

"Cutting off its legs? That was the best you could do?"

"I knew for certain it would work."

"Don't you see how cruel—"

"Come on, Jason, it's only a turtle."

He swallowed. "Maybe we ought to see what Paige thinks of it?"

"Don't tell her."

"Why not?"

"I don't know, maybe she'll think it's bad."

"It *is* bad."

A few moments of silence, then: "If you love her, you won't tell."

"Oh, is that right?"

She nodded. "It'll just upset her, maybe even make her sick."

"I think she'll be able to handle this."

"How do you think she'll handle hearing about you and Brooke?"

"I haven't a clue as to what—"

"Don't lie. I'm not Paige."

Silence.

"Besides, I was practically standing right there. I saw Brooke's shirt open, her little pancake tits sticking out, waiting for you to suck on 'em. I saw her hands in your jeans ... my gosh, that's what I couldn't figure out at all, Jason, what were they doing inside your jeans? Maybe when I tell Paige, she'll know."

Jason's trembling hands came toward her.

"Don't. If you do, I'll scream."

Chapter Twelve

"This is Hillary Egan," she spoke into the phone.

"Jason Bennett, here. Lily Parks' guardian."

"Oh yes, hello, Mr. Bennett. We never did get to meet."

"Right. I was wondering if we could remedy that, maybe get together tonight. I'd like to talk about Lily."

"Is there anything specific?"

"You're her therapist. Frankly, I'm interested to know what your opinion is of her."

"Well, as for a psychological diagnosis, it's a little premature. I won't be testing her for several weeks yet. And since I've only been seeing her for such a short time I'm afraid I couldn't—"

"Okay, look, what about her background? I assume you've made a little headway there, begun to talk to her about her past?"

"If so, I couldn't tell you about it."

"Why not?"

"I explained all this to your wife when we first met. I would have thought she'd have mentioned

it to you. The thing is, I believe in giving my
clients privacy, complete confidentiality. What
they say to me in the confines of the therapy
room goes no further."

"But she's only a kid."

"You make that sound subhuman."

"That's not how I meant it. It's just that parents, guardians have certain rights, too. How are
they to help out if they don't know what's
happening?"

"I'm sorry, Mr. Bennett. As a professional
with a reputation to consider, I'm not about to
change my mind on this. I can only help Lily if
she reaches out and puts her trust in me. And
once she does that, I refuse to betray that trust."

*I'd like to see how that philosophy holds up
against a court subpoena ... Easy, Jason, don't get
crazy. The truth is, the uptight therapist probably
knows less about Lily than you do.*

Hillary hung up the telephone, sat there in the
kitchen over a cup of steaming tea. Actually she
wasn't sorry she was abrupt with Mr. Bennett.
As a professional, she had done the only thing
she could have done. Certainly she had formed
opinions based on her observations. What therapist worth his salt would not have? But testing
was an integral instrument in any diagnosis.

The issue of confidentiality aside, what use
would her observations be to the Bennetts, what
purpose would they serve? The complexities of
the psyche often tended to confuse and alarm
lay people—needlessly. And it wasn't as though
Lily were creating havoc in their home, not at
all. On the few times Paige had come to her

office to discuss Lily, she had made that abundantly clear—the child's behavior was exemplary, doing what was expected of her.

Taking it all into consideration, Hillary had no wish to give the Bennetts a basis for misinterpretation which might result in their removing Lily from their home. The longer Lily remained in their capable care and custody, the longer she would remain Hillary's patient.

Already aware of the extensive violence and abuse in Lily Parks' background when she took her on as a patient, Hillary knew it would be an intriguing case, perhaps even one that would win her acclaim as a clinician. Now, having had some opportunity to work with Lily, she didn't expect to be disappointed.

She went to her bookcase, took out the *Diagnostic Manual of Mental Disorders*, went straight to the section, "Sadistic Personality Disorder," and read: "A pattern of cruel, demeaning, and aggressive behavior, to intimidate and establish the dominant role in a relationship. Amused and fascinated by the physical and/or psychological suffering and humiliation of humans and animals."

Brooke was clearly surprised to see Jason standing at her door. She let him inside. "Paige usually calls about this time . . ." she said. "What are you doing here?"

"I need someone to talk to, and right now you're about all I have."

She nodded, hobbled back to the sofa—she was wearing a shorter, knee-length cast.

"All right, what is it?"

"Lily."

"Lily, Lily, Lily. God how I've grown to hate that name. Paige and I go out of our way not to mention her, considering how I'm not one of her fans. But we might as well not bother, she's there between us like the goddamned Berlin Wall. Did a German need to talk about the wall to know it was still in the way?"

Jason sat down.

"Answer me something—do you think you'll be able to get the kid away from her come April when you bring her and the baby home?"

"You think not?"

She shrugged. "At the start of this, Paige was a cheerleader for Mother Anna. Now I don't know. Now I hear doubts in her voice, like maybe this lady isn't so darn swell after all. Not the right kind of mother for Princess Lily."

Jason sat looking down at the carpet, his shoulders and back hunched and his hands resting on his knees.

"It's so hard to imagine this happening. I keep wondering if someone is about to tap my shoulder, tell me I've been watching some lousy surrealistic movie, fucked up in the shooting."

"She's only a kid, there must be some way to maneuver her out of there."

"It's worse than you think."

Silence.

"She was there that day."

"What day?"

"Us. In the woods."

A slow intake of breath . . . silence, then: "Has she told Paige?"

"Use her ace in the hole? Uh, uh, too savvy for that, much better to wave it over my head."

"Oh, come now, you're not saying she's blackmailing you?"

"Remember that turtle?"

A nod.

"Last night I discovered the turtle didn't have any legs. She actually went and cut them off so it couldn't climb out of the tank. It was when I threatened to tell Paige—"

Brooke's mouth dropped open, then suddenly as though a spasm gripped her, she began to laugh. Louder and louder until finally Jason went over and shook her, making her stop.

"How can you think this funny?" he said.

"I don't. It scares the shit out of me . . . Jason?"

"What?"

"You think she's the one who cut the branch, don't you?"

"I do, but what good does it do me? I have no proof, it could just as easily have been caused by the storm. Besides, do I chance suggesting it to Paige when Lily could blow any degree of calm Paige has finally managed right to hell?"

Lily had been playing with the steel box and puppets in Hillary's office since the beginning of the session. Hillary checked her watch—so far now, it was twenty-five minutes since the session had started. The child had gone through the same routine over and over: placing each of the four puppets—each representing a member of a fabricated family—into the box, locking the box, then smashing each one with the hammer.

"They must be a very sad family, always to get hit like that," Hillary said.

"Uh, uh, punished."

"I see. What was it they did that was so terribly naughty?"

"*You* must be a very sad family," Lily said, not bothering to answer Hillary's question.

"Why would you think that?"

"The old man upstairs drools over his shirt and pisses his pants, and you'd love to be rid of him."

Hillary made an effort not to let the taunting get to her. Instead, she said out loud what for so many months she'd said silently.

"Though Father may do things I don't like, it doesn't mean I don't love him. If he were able to change those things, I'm sure he would. A baby, for example, regularly soils himself . . . would a mother love the baby any less because of it?"

"A baby can be useful. If it's a good one, it'll grow big and strong and brave, maybe even smart. Old people just get weaker, smellier, dumber, and more scared. Real, real scared."

"Of what?"

"I don't know, anything, everything."

"Did you ever know an old person?"

She nodded.

"Who?"

"My mother."

"But your mother is young, in her early thirties I remember Paige telling me."

"No, but it's not like that. Old is the man upstairs, scared and weak and used up."

Silence, then: "I think I see now. Old has

nothing to do with age, it has to do with strength."

"Right."

"Well, what do you suggest we do with these old people?"

"Put them away."

"I don't quite get what that means."

"Kill them, bitch. Do you get it now?"

After Lily left that afternoon, Hillary hunted up the key to Father's bedroom and added it to her silver dollar key ring. From here on when Lily was at the house, she'd lock Father's door. Not that she really thought Lily would bother him.

"The question: is the patient dangerous to those around her?" Hillary said as she lifted the tape recorder microphone from her desk drawer and spoke directly into it. "No, I think not, not as long as the child's fantasies are being played out under professional guidance. Though violence is basic to sadistic personality disorder, this patient has not stepped beyond the fascination stage. . . .

"I base this conclusion on two factors: one— the child is young to be acting out violence. Two—aside from therapy where Lily is able— and even encouraged—to show her troubled side, the girl is apparently polite, cheerful, easy to get along with. Even helpful. Since her functioning in the outside world is appropriate, there is no reason to believe there will be any sudden change.

"The locked door is simply a precaution."

It was after Thanksgiving and Paige and Lily

had taken on the project together—clearing and cleaning the bedroom next to Lily's, painting it, and making it into a nursery. Lily and Paige even picked out Sesame Street character curtains and decals for the wall.

"What does My Boy's room in the city look like?"

"Well, let me see . . . The furniture is white. Jason wallpapered it with jungle animals."

"You don't think he'll be scared, do you?"

"Not at all."

Lily stretched her arm out. "Do you think he'll like this bedroom as much?"

"Oh, I'm certain of it. And we'll have to tell him right off who played such a big part in creating it."

She smiled, then dipped the paintbrush in the pale yellow paint.

"Can I take care of him, even when he's real little?"

"Are you kidding? I'm counting on you. Joshua is going to look on you as a big sister."

"He is?"

Paige nodded. "I know you won't live here, but you'll visit often. Girls and boys go off to camp, boarding school, college, things like that. It doesn't make them any less remembered or loved by their younger sisters or brothers."

"Paige, do you have any sisters or brothers?"

"No . . . no I don't, Lily."

"Are you sure?"

"Of course I'm sure, why?"

"Just that you looked a little funny."

"I guess I always wished I had one. Being an

only child can be lonely. But then I don't have
to tell you, do I?"

She nodded. "Paige, I wish—"

Paige went over, put her finger to Lily's
mouth, then bent down and put her arms around
her.

"I know, sweetheart, I wish, too. But some
things just can't be. Besides, it wouldn't be right
... If Jason can get your mother out of prison,
she'll need you with her."

"But if I'm afraid?"

Paige pulled back. "Of your mother?"

"Tell me about Lily," Jason said to Anna at
the prison.

"That's a strange request."

"Is it?"

"She's living with you. I would think you'd
know."

"I don't, you tell me."

Anna shrugged. "My baby's a good girl, she
was always helpful, never refused me anything."

"What about him?"

"Who?"

"Maynard, her father."

"I don't understand."

"Let me spell it out more clearly for you ...
did he ever hit her, beat her, abuse her—sexu-
ally, physically, psychologically?"

"Not that I saw."

"You were living with them?"

"Of course."

"Then you did see?"

"Yes, and there was really nothing ..." Anna
stood up, stepped to the window, stared into the

courtyard where a volleyball game was getting started. "She handled him," Anna said finally. "Almost through instinct, she always knew the right words to say to him, how to act around him to keep him off her back. Almost like he was a piece in a jigsaw puzzle she had already put together a hundred times over."

On the drive back to Briarwood, Jason thought about it. He guessed he had expected a little more. More reasons why a kid would be so messed up. Not that what Lily saw go on between her parents wasn't reason enough, but according to Anna, she was spared worse. And mostly because she knew how to work the monster . . . Yet she hadn't learned by example, certainly she hadn't been emulating her frightened mother. Anna had simply called it instinct. . . .

Could it be Lily understood the monster because she was so much like him?

"Jason?" Paige said, trying to get him to turn toward her, but he continued to read.

She tried again. "When will you talk about it?"

He gave her a quick glance, then back to the papers in his hand. "What's that?"

"Whatever it is bothering you."

"Look, I'm simply trying to get through this complaint."

"I'm not talking about this moment. It seems in the last week or so, you've been in your own world. And no matter what I do, I can't seem to get entrance."

"A lot on my mind."

She played her fingers through his hair. "Share it with me," she said.

"You don't want to know."

"I do, even if it's about Anna and the trial."

"How good of you."

"Oh, come on, I didn't mean it to sound like that."

Jason put the complaint down, turned over, propped his head on his hand.

"I'm going to Laurel Canyon tomorrow."

Somehow just the mention of Lily's hometown and knowing Jason could drive there so easily seemed to make what happened there that much more real. "Why?" she asked.

"I want to talk to the neighbors, people who knew the Parks."

"What exactly are you looking for?"

"Witnesses to Maynard's violence."

"You might find that Anna's not as innocent as we thought," Paige said.

One eyebrow lifted. "Oh?"

"Just something Lily said . . ."

Paige—not certain herself how accurate Lily's recollection was—would rather not have gone into it with Jason, but she had started it, and now he was waiting for the rest.

"She inferred she was scared of her mother."

He didn't say anything—it was just his body language that spoke annoyance. "Look, Jason, I did try to pursue it, but she closed right up. I've noticed before, she hates to say unkind things about her parents. As soon as she realizes she's doing it, she buttons up and changes the subject. She's determined to protect them."

"My, isn't she the little martyr."

"I don't see it that way."

"I didn't suppose you would."

"Why would Lily be afraid, Jason?"

"You're going on the assumption she is. I don't believe it for a minute."

A long pause, then: "But what if it is true, what if she has reason to be scared of her mother?"

"You know, Paige, the bottom line is, it doesn't make a difference. What you're suggesting—and not very subtly—is, I dump Anna Parks off at the nearest weigh station. Sorry, too late now for that. She's my client, and I'm going to do whatever I can to see she goes free. No matter what Lily infers or what you think of her mothering skills."

Paige shook her head. "It amazes me—only a few weeks ago you and Lily were outside building an igloo together. You were really going out of your way to get along. In fact, if I closed my eyes, I could almost believe you liked her.

"And then suddenly we backed up, started from scratch. Right about the time you scolded her, saying she wasn't feeding her turtle regularly ... Surely you aren't still angry at her for that?" Paige shook her head. "No, uh, uh, I refuse to believe that's what it is ...

"But then what, Jason, what was it I missed?"

The house the Parks had lived in was four tiny rooms on a deserted country road, the kind of simple house that kindergartners draw or travelers occasionally pass by and wonder, does someone really live there? Lots of empty land, a dozen or so junk vehicles scattered in parts over

a grassless area. Trees and bushes and lots of woodland, now being covered by a dusting of fresh snow.

Right now there was a For Rent sign out front. Was the realtor serious? Jason walked up to the low window, peered in through the dirty chipped glass: no shades, a grease-stained five-and-dime carpet, a sofa left behind, the yellowed stuffing fallen loose and spilling out. He walked around the back. There was a doghouse out there, big enough for a Saint Bernard . . . When he gave Lily the turtle, he remembered her saying she'd never had a pet.

Jason got back in the car, drove about a half mile, stopped when he came to a mailbox labeled Greta Sinclair. A middle-aged woman with good skin and a silk flowered scarf wrapped around her head came to the door. "Can I help you?" she said.

"Ms. Sinclair, my name's Jason Bennett. I'm looking to talk to someone who knew the Parks family. You might remember, they lived up the road about—"

"I know where they lived. Don't you reporters ever give up?"

"I'm a lawyer. Anna Parks' lawyer."

"A little late, aren't you? I read somewhere where she got a mighty stiff sentence."

"You think, too stiff?"

"Well, I'm not a judge."

"But you knew her?"

"Not really, but—"

He gestured to the door between them. "Do you think maybe I could come inside?"

She studied him, his face, then his clothes

down to his shoes—finally she unlatched the
door and opened it.

"Call me Greta. And God help me the day
serial killers begin wearing cashmere and im-
ported leather."

"A good eye. Retail clothing?"

"Manufacturing." The large picture window
in the living room had a blue flowered drape
cinched back over white sheers, the same soft
flowery material used for the upholstery on the
sofa and one of the chairs. She gestured for him
to sit. "Head seamstress at Yves St. Laurent for
thirty-five years."

"You must have started at age ten."

"I could learn to like you, boy."

Jason smiled. "About Anna Parks—"

"Yes, yes, Anna Parks. Well, as I started to
say, I didn't really know her. It'd be more accurate to say I knew of her. My sister's an emergency room nurse at Fielding Hospital. Anna was
treated there a number of times. From what I
understand, she was beat up regularly . . . But
then, I shouldn't have to tell you that."

"Why do you suppose she stayed with the
husband?"

"According to my sister, he had her mesmerized. As much as the bastard beat her, in some
peculiar way, she felt she needed him. I guess
there's women out there who are scared to make
it on their own, will put up with about anything.
And then—who knows?"

"Can I talk to your sister?"

"Sure, here, I'll give you her address." She
wrote it out on a slip of paper and handed it to
him. "You appealing the case?"

"Actually I'm trying it." He walked to the door and she followed, her eyes still looking him over.

"How'd a fellow like you get involved in this case?"

"Why do you ask?"

"You don't look like a country lawyer to me; in fact, you look like you might cost a bundle. And as far as I know, the Parks were poor as church mice."

"You know, when I meet a perceptive person like yourself, I say to myself: 'Hey, Jason, don't walk away till you pick some brain.' Now let me ask you, Greta, if you were in my place, wanting to get Anna Parks out of this fix, what would you do?"

"I'd go find the kid, ask her."

"Why?"

"According to everyone around, my sister included, the girl was amazing: bright, caring, helpful, responsible, old before her time you might say. Usually it was she who brought the mother to the hospital for treatment. Drove, too, on occasion, can you imagine? She knew all about cars from the father. I guess it just strikes me that a kid like that ought to be able to describe exactly what was going on in that household. That is, of course, if such a kid exists."

"She was found, you know."

"Yes, I read it in the papers. Actually I was referring to her faultless reputation. Look, I've never had a kid, but I've got twelve nieces and nephews, twenty-seven grandnieces and nephews. Good solid homes, lots of love, attention, smarts to go around and around. And yet I haven't seen a perfect kid rise out of the bunch."

"You're saying the kid's too good to be true."

"You tell me, you're the one who found her, aren't you?"

When Ruthanne telephoned Paige at about four o'clock, Paige was just putting a roast in the oven.

"Paige, can you come over?" she asked.

"Could it wait a little. Say about—"

"Please now . . ."

"Ruthanne, are you crying?"

She left Lily at home and hurried over—snow had begun to fall. When she got to the house, she found Ruthanne sitting alone in the darkened living room. Paige went to the sofa, knelt down, and took Ruthanne's hand in hers.

"What is it?"

"Roger," she whispered.

"What, is he sick?"

Ruthanne took a deep breath, then: "I walked into the baby's room earlier . . . and found him putting a pillow . . . over the baby's face, Paige." Big tears started to slide from the corners of Ruthanne's eyes over her full cheeks, and Paige hunted through her purse, came out with a wad of tissue, and handed her some.

"The baby, is she all right?"

She pressed her lips together, nodding.

"What if I hadn't walked in, what if—"

Paige put her arm around her. "But you did, Ruthanne. And Carolyn wasn't hurt."

"I keep thinking suppose I had gone down to the laundry room, or into my bedroom to put away the folded clothes or—"

"Don't torture yourself this way, it won't help.

Ruthanne, did you talk to Roger about it, ask
him why?"

"I couldn't. I mean, I screamed and cried and
carried on, but couldn't pull myself together
enough to talk. And Charlie, my Charlie is as
good-natured as they come, the salt of the
earth—sometimes I think he just popped out
knowing the right thing to do—but as for getting
through to kids, he's worse than hopeless."

"Why do you suppose Roger would—"

"I don't know, here I thought everything was
going so wonderfully, he didn't seem one bit jealous of his baby sister. Did he seem jealous to
you, Paige?"

She shook her head. "Still, there's got to be
some reason."

"Oh, I know, I keep telling myself that. Paige,
what about you, could you talk to him?"

"Me, why me?"

"You deal with children in school, and you're
wonderful with Lily. Just try to find out what's
going on in his head. If I send Charlie in, he'll
just stand there looking disappointed at him . . ."
She held up her hands, her fingers trembling.
"And just look at me, I'm in no condition to talk
to anyone."

Paige knocked several times before Roger came
to the door and opened it. She went and turned
on a bedside lamp, then sat on the bed: Roger's
face was red and splotchy.

"Can we talk?"

He shrugged.

She patted the mattress. "Come on, sit."

Roger sat down and waited for her to talk, his
eyes on his shoes.

"Your mother is worried about you, Roger. She wanted to talk to you herself but she's too upset over what happened today." A pause, then she said, "Roger, I've been around here enough to see how much you adore your sister. That's why it's so hard for me to understand why you'd want to hurt her . . ."

"I didn't want to hurt her, not really."

"Then why? You know when a pillow is held over a person's face, it stops his breathing. If you had held it there too long, Carolyn would have died."

"I never would have held it that long."

"Why do it at all, Roger?"

"I guess to punish her."

He started to cry, buried his face into the spread, and wept. He obviously felt terrible, if only Paige could have peeked inside his head to see what was really going on. She reached over, placed her hand on his back, rubbing it while he calmed down.

"Why would anyone want to punish a little baby?" she asked when the tears finally stopped.

"Carolyn isn't perfect, she doesn't do everything right."

"No one I know does."

"But I'm her big brother, so when I see her do something bad, it's up to me to teach her."

"What kind of bad things?"

"She screams in the middle of the night, wakes up everyone."

"Babies need diapers changed and to be fed often. Since they can't talk, they have to cry in order to let you know when."

"Mommy said, when I was her age, I was already sleeping right through the night."

"Well, babies develop at different rates. But the important thing here is, babies don't get punished. They're way too young to even know what it means. And when a child is old enough or if it becomes necessary, well, punishments should definitely not be hurtful. . . . That's why those things are best left to moms and dads."

"My folks don't know about punishments."

"You mean, you've never been punished?"

"Uh, uh."

"Sounds to me like you think a lot about them for a boy who's never had a punishment. Who's been talking to you about them?"

Silence.

Paige cupped her hands over Roger's shoulders. "Tell me Roger, who?"

"Lily."

As soon as she got home, Paige sat Lily down.

"This afternoon, Roger put a pillow over the baby's head. Thank goodness, Ruthanne walked in before Carolyn was hurt. Lily, do you know anything about this?"

"How would I? I was upstairs doing homework. Doesn't he like the baby anymore?"

"Of course he likes the baby," Paige said, trying to steady her nerves. "Lily, I questioned Roger about this, and he's very confused. It seems he was trying to punish the baby. Apparently you had been talking to him about punishments?"

She nodded.

"What was it you told him?"

"You said I wouldn't have to talk about it."

"But you talked about it to Roger."

"He's different, he's just a kid."

"Lily, it would help me understand."

Silence.

"Please, sweetheart."

"Mommy would get punished, and I'd have to stay there and watch the things . . ."

"What kind of things?"

A sigh, then: "Oh, he'd hang her by her wrists from the shower pole, or stuff her head in a tin wastebasket, make her stand outside while he'd practice throwing balls at the basket. He'd make her eat animals he killed in the woods. She'd throw 'em up, choke, then he'd force her to swallow it back—"

"Oh God."

"So sometimes I'd eat for her. Raccoon meat is bitter, it leaves a coat on your tongue so thick that—"

"Stop it!" Paige gathered the child in her arms, her eyes shut tight as though to wipe away the freshly drawn pictures. "I'm sorry, Lily. You don't have to talk about it, not if you don't want to."

Paige ate very little at dinner. She had spoken to Ruthanne and explained everything the best she could. It wasn't as though Lily had told Roger what to do or even suggested he do it, but somehow in a child's head things got confused. . . . And for some reason, perhaps a bit of sibling jealousy, Roger had decided to try out punishments.

The kind of sick punishment the monster

thought up for Anna, the kind that perhaps aroused little boys' imaginations.

The nurse's name was Mona and Jason caught her by surprise as she was putting on her fluffy fake fur coat and boots.

"I don't have much time but you can walk me to my car if you want. Normally I'm on till eleven, but tonight my granddaughter's the lead goose in the first graders pageant. There's no emergency gonna make me miss that."

"That wouldn't be a Christmas goose, would it?"

Angela smiled and looked at the business card Jason had handed her. "So Sis gave you my name, huh? Okay, what can I do you for, Jason Bennett, attorney at law."

"I represent Anna Parks."

"Really? Interesting."

"Why?"

"I don't know, I guess I felt sorry for the woman, though I didn't have much sympathy with her not walking off years before, leaving the miserable bastard."

"Why do you think she didn't?"

"I don't know, scared of him, scared to be on her own, maybe some of both. She was pretty much alone, except for the sister, of course."

"You knew the sister?"

"Oh no, never met her. But Anna talked about her a lot. Her name was Nora, I believe. She lived in the next county, but apparently visited often."

"Sounds like they got along pretty well."

"That's certainly the impression I got."

Jason paused a few moments, wondering why Anna had lied, then asked, "What do you think made her finally kill him?"

"I'll tell you, I've often thought about it, and the way I see it, Anna would have had to be driven out of her mind to do such a thing."

"Why's that?"

"I just couldn't picture it any other way. Something monumental had to have spurred a woman that insecure and passive to suddenly kill. Not that he didn't deserve it. But the worst crime committed here, I'm afraid, is to that little girl."

"Why's that?"

"All of the obvious reasons. Here was this kid trying her best to take over for the mother, meanwhile being robbed of a normal childhood. No kid contracts out for that kind of deal. Yeah, if I have to say anything, I felt more sorry for the kid. Real sweet. Once in a while I'd catch some anger showing in her expression, but listen, put in her shoes, wouldn't you be angry, too?"

Sure, he'd be angry, but right now his mind was on Mona and what a good character witness she'd make for Anna—a professional who saw the hurt and bruises firsthand. She was bright, observant, certainly had no reason to flower up a story. If she could say it to the jury just as she had said it to him, it'd be fine—Anna would have had to be driven out of her mind to do such a thing.

And he was also thinking about Anna's sister. Though he'd promised Anna he wouldn't try to find her, under the circumstances, he was about to break his promise. He went back to

the hospital, to a phone booth, and called his office. From the brief investigation conducted earlier, he knew Nora Kalish had indeed left the area, but that's as far as it had gotten. Now he told Pat to put out some fresh feelers.

Once Paige hung up the phone with Hillary, she felt oddly disloyal, but that was only because her mind was charging on emotion. After all, how was Hillary to really help Lily if Paige didn't do everything she could to cooperate? And surely those punishments the child admitted she was made to watch were something her therapist ought to know about—that is, presuming she didn't already.

Paige also mentioned to Hillary the discrepancy in the two stories Lily had told her: not so long ago Lily had told of her mother forcing her to eat food she didn't want. Which was it, was she scared *of* the mother or *for* her? Did Lily herself know?

She got up, went to the bathroom, then into Lily's bedroom. As always, Lily was on the floor mattress, sleeping with her one leg peeking from the covers. Paige stooped down, drew up the quilt, tucked it securely under her chin, then kissed her cheek. As soon as she heard noise downstairs, she tiptoed out of the room.

"Jason?"

"Down here."

Paige went down and kissed him. "Want something to eat?"

"I stopped on the road."

"I think I was wrong about Lily being scared of Anna."

"Oh?"

"What she seems scared of are the memories, the abuse she was made to witness."

"Anna?"

Paige nodded.

"She talked about it?"

"Some."

"Then she can testify."

"Is that all you can think of?"

"It's my job, Paige. And it's her mother's life."

Say it, wimp. Just come straight out and say it: Paige, I had a couple of romps in the hay with your best friend. Not a big deal, no way ... As soon as I took hold of my senses—stop, over, the end. So you ask, where was my mind? What is it, how do they say, stuck in my pants zipper? And never before, hey I mean never ever did I so much as lay a finger ... But still even this, it was nothing, I swear to God it was nothing. Less than nothing.

And I wouldn't even be bothering to mention it, if not for your little poisoned pal. Would you believe, she's not your pal, not my pal, not anyone's. Watch her, don't take your eye off her, she's got evil tricks frying in her head, splattering up and down her sleeves. Who says? Me. Hey, you remember me— husband, lover, friend.

Any of them sound familiar?

"Jason!"

His attention snapped back. "What?"

"Where've you been off to?"

He shrugged.

"You've had the oddest expression ..."

"Just wondering ..."

"What?"

"When's your next doctor appointment?"

"All that mystery for that? Monday. Which incidentally begins my ninth month."

Okay, suppose he came clean, told her, what then? Be honest, totally honest. She'd be hurt, angry, no, enraged. . . . Not good for the unborn baby, not good for Paige. Certainly not good for him. And the quadraplegic turtle? Up against an affair with her best friend, mightn't it seem like childish folly?

Chapter Thirteen

"How did our picture of young Joshua come out?" Paige said to Dr. Barry, eager to see the sonogram just taken.

He handed her the picture.

"You'll be able to make him out with far less difficulty this time."

Her mouth opened. "Oh my gosh, yes!" She zoomed in on the baby's head, face. "What is this? Oh, no, tell me it can't be, he's sucking his thumb? The oral fixation already in the womb." She laughed. "Wait'll Jason sees, I'll definitely get more than my share of blame for this particular trait." She studied the picture further, finally sliding it into the envelope the doctor handed her.

"How's that little girl coming along?" the doctor asked.

"Oh, Lily's fine, so excited about 'My Boy,' as she calls our little Joshua. She and Jason are—" Paige put up a level hand, then rocked it. "Well, suffice to say they have their ups and downs. And of course, she has a lot of unpleasant memo-

ries to deal with. Memories seem to be surfacing, but one doesn't always coincide with another."

"Because of the frightening nature of them, recall is apt to come out in disconnected pieces, one here, one there. The psyche has amazing protective powers."

Paige nodded. "Well, she's going to a therapist. Hopefully she'll be able to sort them, make some sense out of the horror. If that's possible. You know, I'm determined to make this Christmas special for her. I doubt we'll have her for another . . ." Paige sighed, shook her head. "No, I refuse to dwell on it, get myself all upset." She slipped into her fur-lined jacket and red wool hat and lifted the manila envelope holding the sonogram. "So what do you think is a good present for an eleven-year-old?"

She looked at her watch. With Lily going after school today to Hillary's, it was a perfect time to shop.

Hillary had given Father his newspaper—promising as always to be back at four-fifteen, which in the last several weeks had become their tea time—and locked the bedroom door before looking up to see Lily standing there. She dropped her silver dollar key ring in her black leather purse, then stepped across the hall and hung the purse over her bedroom doorknob.

"What're you doing up here, Lily?"

"May I use the bathroom?"

"Of course. Use the half-bath downstairs."

Once in the therapy room, Lily headed straight toward the easel. She painted a baby in a circle. "Why the circle?" Hillary asked.

"That's the mother's stomach."

"I see. Then this baby isn't born yet?"

"No and it won't get born till you stretch the mother's legs way apart."

"Did you ever see a baby born?"

"Just a bloody one, that didn't count. But I'm going to see My Boy born."

"My Boy, that must be Paige's baby?"

She nodded.

"Is Paige planning on delivering at home?"

"I don't think so."

"Then how will you watch?"

"I don't know, how will you watch?"

Silence, then: "Lily, didn't you just say—"

"No, I didn't just say anything. I think sometimes you hear things you shouldn't. But know what, Hillary—I'm going to take care of My Boy. Paige is going to let me."

"What will you do for him?"

"Change his diaper, rock him, feed him, teach him to talk, to read. What did you think I would do, sandpaper his feet?"

"No, I certainly wouldn't have thought that. Lily, tell me about the other baby."

"I told you, that one didn't count."

"Everything counts."

"Only if I let it."

"Well, you must have let that baby count at one time."

"Know what? Before I bagged it and tied it, and threw it away, I looked all through that blood. Still I couldn't tell if it was a boy or girl baby. I looked so hard because I thought for sure Mommy or Daddy would ask. But neither of them did."

* * *

Hillary had been speaking into the tape for several minutes when she looked at her wristwatch: tea time, Father would be expecting her. She hurried on to finish. "The aborted fetus seems to play a significant role in the patient's development. Feeling alienated from her mother and father, she apparently anticipated a brother or sister to fill the void, someone on whom to shower affection.

"This loss coupled with the violence and cruelty she was forced to routinely witness and somehow process into her psyche, likely immobilized what was already an unstable emotional blueprint. The feelings she now encounters are scrambled, unreliable, impossible to keep and restrain other than for a limited time period. Thus, she is never able to direct those feelings in any positive path. In this type of patient, anger and violent thoughts radically escalate when feeling abandoned. This patient has felt abandoned most of her life.

"While it is imperative that the therapist pursue this avenue—considering that the child's domicile is precarious at best—the testing material has arrived and I will begin with it at our next session."

Paige dragged the large cardboard box toward Ruthanne's back door. Ruthanne stuck her head out.

"What in the world? Wait right there, let me help you with it." She put on a jacket, came out, and took hold of the box. "Okay, where're we taking this?"

"You tell me, it's a ten-speed bicycle for Lily. I don't want her seeing it before Christmas."

"Okay. Well, let's put it in the storage shed."

Once it was hidden away, Ruthanne insisted that Paige come inside.

"Just one short cup of tea. I've got something I need to say."

"Sounds mysterious."

"Not so. Paige, I don't even know how to begin this."

Paige followed her into the kitchen and sat down. "For goodness sakes, whatever it is, just say it."

"It's Charlie. I tried to talk him out of it, but no matter what I say, Paige . . . he doesn't want Roger playing with Lily."

"You mean, because of yesterday?"

Ruthanne nodded, then sighed. "I know it wasn't her fault, it wasn't anyone's fault but . . ."

"But let's blame Lily."

"Well, if she hadn't talked about things like punishments, Roger wouldn't have thought of it himself. Paige, I hate this, I really do. I know what kind of awful life she had before, and what you've been trying to do for her. And I think it's great."

"Please don't talk about her like she's some miserable charity case."

"I didn't mean to."

Paige stood and Ruthanne followed, reaching out to Paige. But Paige shrugged off the attempt and headed for the back door.

"I never expected you, of all people you . . . Listen, I think I'll take the bicycle with me, I can hide it in my basement."

"Oh, Paige, please, don't. Leave it here." But when she saw her head toward the shed, "Look, if you insist on taking it, Charlie can drive it, carry it inside for you . . . Can we talk about this more? Please, stop it, you shouldn't be lugging a big box like that yourself!" Tears were running down Ruthanne's cheeks.

Paige had already pushed, dragged, and bumped the box to a downstairs corner before she stopped, covered it with some rags, caught her breath, then leaned against the filthy oil burner and burst into tears.

She had really enjoyed Ruthanne's company and had started to count on her friendship— country girl, unsophisticated, uneducated, yet in many ways Paige had more in common with her than with Brooke. Maybe because of the pregnancy, the children, the circumstances. Who knows? But now, it was spoiled, she couldn't overlook this.

She understood how the incident yesterday with the baby had terrified her, but still it was no excuse to shift the blame to Lily. The classic small-minded parents who refused to accept their child's participation in wrongdoing. And in this case, it was not only participation—whatever Lily's horrid reminiscence might have suggested, it was Roger alone who had put the pillow over Carolyn's face.

"Paige!"

It was Lily. "Down here," she said.

Lily bounded down the steps, turned the corner. "Why're you down here?"

She shrugged.

Lily came closer, her finger touched her cheek. "You crying, Paige?"

Paige wiped away her tears with her jacket sleeve, sniffled, and attempted a smile. How would she ever break the news to Lily?

"Just some silly tears over nothing," she said finally.

"If someone hurt you, you'd tell, right?"

Paige hugged her, then put her arm around her.

"Guess what. I bought prepackaged cookie dough, holiday-shaped cutters, jimmies, assorted candy mix, and tubes of frosting. Let's go up and see how creative we can be." Then looking at the tank as they passed by, she shook her head. "Just what is it you give that turtle of yours to drink—vodka?"

Paige and Jason were playing Scrabble when the phone rang. Lily was busy upstairs and Jason picked up, talked a moment, then held it out to Paige. "Ruthanne."

Paige stood up and headed to the kitchen for a glass of juice.

"Tell her I don't want to talk."

"What?"

"You heard me."

He put the phone to his ear. "Ruthanne, can she get back to you?"

Finally he was in the kitchen, his arm around her. "Okay, what happened?"

She put the empty juice glass in the sink. "Nothing, I just don't want to talk."

"You girls have a squabble?"

"I'm not a child, Jason."

"Well, you sound about eight. Look, if you don't tell me what happened, I'll call Ruthanne and ask her. And if she doesn't tell me, I'll ask Charlie. He doesn't strike me as a guy who beats around the bush."

"Okay, I'll tell you. But if I do, you've got to promise not to jump to conclusions."

He nodded. "What?"

"I told you yesterday how Lily spoke about her father punishing Anna, how she was made to watch."

"Yeah."

"Well, she talked to Roger first. And I guess she was pretty graphic. In any event, Roger got the insane idea that maybe he ought to punish his baby sister."

"How?"

"Ruthanne found him in the nursery putting a pillow over her face."

"Lily told him to do it?"

"That's just it, she didn't. She told him about some of the sick stuff her father put her mother through. And I guess what it did was fire his imagination."

"He's not that type of kid . . ."

"What do you mean?"

"I mean, I don't picture Roger as being the type of kid to do something like that. He seems like a big, happy, friendly kid, the kind who wouldn't hurt a fly."

"But he *did* or at least, tried to. Ruthanne caught him in the nursery, with the pillow."

"Maybe there was more to it."

"You mean, maybe Lily suggested he do it, maybe she was sending out radar signals? You

might as well say it, not just stand around thinking it. Must you be so predictable?"

He shrugged. "Well, you might not like the idea, but did you at least consider it?"

She headed upstairs.

He gestured to the Scrabble. "What about the game? I never knew you to quit when you were ahead."

"I'm going to bed."

"Look, Paige, I don't want to start—"

"Jason, I spoke to Roger myself. And all he said was Lily told him about punishments. Can't you accept that she did nothing intentional or illegal? Nothing except let out a little of her pitiful past to some playmate."

The trail on Anna's sister was stone cold—Pat had checked with the Department of Motor Vehicles and the hair salon where she had worked as a manicurist for thirty years. None of her neighbors, former friends, or co-workers knew where she was hiding, or if they knew, they weren't telling. The question was, why would she hide out? But it was a question that probably wouldn't get answered, at least not in time for the trial.

Today Jason was in the Albany Women's Prison preparing Anna for her testimony. He had already gone over most of the Parks' sixteen-year marriage, beginning when Anna was sixteen and Maynard was thirty.

"Okay, now let's talk about what happened that day."

"I can't, I don't want to. It gets me sick to even think of it."

Jason sat down and took a deep breath. Finally, he looked at Anna.

"Look, I can't do this myself. I need at least to know what precipitated the murder, your striking him. According to Wendell, you remembered that much."

She nodded and licked her dry lips. "Sometimes when I think of it, I get mixed up, I forget . . ."

"What about reconsidering hypnosis?"

"No, no, no, I'm frightened of that kind of thing. A mind shouldn't be tampered with like that."

"Okay, forget it. I'll get Lily to fill in the blanks. I'm sure she'd agree to testify—"

Anna's eyes narrowed. "Mr. Bennett, you promised she wouldn't have to."

"Please understand, I need to create a picture for the jury—the fury you felt when you lifted that sickle to your husband, when you brought it down on him. What he had put you through that day of the murder and all those days before. All those beatings, those sick punishments, Anna. And the only observer was Lily."

She lifted her eyes to the ceiling, closed them, and took a deep breath. Finally she looked at him. "She told you?"

"Not me, my wife. And then only some of it. But the important thing is, she could be a big help to our case."

"No, I don't want her on the stand, I don't want her at the trial. Can't you see how important that is? Lily's been through enough, she mustn't be put through more. I will not allow it. Please, Mr. Bennett, those are my wishes . . ."

"You agreed to cooperate."

"I'm sorry, really I am, but that wasn't part of the deal. If you try to bring my baby to the courtroom, if I hear that she's even outside the courthouse, I'll change my plea back to guilty."

Great. Anna Parks was pulling out her tough act, just in time to compromise her chances at trial. Lily was counted out, so was hypnosis, and by the looks of it, Anna's sister was, too. Jason picked up his notes.

"Okay, we'll do it your way. Let's go over what you remember."

It was 2:55 when Hillary entered the therapy room—Lily had been waiting for only a few minutes. Though the child would normally sit down and wait for her in one of the chairs, today she was in the chair behind Hillary's desk.

"Lily, what are you doing there?" she asked.

Lily looked up, surprised to see her. "You're early."

"Yes, by a few minutes. What are you doing there?"

"Pretending I was you."

"I see. Well, I'm flattered. But my desk is private, that means it's off-limits, all right?"

Lily stood up, moved to her seat.

Hillary sat down herself and opened her bottom desk drawer. "Lily, today we're going to begin some testing. It's actually quite simple—I ask the question and you—" She stopped and leaned down further, looking. "Now, that's strange, I know I put them right here." She got off her chair, stooped down, and began to hunt through the drawer.

Finally Lily stood up, went to the wastebasket and reached down—when she stood up she had a pile of scrap paper in her hand.

"Is this what you're looking for?"

"No, what I'm—" She stopped, looked at Lily, then reached over and took the torn test papers. "Lily! Why would you do this?"

"But I thought you wanted them."

"You know what I mean."

"Oink oink, you know what I mean, know what I mean," she parroted. "Now, how would I know what you mean when you oink oink oink like a dirty old pig. Goodness me, you're getting just like the poor ugly old man you keep locked upstairs, stiff and oinky and stinking of shit. Do those sicknesses run in families? Because if they do, soon we're going to have to lock you—"

"Stop it this instant."

"Oops, that's it, isn't it, why you treat him so mean? He's not even your real daddy, is he?"

Before she knew she was doing it, Hillary's arm swung out, her hand stopping just inches short of Lily's face. A long silent pause as she withdrew her hand, then in a voice that seemed to have lost its pitch: "I'm so sorry, Lily."

Silence.

Hillary took a deep breath. "Maybe for today, it would be better . . ."

Smiling. "Want me to go, Hillary?"

Once Lily left, Hillary sat down, trying to regain her bearings—what had she done? She had never struck a person in her entire life. Not even when she was a child had she hit a playmate. Violence was wrong, Mother and Father had instilled that in her from the moment they took

her in. But now here she was a fully grown adult—a professional—and she had nearly struck an eleven-year-old patient!

She had been pulled into the war zone, something Hillary had been trained to guard against. Today Lily had reduced her, taken the reins, and it must never happen again. She looked at the bottom drawer of the file cabinet—apparently Lily had gone through it, found Hillary's adoption papers . . . If she found those, what else had she found?

She looked at the drawer above—had she found the envelope with the tapes?

Paige told Lily that Ruthanne didn't want her playing with Roger and why. Lily was quiet for a few moments, then without wallowing in feelings of anger or dejection, announced that it would give her more time to build the sled for My Boy.

"I didn't know you were considering such a project," Paige said.

"I don't tell you everything, Paige."

"But how will you build it?"

"I saw two old sleds downstairs—they're broken, but the runners are good, just need to be sandpapered and soaped. And then I can use some of the plywood standing against the back wall. I want to paint it yellow. My Boy will like that."

"I didn't know you could build."

She nodded. "Daddy taught me. He taught me about cars, too. Did you ever see the squirrel cage I built?"

Paige shook her head, thinking how strange it

was that the monster Maynard apparently had a productive side to him. He'd had a relationship with his daughter, not all of which was negative.

"No, I never did see it. But as I remember, Jason did."

"Yeah. Well, wait'll you see the sled. I'm gonna build sides and a roof so the wind won't get in his face."

"Joshua might be a little too young for it this winter."

"I don't think so, Paige. Wait, you'll see."

Lily went off and Paige sat there a few moments alone. She looked into the living room where she had stacked a bunch of wrapped packages waiting to put under the tree. Tonight Jason would chop down a tree and they would all decorate it. There were ten days until Christmas, and Anna Parks' trial started the eighteenth of December.

Though Paige hadn't whispered a word of it to Lily, it was conceivable that by Christmas, Anna Parks would be free. Only a slim chance, she supposed, but still something she had to consider. In any event, Paige had picked up little gifts for Anna: clothing, lingerie, perfume, things that a woman locked in prison might miss.

Things a daughter could give a mother. It was time Lily forgave her mother for whatever her inadequacies, and most of all, it was time—the hardest for Paige, too—that she thought seriously about leaving. . . . Soon Paige would talk to her, try to excite her about the prospect of going back to be with her mother.

She heard the hammer already pounding the

wood downstairs. Lily was one remarkable little girl.

That night, true to his word, Jason, carrying an ax he had just purchased, took Paige and Lily out into the light-falling snow to find the perfect tree. Paige brought along a camera, insisting that even in the darkness this would be too good a picture to miss. Lily looked on as Jason swung low on the huge evergreen and Paige snapped the shutter.

"I wish we had thought to do this weeks ago. Then make the picture a Christmas card."

"Without you in it?"

"Well, we could have rigged something. Right, Lily?"

"Right, Paige. Maybe next—"

Silence, then: "How's that sled coming along? Jason, wait till you see the wonderful sled Lily is building for Joshua."

Once in the house, they worked for forty-five minutes getting the tree to stand straight, then the lights strung and blinking. Finally Jason sank into a chair.

"I've had it."

"Oh no, let's finish the tree," Lily said, pulling him back to his feet.

They decorated the tree and hung pine cones on the door. And it wasn't until much later, after the music and hot chocolate with marshmallows and homemade Christmas cookies that Lily went upstairs, and Paige sat next to Jason.

"Have you seen Ruthanne?" Jason asked, breaking the warmth of the mood.

"Why do you even bring up her name?"

"Because she was a friend of yours, or so it seemed."

"The operative word is, *was*. Things change."

"They don't have to change. Don't let it happen. So Roger and Lily won't be pals, big deal, they'll find other kids. That doesn't mean while the kids are in school or busy with something else, you can't drop over and see her."

"Let us assume for a moment that this was Joshua, not Lily. Would you suggest we remain friends with people who thought our son wasn't good enough to play with their son?"

Silence.

"It's just not workable, Jason: the tension would be so strong you'd have to cut through it. And don't think I haven't missed Ruthanne enough to think about it."

Jason suddenly sat forward, looking toward the kitchen.

"What is it?"

He stood up. "Where's the ax, I left it—"

She stood up beside him. "Don't panic, I know where it is. I brought it down to the cellar."

He headed for the cellar. "Whereabouts?"

"Near the water heater. Why?"

"I wanted it in the attic."

"What's the difference?"

"No one goes there, I'd feel better."

He hurried downstairs, and she shook her head as it dawned on her ... why hadn't it sooner? All that warmth and closeness and holiday cheer was a farce. Jason was right in there with Ruthanne and Brooke, and for that matter the physical education teacher. Though Lily hadn't done one thing to warrant it, none of

them could put aside her parents' sins, and put some trust in her. Paige was closer to Lily than any of them, they spent lots and lots of quality time together. . . .

The phone rang, she lifted it on the first ring, startling Brooke. "Hello," she said.

"Paige, I . . . did it ring?"

"Yes, once. What do you want?"

"Well, I just called to say hi. Am I calling too late?"

"Yeah, I think maybe you are."

Paige hung up the receiver, then pyramided both hands over her mouth. Oh God, what was the matter with her?

Chapter Fourteen

The night before Anna's trial, Paige sat Lily down. "We've got to talk, young lady."

"What'd I do?"

"Not a thing."

"Then what?"

"Your mother's trial begins tomorrow."

Silence, then: "But you said it wouldn't be for a long time."

"If Jason had to appeal it, but that might not even be necessary. He could win right then and there."

"Will he?"

"I don't know, but he believes he has a chance."

"I don't want him to win."

"Don't say that."

"I mean it. I want to stay with you."

"We're talking about your mother, Lily. She loves you."

"So do you."

She felt a lump rise in her throat. . . .

"Well, don't you?"

Paige took her in her arms. She mustn't break down, she mustn't let Lily see her cry.

"Of course I do," she said, her voice coming out all chipped and whispery.

"Still, Lily, she's your mother. And you belong with her, not me."

Lily pushed away, got up, and went to her room. That night while in the bathroom, Paige heard cursing from Lily's bedroom, words she hadn't heard since the first days of Lily's arrival. Paige went in, kneeled down next to her, but Lily turned to the wall.

"I want your happiness, sweetheart. And if your mother gets let out ... Not that I know she will. But either way, Lily—" She sighed, stopped, and finally stood up and left.

"What's going on?" Jason asked as she got into bed.

She turned away, pretending she hadn't heard. She didn't want to discuss this with Jason—at least not now with Lily so hurt and angry and she herself so emotional.

"I set the alarm a little earlier than usual. The weather predicted six inches of snow and with the trip to Laurel Canyon ..."

"Take the four-wheeler."

"No, I'm leaving it for you."

"I have three weeks to go yet, Jason."

"Nothing's certain, I'm leaving it. Oh, and if for any reason you need me—"

"I'll be fine."

"Just call the Clerk's office."

"Jason ..."

*   *   *

It was when Paige woke the next morning—
Jason had already left—that she felt the twinge
in her back. She went to the window and looked
out: he had left the Pathfinder, but by the looks
of the clear sunny skies, the forecast was off.

When she got to the kitchen, Lily was just
coming up from the basement, about to pass her
by with no greeting.

"What're you doing down here so early?"
Paige asked.

Ignored.

"Lily?"

"Working on the sled," she answered finally.

As Lily headed out of the kitchen, Paige noticed that her back jeans pocket was bulging.

"Hey you, wait, what about breakfast?"

"Had some," Lily said going upstairs.

"What's all that in your pocket?"

Ignored again.

Paige poured coffee and took a bran muffin.
Lily went off to school without so much as a
wave good-bye . . . and to make it worse, she
wouldn't be home until late afternoon: today was
Lily's therapy. Paige took another muffin, this
one blueberry. Finally she got up and went inside to admire the tree. She looked at the telephone, then away. No friends, not on the best of
terms with Jason, and she and Lily not even on
speaking terms.

Maybe after she picked up around the house
she'd go to the mall, have lunch, shop around,
look at the holiday decorations. She had already
shipped out tons of gifts to Jason's family in Illinois and gotten Jason a half-dozen shirts and
sweaters, ties, a warm-up suit, an electric saw,

two books, and the Neil Diamond CD collection. But wouldn't he love a cellular telephone for the car?

She had already bought the baby a crib mobile and music box, enough stuffed animals to fill a zoo ... and Lily a dozen gifts, one of which was a dual tape deck not yet wrapped. Still a stone-washed jean jacket might be nice for the spring. When Paige was a girl, jeans jackets were a hot item—but she could only dream of owning one.

She arched her back, and with her fingers rubbed the small of it.

The little courtroom looked very much like it had before, with the same players, that is except for Sam Bender, the public defender, no longer needed. Also, this time the only spectators were the twelve men and women the D.A. and he had elected for the jury.

Jason had subpoenaed Anna's medical records from Fielding Hospital, and a hospital spokesman came in, testified as to Anna's emergency room visits, reading off the date, diagnosis, prognosis, and treatment. It wasn't until late morning that Anna took the stand.

It was at least forty-five minutes into her testimony when Jason directed her thoughts to the small wooden structure that stood behind her house in Laurel Canyon.

"Can you tell the Court exactly what it was, what it was used for?"

"Boss built the penalty box ..."

"Excuse me?"

"Boss. I always called my husband Boss."

"Did he ask you to call him that?"

She ran her tongue over dry lips, then pushed back hair that had fallen to her forehead.

"It started when we were first going together. I'm not sure if he asked me to, or I just started callin' him that because he was so bossy. Either way, it stuck."

Jason looked at the court reporter. "Let the record show with respect to the defendant, the names Boss and Maynard will be used interchangeably." Then, back to Anna. "Now, you mentioned a place called the penalty box. Please elaborate for the Court."

"He drew it all out on paper first to show me, had the name of it lettered across the top of the paper. I even watched him build it." A long pause while she fidgeted in her seat, then: "He'd make me go inside, stay there till it was time to come out."

"Why?"

Tears started to fall. Jason handed her a handkerchief.

"Because he said I did wrong," she said. "Maynard didn't want me answering him back or defying him. He'd set rules—if I stuck to them, he was nice as pie. But if I bent them, even a little . . . well, he said he needed to teach me."

"I see. Will you kindly describe the box for the Court."

"I'm not so good on measurements. But it was maybe twice the size of a doghouse. It was like a doghouse with only a small hole to crawl through to get me inside or out. And not even a window."

"Could you stand inside it?"

"No, just kneel or sit. Or pray. Boss used to say it was a good time for me to pray."

"I imagine it'd be stifling in—"

"Objection," the D.A. said.

"Sustained," Kraft ruled.

"Mrs. Parks," Jason began, "would you kindly tell the Court what it was like, what it felt like being trapped inside that doghouse. Pardon, penalty box."

"Well, it was dark and close. I mean there were times you'd want to scream to get outside where you could see daylight and breathe normal and stand up straight. And whatever the weather was—hot or cold—it was a hundred times worse inside there."

"Did Maynard stand around, guard you? You know, to make sure you wouldn't get out?"

"Oh no, he wouldn't do that. Sometimes if he thought I needed to work up a lot of remorse, I was there for days."

"Days?"

A nod.

"Nonstop, no letup? Like you were living there?"

"Yes."

A long pause to give the jury time to let some of the horror of it sink in, then: "Well, if Maynard didn't stand guard, I suppose you had an occasional opportunity to get out?"

"No."

"Why not, what was to stop you?"

More tears fell—she lowered her head, trying to hide her face from the jury.

"I was hooked in by a short steel chain . . . it

went to a locked collar around my neck. I'd get unhooked for meals . . . and bathroom privilege."

Jason nodded. "Okay," he said. "Describe those meals for the Court."

"Boss'd usually come carrying the tray out himself. He'd unhook my collar, have me crawl outside, then make me watch as he uncovered the food—"

Jason followed Anna's stare to the back of the courtroom. A thin, graying woman in a dark blue suit had just come in. She took a seat in the last row. He turned back to Anna.

"Please continue—"

Anna put one hand to her stomach, another to her chest. "I can't, I feel sick. . . . Please, let me stop."

"Your Honor," Jason said, addressing Kraft. "If we could have a short recess?"

The judge looked at his watch. "It's fairly late, why don't we just adjourn for lunch." He lifted his gavel and banged it loudly. "Court to reconvene at two-thirty."

A woman officer came and took Anna, and Jason turned to the back-row spectator. But she was gone.

The intermittent back pain that had started earlier was still occurring at two o'clock when Paige sank into a booth at the mall luncheonette and ordered a tuna salad and tea. She looked out the window and poked at her food—it was snowing, but small, light flakes, certainly not what had been forecast.

She took a taste of tuna, put the fork down . . . She'd found both gifts she'd started out for, so

she ought to feel good. Mission accomplished. Then why was she suddenly feeling so anxious, so jittery? Did it have to do with the back pain? Or maybe to do with the Anna Parks trial going on right this moment.

She got up, went to the phone booth, deposited some coins, then after checking her address book, pressed in Dr. Barry's number. His nurse picked up.

"Lenore, this is Paige Bennett."

"Hi there, Paige, what can I do for you?"

"I've been having back pain since early morning. I just wanted to check it out."

"Describe the pains."

"Well, more discomfort than pain, I guess. Every so often I get a twinge."

"Can you tell me how often?"

"Not really, it comes and goes."

"It doesn't sound like anything to be concerned about. The doctor will be in at three, and I'll pass on your concern. Meantime, if it gets worse or anything more develops, you get right back to me, hear? If necessary, I can reach the doctor. But it sounds like typical aches and pains most expectant mothers get, particularly in their ninth month."

"Good, I feel better already."

She put down the phone and went back to her seat. She looked out the window at the snow falling, just a little bit heavier than before. She had told Lenore she felt better, but she didn't really. In fact, she felt about ready to shed her skin.

It was silly, but she wished Jason were home.

*   *   *

Jason hung up the telephone receiver. This was his fourth try; apparently Paige had gone out. Going back to the courtroom, he glanced through the large lobby windows at the snow falling, sticking to the ground, and wondered if it was coming down in Briarwood, too. Fortunately, he had left Paige the four-wheeler.

He had briefly questioned Anna right after recess began, but she swore to him she'd never before seen the woman who'd entered the courtroom. His first guess would have been her sister and he said so, but Anna quashed that idea right off. Seeing how upset she still was, he let the guard take her to the prisoner's room to have lunch and rest while he waited to see if the woman would return.

Now sitting alone in the courtroom, with the turkey on rye he'd had sent in, he went over the list of witnesses he hoped to get on after lunch. When he heard the door, he turned, then got up just as she was about to back off.

"Hey, wait, don't leave," he said rushing toward her.

He caught up with her in the lobby and put his hand over her shoulder to stop her.

"Hey, look, if we could talk just a couple of minutes. I'm Jason Bennett, the defendant's attorney."

She nodded. "I know who you are."

"Then you have me at a disadvantage. Come on inside, we'll sit and talk."

"I don't know, I don't think—"

"Please."

She followed him; he led her to the front table, and they sat across from one another. The

woman was small and thin; she looked to be in her midforties.

"How do you know Anna Parks?"

"What makes you think I do?"

"Her response when you walked in. She was mighty upset when she saw you."

"Yeah, I suppose she was. I'm Nora Kalish, Anna's big sister."

A pause, then: "I've been trying to find you."

A lift of her narrow shoulders. "Anna wanted me away, she pleaded with me not to show my face. I never could refuse her anything. . . . But now when I read in the newspaper about the trial, I figured maybe it'd be a chance for her to have a life again."

"Why'd she want you gone so bad?"

"Because I know about the kid."

"Lily? What about Lily?"

"She was part of it, I mean the abuse and all. Anna tells you how Maynard put her inside that box with only a lousy hole for her to breathe from? What she doesn't tell you is how Lily was the one who locked the collar around her neck."

Hillary had been taking occasional glances out the front window, watching the snow accumulate . . . so this time she saw Lily standing inside the front gate. With one hand held like a visor at her forehead, Lily's other hand waved toward the upstairs window.

Hillary opened the outside door, and despite the cold, went down the front steps and glanced up at Father's window. Knowing how much he loved the outdoors, especially to watch a good snowfall, she had earlier pushed his bed nearer

the window. But the eyes that stared back at her had only fear in them.

Hillary gestured to Lily. "Come inside, I'm afraid Father is still nervous seeing a stranger in the house."

Lily came inside, stamping her snowy sneakers on the mat.

"My goodness, it seems to be getting bad out there. I wasn't sure you'd show up."

"I had to."

"Oh?"

"Yeah, today is special. I have to tell you something."

Hillary smiled, pleased that the near-disastrous session they had had last time hadn't destroyed any of the trust she had worked so hard to build.

"Let me run upstairs to calm Father. I'll be right back."

"Okay, sure."

Hillary hurried upstairs and Lily stuck her hand in her back pocket, pulling out a book of matches. She lit one, held it, and watched it burn right down till the sulphur marked her finger, then finally blew it out. Hearing Hillary's footsteps come closer, Lily slid the burnt match and matchbook back into her pocket.

Nora and Jason sat at the courthouse coffee shop while he questioned her about Lily. According to her, since the age of five, Lily had been in on the abuse.

"It started out innocently enough, I suppose," Nora said. "I mean, the child was simply trying to save her own hide. No one else was able to do

it, least of all, my sister. And then it got to be something that gave her pleasure."

"How do you know that?"

"I don't, Anna and I fought about that a lot. She hated me for saying it to her. Actually I think she was almost as scared of Lily as she was of Maynard. I know it sounds crazy, she's only a kid. But I once saw Lily strap her mother to a chair under Maynard's orders. She strapped her tight, so tight that she nearly cut off her circulation. . . . And there was a sparkle in those eyes. . . . The same kind of sparkle as in his."

"How could you watch and do nothing?"

"As I said earlier, it wasn't easy for me to refuse my sister. I pretty much brought her up. My mother was sickly, my father left us before Anna was born. When Anna ran off, got married, only a sophomore in high school, I nearly had a stroke.

"I hated Maynard, he was way too old for her. What kind of thirty-year-old fools around with a kid only sixteen? But my sister was mesmerized by him. He could do or say no wrong. She even accused me of being jealous that she had hooked herself a guy while I hadn't. I never had a lot of dates; early on, I guess it did bother me. But once I saw what kind of life Anna married into, I considered myself lucky."

"It still doesn't explain how you'd allow it to go on."

"Simple—Anna told me it herself—either I keep my mouth shut about what went on between her and her husband or I could forget I had a sister. So if ever a fight would start up

when I'd be there, I'd pick up my bag and leave. Sometimes I saw more than I wanted to see, and I'd cry all the way home." Her voice now a whisper, she put her fisted hand to her mouth and twisted it. . . . "But this I kept locked."

"So why now, what convinced you to speak up now?"

"Her threats don't mean so much now. With her in prison, I might as well not have a sister."

Jason excused himself and got up to go to the telephone—the third try home since they'd been there, but still no answer. Paige knew how to reach him if necessary. . . . He looked at his watch: almost time to reconvene, he went back to get Nora. He dropped a few bills on the table, then gestured for her to come along.

"Do you want me to testify, tell the Court what I know about Lily?" she asked him.

"I don't know if it'll help any. Do we need two abusers rather than one? Will that provide a double amount of tears or will the jury decide it's a house of freaks and turn to ice? I don't know, I need time to think about it. To be blunt, I want to get a postponement and get the hell home."

"You're the one's got the kid, aren't you?"

"Yeah, I'm the one." He led her back to the courtroom.

Jason was right all along—the four-wheeler handled beautifully in the snow, passing other cars already caught in slides. And the snow seemed to be getting heavier. In fact, she didn't like the idea of Lily walking home from Hillary's in this weather. . . .

What if Jason got Anna off and she refused to let Lily stay for Christmas? Would Paige have to pack up all those gifts, send them off with Lily, and never get to see her excitement or the joy on her face when she opened them?

The moment she got home she drank a glass of milk trying to calm a mind that wanted to flit in all directions. She went to the telephone, picked up the receiver, looked at the clock, then put the receiver down again. The therapy session had already begun and she hated to interrupt. She'd call at four, as soon as they were done, to tell Lily to wait to be picked up.

She went to the window, watching the snow come down. It would be much more beautiful if she didn't have to think of Jason taking that long drive home.

After long and difficult deliberation, Hillary had decided not to mention the tapes unless, of course, Lily herself brought them up. There was a good possibility that Lily hadn't seen the manila envelope containing the taped therapy sessions and Hillary's evaluations. After all, the envelope wasn't labeled, so unless she opened it to check the contents, she wouldn't have known there were tapes or that they pertained to her. And taking the worst scenario, if she had listened to excerpts from the tapes in those five or ten minutes she usually had alone before sessions, how much of it would she have heard? Or understood?

But Hillary had locked the file cabinet this time. So if there was any significant statement needing to be said about Lily's misbehavior at

the last appointment, it was said in that single act. Lily knew it, and if she wished to discuss the word "privacy" more fully, the therapist—as always—would be ready to talk. Hillary had reordered the tests; hopefully this time they wouldn't take so long coming.

For the first ten minutes the girl sat silently, and though Hillary was eager to hear more about that something special Lily had spoken of earlier, she didn't dare to pass over control by appearing too anxious. Suddenly and for the first time, Lily lifted one of the puppets and put her hand inside the body, then with her fingers manipulating the arms and head, said in a deep, resonant voice, "Hello, Hillary." And Hillary realized immediately that this was the way Lily would tell her the special news.

"Hello, what's your name?" Hillary asked.

"Boss."

"So good to meet you, Boss. Are you a friend of Lily's?"

"No, Lily has no friends."

"Really? What about Paige?"

"Not her. She might of been her friend if she didn't have stupid old Jason sniffing around after her, always telling her bad things about Lily so she'll kick her out."

"I don't understand. Are there plans for Lily to leave the Bennetts?"

"Not yet."

"I see, then what you're worried about, is her future. Maybe it'd be better for her to wait and see—Paige certainly seems to like having Lily around. And she seems the type to make up her own mind about things."

"No way. He yells at her, beats her up, makes her do what he wants her to."

"I find that hard to believe."

"I don't care what you believe, bitch. You just listen here because I'm boss!" Lily sat forward, and pressed the puppet's hands to its stomach. "Uh, oh."

"What's wrong?"

"Gotta go shit."

"Who, Lily or Boss?"

"Both."

Hillary nodded. "You both go, I'll wait." Lily returned a few minutes later and held up Boss.

"Ready, set, go," it said and Hillary gave her full attention.

Lily looked at the puppet and in her own voice sounding as close to real sadness as Hillary had ever heard it, said, "I miss my daddy."

Hillary looked at the child's eyes—they were actually moist with tears—the first real display of emotion she'd seen, but still Hillary knew it would be short-lasting. However, in that one instant, Hillary felt what Paige Bennett must have been feeling all along. She so wanted to be able to wipe the child's slate clean, extinguish the evil and begin her again at day one— a total life recycle. But that wasn't how it worked.

Lily put down the puppet. "Hillary?"

"Yes, dear?"

"I think I smell smoke."

Hillary's head shot up, she sniffed, then leapt from her chair. Running upstairs toward Father's room!

*   *   *

What the hell was taking so long? It was after three, more than a half hour past starting time. Though the jury was in place—looking annoyed and bored—the judge, clerk, D.A. and, in fact, Jason's client, were among the missing. Jason went up again to the bailiff.

"Can you tell me what is going on here?"

He shrugged. "The judge is in chambers. Last I heard, he'd be in momentarily, 'course that was ten minutes ago. He gave orders, though, no one's to leave."

"Look, I'm heading to the lobby to make a brief phone call. Will you let me know if he's about to enter?" He nodded and Jason hurried off to the phone booth and quickly pressed in his home phone. Paige picked up immediately.

"Where the hell were you?"

"Jason, what's wrong?"

"Nothing. I tried to get you a dozen times. I was worried, is all."

"Actually I've been worried about you, too. The snow is beginning to pile up, it's already three, four inches. And the winds. Well, I don't like you driving in this. I wish you had taken the four-wheeler."

"Where were you earlier?"

"At the mall."

"In that case, it's good I didn't. How did it handle?"

"Beautifully, though I hate to admit it. Jason, what's happening with the case?"

"I'll tell you when I get home. Paige, you're okay aren't you?"

"I'm fine, I have a slight backache, but other than that—"

"A backache?"

"Yes, but it's nothing. I called earlier, spoke to Barry's nurse. She assured me it was run-of-the-mill stuff."

"I'd feel better if you went to the hospital."

"That's crazy, Jason. It's not that bad. Really."

"Will you promise if it gets the slightest bit worse, you'll go. Even if you think it's for nothing ... So you'll spend the night there, what's the big deal? I'll send you yellow roses. Then tomorrow I'll take the day off and—shit!"

"What Jason?"

"He's calling me."

"Who?"

"The bailiff, I've got to get back. Promise me if it worsens at all, you'll go."

"Jason, I know it won't—"

"Please, Paige, it's important to me!"

Silence, then: "Okay, I promise."

When Hillary reached upstairs, smoke was coming from under Father's door. She rushed to her purse, pulled it off her bedroom doorknob, and dug her hand in for the key ring. Unable to find it, she tipped the purse, shook it out, then crouched on her knees, raking her hands through the contents. No keys!

She ran to the door, put her hand over the hot knob, turned it—nothing. Of course, nothing, what did she expect? She smashed her body up against the door, pounding it with her fists. . . .

"Why don't you just open it?"

Hillary turned to see Lily.

"It's locked."

"Use the key."

"I can't find it. Oh, dear God," she screamed. "I can't find it!"

"Want me to look?"

"Yes, please!" Hillary, now beginning to function, ran to the telephone, called the operator. "A fire at 22 Hoppington Road," she cried. "There's an invalid trapped in the upstairs bedroom. Hurry, hurry!"

Though the smoke was seeping into the other rooms, Hillary bellied along her bedroom floor, sweeping her hands back and forth for the keys when suddenly Lily burst in.

"Hillary, I found them!" she said.

Hillary got to her feet, grabbed the key ring from her hand and rushed to Father's door. Her hands shaking and fumbling, she opened the door and burst into the inferno.... Her eyes fixed on Father—sitting up in bed as though he were watching the snow—except his face wasn't ... Oh, God, his face was gone!

The telephone was ringing, over and over.... She could hear a voice screaming. Was it hers?

Jason was sweating as he headed back to the courtroom. He'd either get a continuance or plead illness, he'd fucking walk right out on the proceedings if he had to. One way or another he'd soon be on his way home.

But the question was, would Paige believe him about Lily, or would Lily be able to talk herself around it? As he took his seat in the courtroom, he noticed the odd look that passed between the D.A. and Judge Kraft. What was coming down now?

And where in the hell was his client? He stood up—

"Just a moment, Mr. Bennett," the judge said. "If you'll please keep your seat."

He sat.

"Ladies and gentlemen, please forgive the delay. But I'm afraid we've had an emergency situation here. At 2:45 P.M. this afternoon, the county coroner pronounced Anna Parks dead."

Jason sucked in his breath as did Nora who was sitting behind him. The jury began to flurry about and whisper.

"Please let me finish," the judge directed to the jury and they quieted.

"She died of asphyxiation. At two-twenty she was found hanging from a shower bar in the washroom off the defendants' resting quarters. A noose made from a ripped bedsheet was around her neck."

Sheriff Buldoon was first on the scene, even before the volunteer fire department. Other than a burn on her hand, which was somehow already bandaged, Hillary wasn't hurt. She looked around, she was in the backseat of the sheriff's cruiser and Lily was beside her, staring at her. The memory of how or when she got inside the cruiser was as foggy as her hand suddenly being bandaged.

"Why'd you lock it?" Lily asked, looking at the silver dollar key ring still fisted in Hillary's good hand.

Hillary looked at her. "What do you mean?"

"You locking your father away like that. I didn't tell the sheriff you did it."

"You didn't?"

"Of course not. You wouldn't want to go to jail, would you?"

Hillary swallowed hard, then a sob came abruptly from somewhere deep; she cupped her hand over her mouth trying to stifle it.

"What did you tell him?" her voice whispered.

"Just that the bedroom door was stuck."

Silence, then: "The keys, Lily. Where did you find them?"

"Next to the washing machine in the basement."

Oh, God, she *had* gone there before Lily arrived; in fact, she did wash at that time just about every day. Could she have taken them with her? Why, when she always kept them in her purse? She didn't remember. . . . What difference did it make either way: Father had burned to death, a horrible, painful, frightening death, and it was her fault. She sat forward, then pushed the handle of the car door.

"Where're you going?" Lily asked.

"I need to be . . . alone." She exited the car and without attracting the attention of either the sheriff or the firefighters, got into her green station wagon. As she pulled away and passed the cruiser, from the corner of her eye she could see Lily still watching her.

By the time she reached Route 9, she was sobbing.

Paige must have let the phone ring fifty times since four o'clock, and still no answer. Where in the world could they be? Could Lily have skipped therapy because of snow? But if

that was so—it wasn't that far a walk home—
where was she now? Besides, Hillary certainly
wasn't about to take her invalid father out in
this weather. . . . Unless he had suddenly gotten ill.

She took Lily's boots from the hall closet,
then hurried into her coat, hat, gloves, and
headed out. As she got to the car, she felt another twinge—she arched her back, it stopped,
and she climbed inside. She pulled out of the
driveway, remembering Lily's anger last night,
then this morning. . . . She would talk to her,
somehow make her understand. And if the
backache worsened she'd head for the hospital
and take Lily along with her. But she'd keep
her promise to Jason, even if she felt foolish
doing it.

One thing definitely not foolish was the four-
wheeler—again she marveled at its sturdiness as
she passed two cars, both slipping and sliding
over the road. Rather than chance the awful
weather, maybe Jason ought to stay in Laurel
Canyon overnight. When she got back to the
house, she would call the courthouse.

That was her last thought before she reached
Hillary's street and smelled smoke. . . .

Still reeling from the news of Anna's suicide,
Jason tried to call Paige. Again, no answer. Did
she go to the hospital? He looked at his watch—
if she did, she wouldn't be there yet. He asked
information for Dr. Barry's number and called.
"Lenore, this is Jason Bennett. Paige's husband—"

"Oh yes, of course. How's Paige doing?"

"I thought maybe you'd know. I'm on the road, there was no answer at the house."

"Well, I did talk to her earlier. She had a back-ache. Nothing specific or regular, in other words it didn't sound like labor. I spoke to Dr. Barry, he agreed. Remember, she's got three weeks to go yet. When the doctor saw her last, which was less than a week ago, the baby wasn't anywhere near position. Usually first-time mothers are late, not early."

"Yeah, that's what I hear."

"Then stop worrying. I'm sure if labor starts she'll call here first thing. Maybe she didn't want to be alone, so she went to a friend's house or to the grocer's to pick up some provisions. That snow out there doesn't look like it's stopping."

"I guess. Okay, thanks." He hung up.

Not likely a friend, but the grocer's, that was a definite possibility. . . . Her sweet tooth simply short-circuiting. He hurried out to the car, took the brush from the back seat, and swept the snow off the Volvo. He looked at his watch: four-fifteen. In normal weather the trip took about two hours. There was already six inches of snow on the ground, and daylight had maybe fifteen minutes yet to go. But the highway ought to be in better shape, the plows should be out full force. . . .

So he'd figure three, four hours tops.

When Paige saw the house in flames—one engine, a dozen cars, at least thirty townspeople fighting it, one of them Charlie Beeder—she

started running toward it. The sheriff stepped out, stopping her.

"Lily!" Paige shouted as a large fist seemed to reach inside and tighten around her stomach. She couldn't tell which was causing it—the baby or the fear.

"She's fine, she's sitting right over here in the cruiser," the sheriff said. Then noticing how she had hunched forward, "Hey, you okay?"

Paige sighed and nodded—Lily was unhurt and the tight discomfort had mostly disappeared once she learned that. Still he took her arm and led her through the snow.

"I was about to drive her home," he said. "But with the wind coming up strong like this, I wanted to first see if we couldn't get this blasted inferno under control."

"Hillary, is she all right?"

"She'll be okay, but I'm afraid her father didn't make it."

"Oh no!"

The sheriff opened the back seat and Lily flew out into Paige's arms, crying. Paige wrapped her arms around her and the sheriff leaned into the car.

"Where's Hillary?" he said.

"I was so scared," Lily said, and Paige—too choked to get a word out—buried her face in Lily's hair.

"Where's Hillary?" the sheriff shouted.

Paige lifted her head and looked at him.

"Hillary was here with Lily last I knew. I wanted to take her to one of the houses in town. . . ."

Paige shifted her eyes to Lily.

"She left."

"For where?" he asked.

Lily shrugged. "I don't know, she didn't say. She just went off in her car."

He opened the cruiser's front door, slid inside, and lifted his radio receiver to get his deputy.

"Merv, Bulldoon here. I wantchata get a plate number for Hillary Egan's car, it's a green Chevy wagon. Then get on out there and find her."

"Why's that?"

"The old man just died in the fire. And she's out there driving around in this damned blizzard, probably not even knowing her own name."

Though the plows were out on the highway, cars were stuck, a couple of cars had even died and been abandoned, making it hard for the plows to get through. Jason made an effort to go slow, the last thing he needed was to end up in some snowbank. . . .

Every so often the thought of Anna's suicide would come to mind, startling him again. She might have even gotten off, who knew? Apparently that was not what she wanted. But she did go along with it, so why'd she suddenly kill herself now? Because of her sister showing up, that's why. Death was better than her secret told?

What about her secret, what did it really mean? One: that her kid didn't give a shit about her? Two: hearing about Lily's mean streak, he and Paige would boot her out? Three: the world would know she was afraid of her own kid?

Wow, afraid of your own kid, pretty god-

damned monumental stuff ... And what's to say
for a kid who'd lock up her own mother, hurt
her? What kind of sadistic mentality does it take
to do that? Even better, what more would a kid
like that be capable of?

Suddenly, he jerked forward, the car
swerved to the left—he went with the skid,
pumped the brakes, then feeling traction,
turned the wheel right. Just in time—the car
stopped only inches from the guard rail. His
fists still clenched, he took a deep breath, resting his chest, arms, and forehead against the
top of the steering wheel.

Why had it taken him this long? It wasn't
Anna who had killed Maynard. ... It was Lily!

Hillary! Hillary! Hillary!
Don't say it like that. ...
Bad Girl, ugly girl, what have you done?
Daddy, don't talk to me that way.
Locked your daddy in a room when he couldn't
even move.
Oh, Daddy, I'm sorry, I never meant for you to
get hurt, to die.
Did too or you wouldn'ta done it.
No, no, I only locked the door because I wanted
to save you.
From who?
From who, from who, she couldn't remember from
who. Suddenly her body started to spin. ... Around
and around and around ...
Lily!

"Eleven cars involved," Merv told Bulldoon
over his car radio. "Never seen such a pileup in
my life. Right now we got three ambulances

from Poughkeepsie Med taking in people, more on the way. I'd say twenty-five, thirty people hurt in all. It all started with the Chevy wagon, went into a triple spin, pitched right across the road, to the southside traffic where that tractor trailer hit it head-on.

"The Egan woman was crushed, died instantly."

Chapter Fifteen

Lily replaced her shoes with the suede boots Paige brought along for her.

"I'm still trembling," Paige said, driving home. "Poor Mr. Egan, what a horrible way to die. And Hillary, what she must be going through. I hope they can find her."

"Me too."

"How did the fire start, Lily?"

"I don't know how, but it came from the old man's bedroom. Maybe he snuck a smoke."

"Why would you think that?"

"I went upstairs to his room to meet him one time, and I saw his pipe rack. Before I left, I saw a tobacco pouch sticking out from underneath his mattress."

"Did you actually see him smoke?"

"No, but it made me think that maybe he did it sometimes when no one was watching."

"Did you tell Hillary?"

"No, I didn't want to squeal. Should I have?"

"I know, squealing isn't one of those things we like to do. But if circumstances warrant it, if

it's something that might be dangerous, then it's important to speak up."

"I didn't know he would hurt himself."

Paige looked at her, put a hand over her hand, and grasped it tightly. "Of course, you didn't."

"Are you mad at me?"

She shook her head. "I'm relieved you're safe. And speaking of anger, how about you? I know you weren't feeling too good about things when you left for school."

"That was way back this morning. Not now."

"Tragedies have an odd way of forcing you to see priorities, don't they?" she said, picturing again the horror Mr. Egan must have suffered at the end . . .

Lily just looked at her, her eyes bright but her expression oddly devoid of the scare she'd just been through. "In any event," Paige said, "I want you to start concentrating on only good things. Because no matter what happens with your mother or where you ultimately go to live, I'm going to be somewhere in the background seeing to it that there's a lot of good going on in your life."

Paige pulled the truck in the driveway, and for a moment they sat staring at one another.

"Look at us, aren't we some pair?" Paige said smiling. "Come on. What do you say we go warm our insides . . . hot chocolate with those minimarshmallows?"

"Excellent," Lily said, opening the door. She jumped out of the truck and into the snow, kicking the powder up as she ran ahead. Just as Paige took the first porch step, she gasped. One of her

hands grabbed onto the side railing, the other went to her stomach.

Lily rushed to her and grabbed her arm. "Is it My Boy, Paige, isn't it too early?"

"Yes, but ..." The intensity of the pain startled Paige but it was gone within twenty or thirty seconds. "Lily, I think it's only false labor, I've been having back pain since this morning. But I promised Jason if it worsens I'd go to the hospital."

"But if it's only false labor ..."

"I know, it sounds silly, but I promised Jason."

"What about the hot chocolate?"

"It'll have to wait."

"It's too early, Paige. We can't let him come yet."

"Lily, I really don't think he is coming, but if I'm wrong, wouldn't the best place for me and the baby be in a fully equipped hospital with professionals?"

"I want you to stay here," Lily whined.

"That's enough, Lily. I'm going inside to call Dr. Barry and try to reach Jason. Please pack me a bag. Throw in a nightgown, robe, slippers, and a toothbrush. Okay?"

Paige went inside, tried the doctor's number, got a busy signal, tried several more times with the same results. Didn't they have a switchboard? She tried information, got the same busy signal. Finally she dialed zero and the operator came on.

"I keep getting busy signals, and I know it shouldn't be, could you check the number?" Paige said and gave her the number.

"No need to check. That's the Briarwood-War-

ing exchange. The phone service up that way is a mess. A lot of busy signals, static, dead lines. You're lucky your phone's even working."

"Because of the storm?"

"Actually, not totally. There was a big accident out on Route 9. Some phone lines are—"

Static took over the line.

It had taken thirty minutes to reach the next gas station. While the car was getting gassed up, Jason rushed to the phone booth, got Sheriff Buldoon's number, and rang it about twenty-five times. No answer. Finally he called Paige . . . the line came up busy.

He waited a few minutes, tried again, then again. Still busy, he called the operator.

"Look, I've got an emergency, could you break in on a line?"

"The number, sir?"

"914–555–3548."

"Just a moment." The operator was back in a few minutes. "Sorry, sir, there's no one on the line, it's temporarily out of order."

"But I get a busy—"

"Out of order, sir."

A sigh, then: "The storm?"

"I guess. Also, there was a major accident reported up that way. Lots of cars involved. I wouldn't be surprised if that wasn't what's responsible for the interruption in service."

Jason put down the phone, stood there . . Take it easy, Jason, don't let your imagination get out of hand—Paige isn't Anna, she wouldn't take guff from the kid. Besides, Lily never even misbehaves around Paige; if anything, she goes

out of her way to watch out for her and the
baby. . . . There's no way she'd ever hurt her. . . .

He paid the pumper and got back in the car.
The best thing he could do was get home.

After hearing about the accident on Route 9,
Paige sat near the kitchen telephone and re-
thought her plan—if it was that bad out there,
four-wheeler or not, wouldn't it be foolish to
travel over treacherous roads? Unless, of course,
she was in labor and had no choice. . . .

But that uncertainty ended quickly when another contraction hit, this one more powerful
than the one that had come less than twelve minutes earlier. . . . They weren't supposed to be
coming this strong so soon, were they? Not with
first labors they weren't. But maybe with all the
tension and anxiety she was experiencing . . .
The big question now was, should she even be
driving?

Ruthanne. She could have Charlie drive her
. . . no, Charlie was out fighting the fire. She
could go back to the fire, get the sheriff's help.
She stood up, went over to the staircase, grasped
both hands around the railing, feeling suddenly
woozy and frightened. Why was it taking Lily so
long up there?

"Lily," she called.

"Coming." Almost a full minute longer, then
Lily bounded downstairs carrying Paige's over-
nighter. When she saw Paige's expression, she
stopped. "What's wrong?"

"I had another contraction, this time a bigger
one. And the telephone isn't working. What I'm
going to do is head back to Hillary's house, have

the sheriff get someone to drive me to the hospital. And he'll take you to one of the houses in town temporarily, I don't want you staying alone in the storm."

Though Paige thought she might complain about the newly devised plan, apparently she was wrong. Lily not only didn't complain, she snapped into action, taking hold of her arm and helping her outdoors, through the snow to the truck. Paige got behind the wheel and turned on the ignition. The engine started, went a couple seconds, then died. She tried again: this time, there was nothing.

"Oh, no. No, no, please no." She took a long deep breath, tried again. Nothing. She looked at Lily. "I don't understand, what could be wrong? We were driving what, fifteen minutes ago? And it was fine then."

"Let me look," Lily said. Paige released the hood lever, and Lily got out, lifted the hood, studied the engine. Done inspecting it, she backed up, knelt in the snow, looked under the vehicle—a look of distress came to her face.

Paige opened the door and leaned out, letting the snow blow inside as she did.

"What Lily?"

"The gas line, Paige," she shouted. "Looks like it snapped."

Evelyn Gear at sixty-six was as spry as a fifty-year-old, in fact, nearly as spry as her daughter Ruthanne. Though she initially argued with Charlie when he insisted she leave her house for the duration of the snowstorm, she really didn't have a choice. Her house was far enough from

the Egan property not to be threatened by
spreading flames, but in fighting the fire one of
the lines had gone out, cutting off the electricity
in the entire neighborhood.

Now, Charlie, in the next room changing to
dry clothes to go back to battling the blaze, was
giving Ruthanne the horrid details of Hillary's
car accident. As if it weren't bad enough with
what happened to poor Lester Egan. Evelyn
stayed in the kitchen, trying to keep her mind
off the tragedies of the day by making more
sandwiches for Charlie to take back to the volunteer fire fighters.

Ruthanne stood in the next room, her fist tight
around the bedpost.

"I say it over and over to myself and I still
can't believe it. Hillary dead, Lester dead, all
those innocent people hurt . . . It's like a nightmare took hold of our town."

"Our phone working?" he asked.

"So far, but there's so much static, it's not
worth much. I tried calling Paige. First it was
busy, then no answer."

"Why bother if she doesn't want to talk to
you?"

"Because I care, that's why."

"Now don't get upset at me again, Ruthanne.
We did the right thing here."

"I know, but that doesn't change my feelings
for Paige. Besides Lily always saw Hillary on
Mondays, I just wanted to see that she was okay.
God, I still can't believe Hillary is dead. . . ."

"Not a scratch on the girl. Paige came down
and picked her up."

"How'd she know about the fire?"

"I don't think she did. She just came to get Lily so's she wouldn't have to walk through the snow, I guess."

"Was Paige upset?"

"I suppose so. Who wouldn't be, seeing that fire, hearing about the old man dead?"

"This isn't good for her, Charlie, I mean, this kind of scare. When she first moved up here, her blood pressure was high, she was overly tense. She doesn't know about Hillary, does she?"

He shrugged. "I don't know how she would of learned."

"Good, it would just upset her more. Is Jason home yet?"

"When I passed the house a little while ago, there was only her car sitting there."

Ruthanne sighed.

"You're going to have to stop worrying. Though you might like to, you can't take care of the whole world, Ruthanne. It's hard enough these days watchin' out for our own."

"I just wish Jason were home so she wouldn't be there alone."

"She's got the little girl. . . ."

"Yeah."

When he left, Charlie took a big brown bag of sandwiches and a two-gallon coffee jug Evelyn had made up.

"When're you going to be home?" Ruthanne called out.

"You girls don't need anything, do you? Stocked up on candles, batteries?"

"No, no, Mom, me, and the kids will be fine."

"Once the fire's out, I may need to go out to

the accident site, they'll be needing helpers there, too."

Charlie drove off—it was just beginning to darken—and from the kitchen doorway, Ruthanne peered into the distance. In winter, with trees bare, she could make out the chimney of Paige's house.

But not today.

Two more pains had hit Paige by the time she got inside the house. Lily helped her upstairs, out of her clothes, into bed.

"Maybe you could dress up warm, run and bring back Ruthanne," Paige said.

"It's already dark outside, and the snow's getting deep. Besides you need me here with you."

"I guess you're right. Oh, I wish Jason were here."

"Don't worry, Paige, I'll take good care of you."

"But there's things you don't know about babies, things you couldn't possibly do."

"I can, I asked the doctor about those things, remember? Wait, you'll see."

"It may not be—" She stopped as another contraction seized her and she cried out.

Lily wedged a pillow at her side, then leaned her toward it.

"Focus on the lampshade, Paige. And breathe in deeply, hold, then exhale. Come on, just the way you learned to do in your class."

"I'm so tense, so scared."

Lily began to massage her feet. "Don't be scared, Paige, I'm here. This help any?"

"A little. Thank you, Lily."

"I'm not Lily, I'm Boss."

"What?"

"Call me Boss."

"I don't understand . . . Oh!" Another one and she began . . . inhale, exhale, inhale, exhale . . . Slow down, slow down . . . She focused on the lampshade and began to count. . . .

"See what I mean," Lily said. "Isn't this better than some dumb old hospital?"

Lamaze didn't work, at least not for Paige it didn't. All she was aware of was intense hurt, pain—like steel barrels crashing back and forth against her stomach walls. Was this what they called hard labor or was this just the beginning with more to come?

A voice was talking, nonstop talking, saying lots of silly things, words Paige couldn't put into logical order. And the strong little hands kept massaging her feet, as if that would make the pain go. She screamed, but even as she heard the sound of her screams in her ears, she sensed it was useless.

"Stop it, Paige." Lily shook her, trying to stop her shouting. "It'll only make things worse."

Startled, Paige looked at Lily, reality crashing down on her. "Oh God, no! Please get a doctor!"

"It's okay, Paige, it'll be okay."

"How can you be sure?"

"Boss knows."

She tried to sit up, she managed to get up a bit, then fell down. She tried again—this time she noticed her hands were immobilized. How did this happen? Lily! But why would she do this to her? Use your brain, Paige, *think*. What

was it Lily said earlier? A crazy thing, so crazy, Paige couldn't remember, wouldn't remember. Strange, odd, peculiar, bizarre, ho, ho, what a joke ... Oh God, if it was a joke, why was it hurting so much? Then forcing herself to speak: "Lily!"

"I'm right here, Paige." She was bending over a big cardboard box. In it were rope, towels, knives, candles, matches, flashlight, Jason's battery-operated radio, dozens of other things.

"My hands," Paige said. She looked to the bedsides—each wrist was encircled by rope, then the rope was pulled and fastened somewhere under the bed. "Why? Untie my hands!"

"No, it's better this way."

"I said untie them now!"

"I'm Boss, Paige."

"I want you to stop talking like that—"

Another pain ground in so deeply, she began to gag. Would she vomit and choke to death? Lily put her hand on Paige's stomach and began to rub it. "Take a real deep breath," Lily instructed. "But if you really have to puke, just turn your head to one side."

The cramp deepened.... Paige could feel lines of sweat roll down her face, into her eyes, making them itch and burn. What was happening to her, was she trapped in a nightmare?

Ruthanne hadn't stopped trying to call Paige. It was an hour later when she got a connection and through the static, recognized Lily's voice.

"May I talk to Paige, Lily?"

"What?"

"Please put on Paige!" she shouted over the noise.

"Just a minute." Ruthanne waited a few minutes, thinking at one point she heard Paige's voice, but then Lily was back on the line saying, "She doesn't want to talk to you. And don't call back!"

Ruthanne started to say something, but Lily had hung up. Besides, if Paige felt that way, what could she possibly say to change her mind? She replaced the receiver. The lights flickered—she had her candles standing in saucers, ready to be lit—but gratefully the electricity came back.

Lily turned away from the phone. With her right hand, she held a small, sharp paring knife to Paige's stomach. She ran the point slowly and gently along her belly, leaving on her skin a thin white line.

"First lesson, Paige: when I'm on the telephone talking, don't shout. It's rude, terribly rude."

Paige's teeth began to chatter so loudly, she could actually hear them. "Why," she said forcing herself to talk. "Why're you doing this?"

"I'm not doing anything bad to you, Paige, honest. What I'm doing is helping you, but you've got to pay attention and listen to me. If I didn't care about you and My Boy, it wouldn't make such a difference. So if the telephone rings again, stay nice and quiet. Okay? And if you mind me, I won't have to do this again."

Silence for a few moments, then: "Paige?"

She looked at her.

"Don't be mad, okay?"

Deja vu ... A rerun of the city scene, the kid holding a knife to her stomach. But this brute was only a little girl, the same little girl she'd grown to love ... The other time Paige kicked, screamed, somehow fought her way out of it, and ran. But now she was too weak to fight, and too scared to scream.

Jason figured he'd gone about ten, fifteen miles in the last hour—it was a lot slower going than he had expected. He pulled into the next service center and went to the phones. He tried four town police departments before he got through to Tuckertown, about twenty miles southeast of Briarwood. He asked for the head cop on duty, then tried to explain his predicament as briefly as possible.

"Look," the officer said finally, "sounds to me like you're overreacting. We're talking here about a little kid who's lived with you and the wife a couple a months now. Okay, so she does weird things, but kids these days are pretty weird, take it from me. It don't necessarily mean they're psychotic."

"My wife's pregnant."

"I understand why you're so anxious, but listen to me, she's gonna be fine. Hey, fella, the bottom line is, I couldn't get there if my life depended on it. I've got all I can do to deal with the mess we got here. Three of our plows down, our main streets not even passable, and don't it figure, we get a call from Briarwood asking us to send volunteers. There wasn't a way in hell we could send our people—"

"The accident on Route 9?"

"That and the fire."

"What fire?"

"I don't know, some house went up in flames, an old man trapped inside, died. The guy's daughter it turns out was the one caused the smash-up on the highway—an eleven-car pileup, would you believe? I gotta say, for one little rinky-dink town, they're sure enough pullin' in their fair share of trouble."

Jason turned, about to leave, then on one dim hope, he tried his home number. Lily picked up on the eleventh ring. There was noise on the line, but he talked through it.

"Lily, put on Paige."

"She's sleeping."

"You're going to have to shout!"

"She's asleep!"

"Is she okay?"

"Yes."

"Lily, you know anything about the house in town that caught fire?"

"It was Hillary's house."

A pulse began to throb at his neck. "Your therapist, Hillary?"

"Yes."

"Then she's the one got killed in that eleven-car pileup out on Route 9?"

Silence.

"Lily?"

"Yes, I'm here."

"Wake Paige up, Lily."

"I'd better not."

"Why?"

"Because she said not to."

"Lily, I don't care what she said. I want you to wake her!"

"No!" Lily hung up the phone.

Jason tried Bulldoon's office again, but still no answer. He tried home again—now it was busy. Finally, he called Ruthanne, and though there was static, he got through.

"Ruthanne, Jason Bennett here."

"Oh, Jason, hello! Is Paige okay?"

"That's why I'm calling. I don't know."

"What? Talk louder"

"I say, I don't know," he shouted. "I'm on Route . . . I got through to the house once—Lily answered, said Paige was sleeping, and wouldn't let me talk to her."

"When I called, Lily said Paige refused to talk. She said not to call again."

"I don't like the sound of it. Could Charlie take a ride over?"

"He's not here, Jason. He's out fighting a fire."

"Shit."

"If I had the jeep, I would—"

"No, I understand. Look, the minute he comes in—"

"Oh, of course, I promise, Jason."

Now, the nausea nearly gone, Paige felt Lily hold a cool, damp cloth to her forehead. She had been staring at the far wall, trying to count each and every lilac on the wallpaper, do anything she could do to take her mind off what was happening. Every muscle in her body seemed so tightly drawn, it ached—somehow she had to loosen up.

Now she looked at Lily, whose expression seemed

one of concern—the same girl who had tied these ropes on her and had held a knife to her not thirty minutes earlier?

"Was that the phone I heard ring?" she asked Lily.

"Yup, Jason called."

"Why didn't you let me talk?"

"You know I can't do that."

"What did he—" Another pain bombarded her, her stare went back to the lilacs, counting, and recounting. Lily was off somewhere rubbing her limbs, her feet, talking nonsense to her. "Jason," Paige said again when the pain began to ebb. "What did he say?"

"Nothing important, just about Hillary."

"About the fire, how would he know?"

"Not the fire, Paige. Hillary was in an eleven-car accident on Route 9. She was killed."

Paige felt as though her breath had been siphoned out of her. "Oh my God," she said in a voice so peculiar she wasn't sure it was hers. "She must have been so grief-stricken, then not knowing what she was doing . . . And so many others hurt . . ."

"I bet she caused it."

Paige stared at Lily—the deep flush as though her cheeks had been scrubbed, the feverish glow in her eyes, making them color purple. Was it excitement?

"Why would you say . . . oh!"

Another pain. Lily put her hand on Paige's forehead and smoothed back her hair while Paige bit down so hard on her lip she tasted blood.

"Better?" Lily asked.

"I'm scared, Lily, please call the doctor."

"The phone isn't working."

"But Jason called. Ruthanne, too."

"There's a lot of static, you can hardly hear."

"Please, Lily!"

"No! Now stop your pestering!"

Paige stopped, and Lily caressed her face. "I'm only trying to take care of you. And the sooner you realize that, the better off we'll be. All of us—you, me, My Boy.

"What about Jason, he'll be home before you know it. Then what will you do?"

"I don't know, but I'll think of something. There's no way he'll ever get the chance to hurt you again, Paige. Not with Boss around to look out for you."

"Jason never hurt me, you know that."

"Oh yes he did, you're just too dumb to face it."

Paige swallowed hard, her throat felt so parched. "What are you talking about?"

"When Brooke came to visit, all that dirty stuff that was going on between her and Jason. And doing it all while they were right in front of you."

She stared at Lily, then shook her head. "No, I don't believe what you're saying."

"Believe me because I saw it with my own eyes. Down at the river. Want me to describe her bare chest? Let me see, she has a round dark mole right about here." Lily pointing to a spot between her own undeveloped breasts.

Paige's mouth opened. . . .

"Then you've seen Brooke naked, too? See, that's why I had to saw through that tree branch,

making sure it would fall when she climbed it. To punish her for what she did to you . . ."

Stunned silence . . .

"Paige, when My Boy comes out, and you're feeling better, can I have one of my Christmas presents? Just one?"

Paige's lips were moving, no sound was coming out. . . . She felt as though she were going to die as the next contraction moved in, encircling her entire lower body. . . . Please, no, she couldn't have the baby, not yet, not with her lying helpless, her hands locked and unable to move, not until someone got here to protect her son from her. *Someone, whoever you are, do you hear me calling?*

Jason and Brooke. Oh, Jason, how could you?

It was already dark, and though Ruthanne could see nothing but snow as she peered out the window, she didn't move from the spot for twenty minutes. Finally she headed to the hall closet and took out her boots, hat, coat, gloves, and scarf.

"What on earth are you doing, Ruthanne?" Evelyn asked, looking up from a shirt of Roger's she was mending.

"I'm going to Paige's house."

"Doesn't Charlie have the jeep?"

"He does, I'm walking."

"In this weather? That's crazy."

She pulled on one of her boots. "Maybe it is, but I'm going anyway."

"If Charlie ever knew, he'd—"

"He'd what? He's not my keeper you know."

"It's cold out there, dark, and dangerous. It

must be a good quarter of a mile over there. And I bet there's a foot of fresh snow on the ground already."

"I'm going, Ma."

"What about the children?"

"Since when can't I trust you with them?"

Evelyn put down the shirt and stood up as Ruthanne pulled on the other boot.

"Why don't you try to call her again?"

"Because I'll get Lily or static or busy signals or nothing. And even if I got Paige, would she talk to me? No."

"Then why are you going?"

Finally she put on her coat, her gloves, wrapped a scarf around her neck.

"Because I know being three weeks from due date, she's probably scared to death there alone. And if she's that scared, well, who knows, she might go into labor. Besides, if I show up at her doorstep, there's absolutely no way she's going to send me away."

"You've got an impossible stubborn streak, Ruthanne. I swear, just the same as your father had."

During the last hard contraction, Paige vomited, but Lily quickly cleaned her up, washing off her arms and chest and wherever else it had splattered. Finally done, she took more rope from her box and looped a length of it around both of Paige's ankles.

"What're you doing?"

"Just getting your legs in position."

"Oh God, you're going to tie them?"

"Don't be scared, I'm going to raise your legs

up, spread 'em wide so it'll be easier for My Boy to come out."

"But he's not ready, I know he's not ready yet."

"Either way, it won't hurt for you to be ready, will it?"

"Please don't tie my legs, Lily. Please—"

But even as she pleaded, Lily had taken a chair, moved it to the wall, taken the left leg rope with her. She pulled on the rope, lifting Paige's leg into what felt like an impossibly rigid position, then secured the end of the rope to a curtain rod. On the opposite wall, she removed a picture, and on the exposed hook, fastened the rope that was tied to her right leg. Paige's legs cramped.

"I feel faint."

"Don't do that, Paige. When it's time I'm going to need your help, pushing. You remember that part of it, don't you?"

"Oh God, my legs . . ."

"Answer me, Paige. Do you remember how to push?"

Paige saw the face come closer, the features grotesque and misshapen like they were being parodied through a trick mirror. She heard the voice, too, but it seemed to come from far away. She forced the words it said through her brain, then nodded.

Now satisfied, the face backed up to the foot of the bed.

"I don't see his head yet . . . when I do I'll tell you. In the meantime, we'll talk so you won't mind the hurt."

Quiet sobbing.

"Okay, then I'll talk, you listen.'
No response.
"Remember how you're always saying that I ought to talk about myself, that when I'm ready, you'll be there to listen? Well, guess what, Paige, I'm ready."

Ruthanne had been gone almost ten minutes when Roger came into the kitchen where his grandmother was fixing his shirt. He climbed onto the counter, then dug his hand into a box of chocolate chip cookies.
"Where's Mommy, Grandma?"
"Off visiting."
"With Daddy?"
"I wish it were with Daddy. No, gone by herself, I'm afraid. And I suspect your daddy's not going to be happy about this visiting one little bit. She's got some darn foolishness in her head that her girlfriend needs her help."
"What friend?"
"Paige Bennett, your neighbor."
"She went there?"
Evelyn nodded as she dipped the needle through the threaded opening, then pulled until it knotted. She lifted the shirt, and with her front teeth, bit off the excess thread.
Roger jumped off the counter, ran to the door, threw it open, then forming his hands into a cone at his mouth, screamed, "Mommy, come back!"
"You get back here yourself, and shut that door before we all freeze to death!" Evelyn got up, pulled Roger away from the door, then slammed it shut. "What has gotten into you,

young man, the snow's blowing right into this kitchen. And if you wake your sister with that shouting, you'll have to answer to me!"

"I've got to get Mommy back here!"

"It's too late, she's gone. Hopefully, she's almost there."

"No, don't say that, she'll be hurt."

"She's a big girl your mother, a strong one, too. She'll be fine in the snow."

"It's not the snow I'm worried about, it's Lily."

"Who're you talking about, that pretty little girl you're always playing with?"

"I don't anymore, Mommy and Daddy won't let me. And I bet she's burning mad at them for making me stop." Tears started to fill up his eyes, threatening to spill over. "And if she's mad enough, Grandma, she might kill Mommy."

"Roger Beeder, I ought to spank your hide good. A little girl like that? Where in tarnation did you ever come up with such a big bad tall tale as that one?"

"She killed her father."

"Why, who said that?"

"She told me. Cut him up in little pieces with a sickle. And said she would do the same to Mommy and Daddy if I told on her."

Chapter Sixteen

Lily held the stopwatch in one hand, and with her other hand she stroked Paige's forehead.

"I told you how I was, Paige, remember that? But still you never did believe me. Sometimes you are just *so* stubborn. What am I going to do with you."

Paige stifled a sob. Another contraction began, and Lily put her monologue aside, going right back to timing, soothing words, touching, and coaching Paige in her breathing. Positioned like she was, Paige had no other choice but to cooperate.

"Good girl, Paige, wow, that one lasted nearly two minutes," Lily said as the pain faded. "You know, sometimes Daddy would let me punish Mommy all by myself. That's when I knew he trusted me. It's a big responsibility to be Boss, at least over someone you care about. It's not like you'd want to hurt them, you just need to teach them.

"Daddy loved Mommy, he did *really*, you could see it when she'd hurt and he'd hurt right along

with her. And she loved him, too—the more he had to lay down the law to her, the more she loved. Weird, huh? Well, people are weird. Even kids." With her fingertips, she drew rolling circles along Paige's legs.

"Oh, you know that girl, Sandy, from school? The one I cut her braid off? Well, after a while, she got to like me, and you know why? Because she used to use that silly red braid to make her feel tough. Once I got rid of it, she didn't feel so tough. And what she needed then, was a friend to watch out for her.

"And at the barbecue, those stupid, pimply faced boys who called me names? I'll bet they won't forget the sound of a hen's neck snapping. If they hadn't run like that, *their* necks might have been next."

An intake of breath.

Lily nodded. "And Old Man Egan . . . I did him and Hillary the biggest favor of all. When he tried to smile, he'd drool, then he'd fart and shit and piss his pants, and poor ugly Hillary whose only dream it was to treat loonies, was the one got the booby prize. Every day, she had to wipe him up again and change his smelly pants. What kind of life was that for a smart one like her, and what person would want to live like that?"

Paige swallowed hard. Who was this monster talking, was it someone she knew? Lily was holding Jason's stopwatch in one hand; with her other hand she was stroking Paige's back, her forehead, her stomach, even squeezing her hand when the pain got too awful.

Okay, but she had taken enough pain, so could she please die now? No, no, there was a little

boy about to be born and she had to watch out that the good-stroking monster didn't get to him. She couldn't go and die now, not just yet.

Oh God, Jason, what have you done? What have I done?

Jason had gone only another fifteen miles when the car spun two revolutions, then skid backward into a snowbank. He got out, tried to push it, then with his feet and on his knees using his bare hands, cleared the snow from around the tires. Finally, he took from the trunk a half-dozen *New York Law Journals*, pulled them apart, slid the pages beneath the back tires, got behind the steering wheel . . .   And prayed.

Slowly, easily . . . ignition, a little gas. The back tire traction took and the Volvo moved forward.

A walk that normally would have taken seven, eight minutes at most now had taken nearly twenty-five minutes and though Ruthanne's feet were nearly numb right through the fur lining and her face red and itchy with frostbite, she was within a hundred feet from the Bennett house. She stopped, took a deep breath, but kept her gloved hands over her mouth, trying to close out the fierce wind.

Paige's car was in the driveway, not surprising, where would she be going? She looked at the house—definitely something strange about it. Though it was only seven o'clock, just about the time Paige served dinner, the house was dark.

Except for the bright lights on in the master bedroom.

*   *   *

Paige had just finished bearing down on a contraction when she heard the noise. Lily heard it, too.

A door, footsteps? Finally, "Paige, it's me, Ruthanne."

"Ruth—" was all she got out when the hand covered her mouth. Then a terry towel was shoved into her mouth. Lily took the knife, went to the door, stood behind it.

"You up there, Paige?"

Footsteps closer. *Go away, Ruthanne, please go away!*

"I walked all this way in a blizzard, so there's no way you're going to send me—" She came into view and her hands flew to her mouth. "Oh, my Lord!"

Her mind unable to grasp quickly enough and react to the horror facing her, she didn't see Lily come at her with the knife. Ruthanne's face registered shock, one shock following another, then her arms pushed out toward Lily, but Lily plunged the knife into Ruthanne's side and stepped back. Ruthanne fell to the floor, blood puddling beneath her.

Dear God, my name is Paige, please let me die, too. And the baby, let me take him with me....

But no, it couldn't be so easy—suddenly her entire body seized. Like a light at the tunnel entrance flashing green for traffic to go through, so was her body directing this child. And though Paige had never felt the real thing before, she knew that the baby was coming now.

Lily pulled the towel out of Paige's mouth just in time to hear her scream, "The baby!"

"I'm here, Paige, don't be scared."

Lily ran to the foot of the bed and her eyes brightened.

"Yes, Paige, My Boy's head, I can see it!"

It had gone well for another twenty miles ... Jason had still forty more to go when the car ahead spun sideways, forged down a six-foot incline into a drift, and the Volvo followed suit.

Jason got out, looked over his position—the snow was coming down as strong as ever, damnit, this time it was surely hopeless. He took the flashlight from his glove compartment, slammed the car door, then putting his coat collar up against the wind, began to walk. Several cars came; he tried to hitch, but they passed. Just as well. If he had a shot at picking up a ride, let him pick up with a winner.

When the plow came, he got out into the middle of the highway, waved his arms. The truck stopped, the driver rolled down his window.

"Hey there, buddy, you'll find that a good way to get yourself run over."

Jason went to the window. "I need a lift."

"Sorry, this isn't a taxi service."

"My wife's pregnant, she's in labor."

He shrugged. "You've got my condolences, but as you can see, I've got a job to do."

Jason pulled out his wallet, counted out two hundred dollars.

"Where're we talking about?"

"Briarwood."

He shook his head. "I get caught somewhere else, I'll lose my contract."

"How much you make?"

"A storm like this will net me eight, nine hundred bucks easy."

"How many of these storms you get a winter?"

"This big? Maybe three, four."

Jason pulled out a checkbook, then a pen. "What's your name."

"Syd Crueger, why?"

Jason filled out a check, all but his signature. He flipped it over, showing it to the man.

"Five thousand bucks, not bad for two hours work, huh? It's likely in three hours you'll be back here plowing, five thousand richer and no one the wiser."

He stared at the check. "How do I know it's good?"

Jason pulled out his wallet, opened it, showing credit cards lined up in the slots.

"Shows I'm a good risk. And hey wait, lookie here." He held up his New York Bar membership card. "I'm an attorney, New York State. I give you a bum check, report me to the Board. They're like the fucking gestapo. If no one else can knuckle you under, they can."

"And that's it, Briarwood?"

"Forty-four Skidder Bay Road, about two miles off Route 9."

He took a deep breath. "Okay, buddy, hop in. I must be loco, but then again, so are you."

At eight o'clock that night, Paige delivered a baby boy—eight pounds, two ounces, twenty-two inches long according to Lily's measurements—with intense dark eyes, a mass of sticky brown hair, and a red face. Calm and exact, Lily cut and tied the cord, even pushed hard on Paige's

abdomen to help her dispel the afterbirth. She immediately took the newborn to the bathroom; when she came out, the baby wasn't with her.

"Where is he?" Paige asked, scared to hear the answer.

"Not to worry, Paige, My Boy's fine. I'm taking good care of him."

"I want to hold him, please let me."

"Of course. First, let's get you cleaned up."

"Ruthanne," Paige said catching at a breath. "Won't you help her, Lily?"

Lily went over to Ruthanne, knelt down, put her ear to her chest, then stood up, and came back.

"She's not dead."

"Then we *can* help."

Lily shook her head. "She deserves what she's getting, and if she could talk to us now, she'd admit it. Who did she and her lousy husband Charlie think they were not letting Roger play with me?"

"They misunderstood, Lily. They thought you were responsible for Roger putting that pillow over Carolyn—"

"I know you're dumb, Paige, but even you aren't that dumb. By now you know I'm the one who told Roger to do it. But he wasn't supposed to kill the baby, just hide some breaths away, so she'd quick learn who had charge of the air."

The concept was so evil, Paige gasped. Would she do that to Joshua? Of course she would. Lily smiled, one of those rare smiles, then went about untying Paige's legs, washing her, changing the sheet, throwing the used one on the floor, getting

her into clean pajamas, then finally releasing one of her arms.

"What about my other arm?"

"No 'thank you' for all I've done? Washing and cleaning and taking care of My Boy?"

"Yes, of course . . . thank you," she said, and in her great relief to be comfortable and relatively free of pain, almost believing her words. But then she thought of Ruthanne on the floor, Joshua—she prayed in his crib in the nursery— and shuddered. "My other arm?"

"No, Paige, you're too scrappy for me to let you free like that. Maybe some day down the road, though, all depending on how quick you learn. It might take a little while. Whenever I got too big for my britches, Daddy'd call me scrappy."

"What did he mean by it?"

"Scrappies want to be bosses, so it stands to reason there can only be one scrappy to a family. Daddy was boss in our family, at least he was for a whole long time. And that was real good because he taught me just about everything I know."

"And then?"

She started to giggle—the very first time Paige had heard her lose herself in laughter. Finally she took a deep breath. "And then I wanted to be boss. So I had to kill him."

After a long silence, Paige found her voice.

"Then there was never a fight, Anna and your father?"

She shook her head.

"Lily, you think I want to be boss?"

"Not really, you just like to play at it some-

times, and you've been playing at it excellent with me to help. But the real boss in this family is Jason, that's why he's got to be killed."

"Lily, no! You mustn't hurt Jason!"

Ignoring her protests, Lily left the room, came back almost immediately, this time with the baby swaddled in damp blankets. She placed him in Paige's free arm. "Want to see him?"

Paige sucked in a breath, tears began to fall down her cheeks. She laid the baby beside her, wiped the tears with her sleeve, then with her fingers, touched the little features, nose, chin, lips, jawline. Like Jason, so much like Jason.

She looked up to see Lily putting on her boots. "Where're you going?"

"I'm taking My Boy home."

"Where, what do you mean?"

Silence.

"There's a storm out there, he's too little to go out."

"Did you forget the sled I made him?"

"But you can't, where would you—" She stopped, bit down on her lip. Finally: "Can I come, Lily, if I promise to do exactly as you say?"

"I don't know if you're strong enough. I was going to wait, come back and get you later."

"Oh, no, I'll be fine. I want to be with you."

Lily stood there a long moment, then sighed. She took the baby from Paige, laid it on the floor next to her, then took Paige's boots from where she'd thrown them earlier, helped her back into them. She untied her bound hand, and at that moment, Paige hauled off, smashing Lily full across her face.

Ignoring the pain, Lily lifted the knife, jumped

on Paige and drew the knife down her arm, cutting through the pajama sleeve. Paige screamed, blood oozed out and suddenly dizzy, she fell backward onto the bed. Lily picked the flashlight off the end table and with the butt of it, smashed it several times across Paige's face. Then she bandaged Paige's arm and put her coat on over it.

Finally, Lily clasped Paige's hands together and tied them at her wrists.

Her own overclothes on, Lily zipped the baby in a bright red legless snowsuit she'd found in the nursery.

"Okay, let's go," she said.

Paige sat up. She could feel pain pounding inside her eyelids, her swollen lip . . .

"What about the sled?"

"When are you going to learn not to question me? It's waiting outside all ready and packed, just like a golden coach."

And it was: the four-runner yellow sled was made of a big square of plywood, with a wood back and sides about a foot high. Four posts anchored a tarp that stretched across the top, sides, and back, and served as a wind protector. The inside was split by a board. The larger section lined with quilts was big enough to sit Paige with the baby, the smaller section held supplies: though it was filled with a number of items, the item that stood out most was Jason's ax.

It was nearly two hours since Ruthanne had left, but it wasn't as though Evelyn hadn't expected her to stay at Paige's and wait till Charlie could come by with the jeep to pick her up. But then, Roger getting so excited and stirring up all

that crazy talk about the little girl, well, darnit, Evelyn just wished that Charlie would get his hide home already to take care of his own family.

So when she did finally hear the jeep pull up, she met him at the door, not giving him a chance to even catch a breath.

"What's this talk about that girl, Lily?" she asked.

"Mind if I get in, take off my coat?"

"Yes, I do mind, it's about time you're home."

"What's going on here?"

"Your wife is what's going on. Ruthanne just picked up and went off to see that neighbor friend of yours, Paige."

"She walked?"

"You know of any other cars around this house she might of used?"

"Why'd you let her go?"

"Why'd I let her? I'm only her mother, and she's not about to listen to me. If you remember back to high school, she didn't listen, even then. Now what's all this craziness about that girl Lily my grandson's been filling my ears with?"

"What'd he say?"

"Only that you and Ruthanne put your foot down to the children playing together. And Lily is mad as a hornet, mad enough to hurt Ruthanne."

"Kids tend to exaggerate."

"That may be, but according to Roger, the girl's capable of it."

"Your wife really in labor?"

"I don't know, I just know she was having back

pains earlier in the day. Mostly, I'm worried that she might be in danger."

"From who?"

"Would you believe an eleven-year-old kid?"

He shrugged.

"Think I'm nuts, huh?"

"Hey, mister, I already know you're nuts. You paid me five thousand bucks for my two-hour round-trip. But hey it's your ride and your time so you say whatever comes to mind. And me, I'll just breeze along, shut up, and nod my head."

Jason looked at his watch . . . he figured at this rate of speed, twenty more minutes.

It was hard crawling into the igloo with her hands tied, but Lily helped Paige inside and onto the tarp. The baby was already lying in a make-shift bed at one side of the three-and-a-half-foot-high, eight-foot round structure. Paige examined the interior, stunned to see diapers, candles, blankets, other provisions. A box filled with two bangle bracelets, a pink plastic change purse, a black stretch belt—the items stolen from school. And a bucket filled with a dead squirrel and two dead rats. Suddenly she started to shake so badly she couldn't stop.

"What's wrong, Paige?"

Strangled noises coming from somewhere deep . . .

Lily opened Paige's jacket for her, laid her down on a pillow, then put a quilt over her. She sat beside her, massaging the back of her neck. "It's okay, Paige, don't be scared."

"The baby, Lily, please let me feed the baby."

Lily unbuttoned Paige's pajama tops, then lifted the baby and placed him at Paige's breast.

"My hands, free my hands?"

"No."

A monster, a murderer, the keeper of her baby ... Oh, God, she hurt so much she could feel tears pressing against the insides of her bruised eyes, not daring to spill out. And so tired, but dare she sleep, leaving Joshua to bear it alone? *I need you now, Jason, Joshua needs you. . . . And Ruthanne, was she lying alone bleeding to death?*

Charlie was at the house in five minutes, looking through the downstairs rooms, calling out for Ruthanne, then Paige. Finally he went upstairs to the master bedroom where he found Ruthanne on the floor inside the doorway. All that blood over the floor, the bed ... *Oh Jesus Christ, what happened here?* He got down, listened at Ruthanne's chest, and thank you God, her heart was still beating. . . .

He rushed to the phone, tried the operator, busy ... 911, busy, too. He threw down the receiver, went over, picked Ruthanne up in his arms, and headed downstairs. Just when he was getting her into the back of the jeep, the snow plow pulled up.

Jason ran over, saw it was Ruthanne. "What happened?"

"I don't know, I found her on the floor. She's been stabbed." He jumped into the front driver's seat.

"Paige, where's Paige?"

Charlie shook his head as he started the car.

"I didn't see her. All I know is there's a lot of blood . . . I'll do what I can to send back help."

Charlie pulled away and Syd, who was now beside Jason, put his hand on his shoulder.

"Hey, look, I figure the money you paid ought to buy a little more time."

From the bloodied condition of the master bedroom and the nursery, it was clear to Jason that his son had been born. At that point Jason lost it, and it was Syd who finally took him by the shoulders and smashed him up against the wall.

"Hey look, buddy, take it easy here, you're no help to either of them like this. So let's take it a little slower. So the baby's born, what would that a meant to the kid?"

Jason stared at him, swallowed, then: "She liked the idea of the baby, she even called him My Boy. She liked Paige, too, she loved her, the one she didn't like was me."

"Okay, we're getting somewhere. So what she wants then is to get 'em away from you. The question is, where would she hide?"

Jason and Syd checked the cellar, the downstairs rooms, finally the attic.

"Oh Jesus," Jason said.

"What?"

"I had an ax here, it's gone."

Silence, then: "Think, there must be some other place the kid knows, would a run to," Crueger pressed.

Only a moment elapsed before it came to him.

"You're right, there is. A fort, more like one of those igloos. I built it for her weeks ago. Down near the river." He began to look around the attic

for tools. "It's a sturdy bastard, has corrugated cardboard insulation, was iced over once, at least, once I know of."

He selected a dirt shovel, a garden spade, what looked like an ice pick . . .

"What about a blow torch?" Crueger asked.

Jason turned. "You've got a blow torch?"

"Propane. The pins in the plow freeze up, I use it to get 'em out."

It was actually warm in there, or did she have a fever? Paige had slept some and when she woke, she realized Lily had untied her hands, taken off her jacket, then tied one of her wrists and connected it to what looked like a long skewer frozen into the ground. Her PJ top was buttoned . . . oh, no, the baby!

"My Boy's right here," Lily said.

Paige looked up—Lily was rocking him in her arms. "I should feed him again, Lily."

"Not yet. You slept awhile, you looked so hot I took off your jacket."

She had begun to tremble again. "I was, but now I think I'm getting cold."

Lily put down the baby in its makeshift crib, took another wool blanket from a pile, and put it over Paige, but still it didn't stop her from shaking.

"What you need is food to give you energy," Lily said.

"That's an idea. Maybe you could go back to the house, get some things . . ."

Lily put her hand in the bucket, pulled out a rat.

Paige shrunk back, foul-tasting saliva rose in her throat.

"What're you scared of, Paige, it's dead." She put the rodent on a board, cut the head off, tossed it aside, then started to slice it.

"I won't, Lily. I can't, I won't!"

Lily cut off a piece of pale meat, then speared it with a fork, and held it to Paige's lips.

"Just try a little bit," she said.

Suddenly there was a noise. . . . Lily, then Paige looked toward the low opening in the igloo. Just the top of Jason's head . . .

Lily picked up the ax.

"No! Watch it, Jason!" Paige screamed.

Jason's head yanked out just as the ax went plowing into the snow.

They had driven the snowplow down, and though it had taken them a roundabout path to get through the trees, with the two feet of snow now on the ground, and the way the headlights lit up the fort, it was worth it. Jason took Syd back a ways.

"There's no way I'm going to get inside there without her claiming my neck first. If you could do the north wall of the fort, use the torch there, weaken it enough so we'll be able to break through it quick."

"Why that wall?"

"Because the way I built it, I figure when it caves in, it's more likely to cave where Lily's sitting."

"Did you see her?"

"I didn't get far enough in to see anyone. But I'm going by process of elimination. . . . Paige's voice came from the south side, so I'm betting the kid's right across from her."

"What if she hears the torch?"

"I don't think so, not with the wind so loud. Besides, I'm going to talk to her, do the best I can to divert her attention.

"Don't go and get your head in too close."

Lily stood over Paige, still holding the ax.

"You shouldn't have warned him like that, Paige!"

"I know, you're right and I'm sorry. The words spilled out without me knowing."

"I don't want to have to gag you, but if you make things hard—"

"I won't, honest I won't. I was just thinking, do we have to kill him? Why can't I just tell him to go away, that the baby and I want to stay here with you."

"Do you think I'm so dumb?"

"Yeah, Paige," Jason's voice came from outside the hole, "you think she's dumb enough to buy a story like that? Christ, she knows I'm not about to leave, at least not without my son. You, well, you're a different story, there's other women who might do as well. Lily knows what I'm talking about, right Lily?"

Silence for a few moments. "Well, either way, I'm not giving up My Boy."

"Hey, I didn't expect you would. You know, it's pretty interesting this setup we got here."

"How do you mean?"

"I mean this igloo, here. I know it was my idea to build it, but if I didn't know better, I'd think it was you who somehow put the idea in my head."

"Why?"

"Well, look around. Sure it's made of ice and

all, but if you ask me, it's a pretty close copy of the penalty box."

Silence.

Jason looked over to Syd—Syd held up two fingers.

"Lily, you still there?" Jason said.

"Yeah."

"I mean, it's a place where you could easily punish someone, at least through the winter you could. What I don't get is, why you and the baby are in there? I mean, Paige is one thing, she must do a half-dozen things a day she needs to be set straight on. And hey, maybe I haven't done such a hot job seeing to it. But I figure you're better in the Boss department than me. Am I wrong about that?"

Another long silence, then: "No, you're not wrong."

"Well, how about we try to strike up some kind of bargain?"

"Like what?"

Syd waved, got Jason's attention, then gestured to the fort and nodded his head.

"I don't know," Jason said, moving back a little. "What do you suggest?"

"I think you ought to tell Anna to keep her mouth shut or I'll come shut it for her."

"I can't do that."

"Why not?"

"She's dead, hung herself this afternoon."

Jason and Syd now stood back and ready—the snowplow's lights directed on the igloo. Jason ran back and together they came forward, rushing their weight against the north wall.

* * *

Paige was watching Lily: her mouth opened, closed, then opened again—her mother had killed herself and she *was* reacting. And then suddenly a wall of snow, ice, all falling, toppling, shooting at them like a pile of heavy wet sand ... first onto Lily's lap, to her chest, shoulders, then covering her ... Paige reached with her free arm to get the baby, but she fell backward as the avalanche shifted to her.

The bright red snowsuit, the baby! Jason had seen Joshua and Paige's positions the moment they'd broken through. He leapt for the baby, dived into the snow, came up holding him. He quickly passed him to Syd to take to the warmth of the truck, and took over Syd's shoveling to Paige. He dug his hands and arms in with maniacal frenzy. Finally reaching her, he cleared her mouth and nose to breathe, the snow from the rest of her face, her shoulders, arms, then tried to lift her out ...

"My hand," she said.

With trembling fingers, he took out a knife, cut the rope on her wrist, then lifted her out of the deep snow. She threw her arms around him, then shaking, crying, her tears mixed with his, she pulled away.

"Lily," she whispered.

Jason stood there, his wet eyes staring into the heap of snow and ice.

"Please, Jason, she can't breathe, she'll die."

One, two, three, four, five, six, seven, eight seconds ticked away in the wind. ... Finally, Jason went over, dug his way through the snow, got down onto his knees, and lifted Lily out.

Epilogue

It was August. Jason had taken a long weekend, and it was the first time Paige and Jason had returned to Briarwood since they'd closed the house after the blizzard. They had invited the Beeders for cheese and wine that night, and though they hadn't seen Ruthanne since her two-week stay in the hospital, they had kept in close touch. Ruthanne's lung condition was uncertain at first, but aside from occasional shortness of breath, the injury had healed.

The wounds were all healing—at least, to one degree or another. Never wholly, Paige supposed. Though Brooke and Jason had ended their brief encounter before Paige even knew of its existence, it was a matter of lost trust, something that would take time and care to rebuild. But as for Brooke, their friendship was over—it had turned into a mere polite, occasional hello when they accidentally passed on the street.

"Paige, have you decided if you'll be teaching this fall?" Ruthanne asked.

"Not yet. The terrible pull career has, you put

so much time into building it, then to just drop
it? Yet, to leave Joshua, just the thought of it
makes me unhappy."

"See, so maybe I'm not so dumb. . . . Maybe
once the children go, I'll begin a career."

"I'm your career," Charlie said, half smiling.

"Pretty feisty words," Jason said.

Paige gave him a look, thinking "scrappy" in
her mind.

Jason put his arm around her. "What's wrong,
I say something?"

"Nothing. Just something silly that reminded
me . . ."

It seemed there were always reminders popping
up, and surely there would be more. Though Lily
did have family, Nora Kalish wanted no part in
her niece's life. And though neither did Paige
nor Jason, they felt a strange sense of obligation.
Either they foot the bill to a private hospital—
they chose Creedmore Children's in Buffalo—
where she'd get quality psychiatric care, or see
her dumped in a state institution.

Actually it was Jason who suggested it, then
insisted.

"The thing is," he said, "I finally understood
her. For one brief moment, I got into her head,
and it scared the shit out of me. The unbeliev-
able fury, the hate I felt when I could have,
would have, sooner seen her buried alive, suffo-
cate in the snow, and the worst part of all—
maybe I even reveled in it. . . . To be only eleven
years old, and to want so much to hurt another
human being."

And as much as Paige had sympathized with
the little girl, she had oversimplified it all, mak-

ing Lily into what she wanted her to be, not willing or daring to believe that a darker side existed. No, Paige didn't understand that kind of hate, and if she lived a hundred years, she didn't suppose she ever would.

Since February, Paige herself had been in therapy. Mainly for the traumas, one after another. Then trying to understand the intense draw to Lily, how it seemed to satisfy her need to mother, to help a wounded child. And then the mind-jarring that began with the attack, snowballing with Lily's questions. No doubt more memories were looking to surface. . . .

In any event, she and Jason would be silent benefactors. If Lily should ever recover—if such a thing were possible—she would never know the part they had played in her treatment at Creedmore. Because the bottom line was—and they had admitted it to each other lying awake at night in each other's arms—nothing a doctor could ever say would diminish their fear of Lily.

It was the next morning and Joshua, now eight months old and already walking, saw the Briarwood postal truck stop at the roadside. He toddled toward it. Usually any mail—which was mostly junk mail—was held for them at the post office, picked up when they got to town.

"My golly, would you look at this fine young fellow," the postman said. "Now, your name wouldn't happen to be Joshua Bennett, would it?" Joshua's fat pink cheeks pumped higher.

"One and the same," Paige said, coming up behind her son.

The postman took a small, plain wrapped

package from his truck—no return address—and handed it to him.

"Looks like a present, and it's not even Christmas." Then to Paige and Jason: "Saw you two here, so I thought I'd bring it on over."

"Thanks," Jason said, kneeling down next to Joshua, and taking it from his hands. The truck pulled away and Jason tore off the brown paper, opened the box. He took out a yellow wooden car.

"That's lovely, looks handmade," Paige said. "No card?"

"Maybe my brother Neil. He used to like to whittle these kind of things," Jason said.

"That doesn't look whittled."

"No, but it's the same type of thing. . . . Look, I'll call him tonight, ask him." He examined the car for any small loose parts, then hoisting Joshua onto his shoulder, handed it to him.

"Here you go, son."

They headed happily into the house, Joshua's strong little hands turning the car over and over, settling finally to the bottom part where little letters were scratched into the wood.

Little letters saying *My Boy*.

ON THE EDGE OF YOUR SEAT!

☐ **SEE MOMMY RUN by Nancy Baker Jacobs.** She became a fugitive from the law and her husband—in order to save her child from unspeakable abuse. (172299—$4.99)

☐ **PRESSURE DROP by Peter Abrahams.** Nina Kitchener has no idea what lay behind the disappearance of her baby from a New York hospital. And nothing will stop her terror-filled quest for the donor who fathered her child . . . nothing—not even murder. (402359—$4.95)

☐ **SOUL/MATE by Rosamond Smith.** A psychopathic serial killer with a lover's face . . . "Headlong suspense . . . What if a well-meaning, intelligent woman should encounter a demonic twin?"—*The Atlanta Journal and Constitution.* "Taut, relentless, chilling!"—*Chicago Tribune.* (401905—$4.95)

☐ **NEMSIS by Rosamond Smith.** "A terror-invoking psychothriller brimming with atmosphere."—*Cleveland Plain Dealer.* "Extraordinary . . . a murder mystery with a literary twist . . . rich in social observation and psychological insight . . . well-written . . . the dialogue has rhythm, pitch, melody and mood"—*Boston Globe* (402952—$5.50)

Prices slightly higher in Canada.

Buy them at your local bookstore or use this convenient coupon for ordering.

NEW AMERICAN LIBRARY
P.O. Box 999, Bergenfield, New Jersey 07621

Please send me the books I have checked above.
I am enclosing $_____ (please add $2.00 to cover postage and handling). Send check or money order (no cash or C.O.D.'s) or charge by Mastercard or VISA (with a $15.00 minimum). Prices and numbers are subject to change without notice.

Card #_____ Exp. Date _____
Signature_____
Name_____
Address_____
City _____ State _____ Zip Code _____

For faster service when ordering by credit card call **1-800-253-6476**

Allow a minimum of 4-6 weeks for delivery. This offer is subject to change without notice.

⌀ SIGNET

PAGE-TURNERS!

(0451)

☐ **STRANGE FITS OF PASSION by Anita Shreve.** Mary chose the small Maine town because it was far away from New York City. And everyone in town knew right away that she was running.... "A finely written literary thriller."—*The New Yorker*
(403002—$5.99)

☐ **EDEN CLOSE by Anita Shreve.** This novel of love, terror and mystery weaves a tale of obsessive passions, and of the shadows cast over life by dark deeds. "Tantalizing!"—*New York Times Book Review.* (167856—$4.99)

☐ **BAD DESIRE by Gary Devon.** "A *very* good psychological thriller!" —Mary Higgins Clark. "More than a superb novel of suspense ... a deep and compelling story of the truly dark sides of love, and ferocity of passion."—Gerald A. Browne. (170989—$5.99)

☐ **WELL AND TRULY by Evelyn Wilde Mayerson.** Loss, redemption— and falling in love again ... "A fine novel that makes for compelling reading."—James Michener (169883—$5.50)

Prices slightly higher in Canada

Buy them at your local bookstore or use this convenient coupon for ordering.

NEW AMERICAN LIBRARY
P.O. Box 999, Bergenfield, New Jersey 07621

Please send me the books I have checked above.
I am enclosing $_____ (please add $2.00 to cover postage and handling).
Send check or money order (no cash or C.O.D.'s) or charge by Mastercard or VISA (with a $15.00 minimum). Prices and numbers are subject to change without notice.

Card #_____ Exp. Date _____
Signature_____
Name_____
Address_____
City _____ State _____ Zip Code _____
For faster service when ordering by credit card call **1-800-253-6476**
Allow a minimum of 4-6 weeks for delivery. This offer is subject to change without notice.

⊘ **SIGNET** (0451)

GRIPPING READING

☐ **BLIND MAN'S BLUFF by David Lorne.** A savage game of vengeance becomes a deadly race against time . . . (403126—$4.99)

☐ **A WHISPER IN THE ATTIC by Gloria Murphy.** In this taut psychological thriller, terror wears a little girl's face . . . (173155—$4.99)

☐ **BLOOD TEST by Jonathan Kellerman.** A child psychologist and a homicide detective hunt through a human jungle of health cults, sex-for-sale haunts and dreams-turned-into-nightmares to find a kidnapped child. (159292—$5.99)

☐ **OVER THE EDGE by Jonathan Kellerman.** The death of a former patient leads Alex Delaware through a labyrinth of sick sex and savage greed, penetrating to the inner sanctums of the rich and powerful and the lowest depths of the down and out. (152190—$5.99)

Prices slightly higher in Canada

Buy them at your local bookstore or use this convenient coupon for ordering.

NEW AMERICAN LIBRARY
P.O. Box 999, Bergenfield, New Jersey 07621

Please send me the books I have checked above.
I am enclosing $_____ (please add $2.00 to cover postage and handling).
Send check or money order (no cash or C.O.D.'s) or charge by Mastercard or VISA (with a $15.00 minimum). Prices and numbers are subject to change without notice.

Card #_____ Exp. Date _____
Signature_____
Name_____
Address_____
City _____ State _____ Zip Code _____
For faster service when ordering by credit card call **1-800-253-6476**
Allow a minimum of 4-6 weeks for delivery. This offer is subject to change without notice.

PULSE-POUNDING READING

☐ **DEPRAVED INDIFFERENCE by Robert K. Tanenbaum.** New York Assistant D.A. Butch Karp has an open-and-shut case putting a group of Croation terrorists behind bars for a cop-killing. But why are the FBI, the Catholic Church and the NYPD all protecting the guilty? (168429—$5.50)

☐ **NO LESSER PLEA by Robert K. Tanenbaum.** A vicious double-murderer has already slipped through the cracks in the system once, and now handsome DA Roger Karp won't rest until he gets a guilty plea. But Mandeville Louis laughs at the law, and even in the security of a mental hospital his killing spree is not over yet . . . "Tough, cynical, funny" —*Booklist* (154967—$4.95)

☐ **IMMORAL CERTAINTY by Robert K. Tanenbaum.** "Tanenbaum's best yet . . . a three-ring extravaganza of crime and punishment that's . . . New York authentic."—*Kirkus Reviews* (171861—$5.99)

☐ **BADGE OF THE ASSASSIN by Robert K. Tanenbaum and Philip Rosenberg.** "Engrossing . . . The accounts of the two murder trials in New York, at which Tanenbaum served as a prosecutor . . . are almost as suspenseful as the stalking and capture of the killers."—*New York Times Book Review* (167988—$4.95)

Buy them at your local bookstore or use this convenient coupon for ordering.

NEW AMERICAN LIBRARY
P.O. Box 999, Bergenfield, New Jersey 07621

Please send me the books I have checked above.
I am enclosing $_____ (please add $2.00 to cover postage and handling).
Send check or money order (no cash or C.O.D.'s) or charge by Mastercard or VISA (with a $15.00 minimum). Prices and numbers are subject to change without notice.

Card #_____ Exp. Date _____
Signature_____
Name_____
Address_____
City _____ State _____ Zip Code _____

For faster service when ordering by credit card call **1-800-253-6476**
Allow a minimum of 4-6 weeks for delivery. This offer is subject to change without notice.

⊘ SIGNET MYSTERY (0451)

MASTERS OF MYSTERY

☐ **MYSTERY FOR CHRISTMAS AND OTHER STORIES**—Edited by Cynthia Manson. Twelve Christmas mysteries—gift wrapped in entertainment and suspense. This clever collection includes stories by John D. McDonald, Rex Stout, George Baxt, Patricia Moyes, and others ... for it's ho, ho, homicide in the season to guess whodunit. (169093—$4.99)

☐ **MYSTERY FOR HALLOWEEN.** Here are 16 haunting Halloween tales carefully selected from the pages of *Alfred Hitchcock's Mystery Magazine* and *Ellery Queen's Mystery Magazine*. (171837—$4.99)

☐ **MURDER AT CHRISTMAS** *And Other Stories.* Twelve frightfully festive stories by John Mortimer, James Powell, Georges Simenon, C.M. Chan, and 8 more of today's best mystery writers. (172043—$4.99)

☐ **MYSTERY CATS.** Sixteen murderously entertaining tales of crime by some of today's best mystery writers: Lillian Jackson Braun, Ruth Rendell, Edward D. Hoch, and other greats. (171012—$4.99)

Buy them at your local bookstore or use this convenient coupon for ordering.

NEW AMERICAN LIBRARY
P.O. Box 999, Bergenfield, New Jersey 07621

Please send me the books I have checked above.
I am enclosing $_____ (please add $2.00 to cover postage and handling). Send check or money order (no cash or C.O.D.'s) or charge by Mastercard or VISA (with a $15.00 minimum). Prices and numbers are subject to change without notice.

Card #_____ Exp. Date _____
Signature_____
Name_____
Address_____
City _____ State _____ Zip Code _____
For faster service when ordering by credit card call **1-800-253-6476**
Allow a minimum of 4-6 weeks for delivery. This offer is subject to change without notice.

There's an epidemic with 27 million victims. And no visible symptoms.

It's an epidemic of people who can't read.

Believe it or not, 27 million Americans are functionally illiterate, about one adult in five.

The solution to this problem is you... when you join the fight against illiteracy. So call the Coalition for Literacy at toll-free **1-800-228-8813** and volunteer.

Volunteer Against Illiteracy. The only degree you need is a degree of caring.

THIS AD PRODUCED BY MARTIN LITHOGRAPHERS
A MARTIN COMMUNICATIONS COMPANY